BORROWED TIME

SUNDOWNERS
a division of
Treble Heart Books
1284 Overlook Dr.
Sierra Vista, AZ 85635-5512

Published and Printed in the U.S.A.

ISBN: 978-1-932695-52-6

Thank you for choosing
a
Sundowners
Western Selection

Borrowed Time

by

Susan M. Ballard

Sundowners

A Division of

Treble Heart Books

Dedication

I dedicate this, my first novel, with love and thanks, to my husband, Brian, who always had enough faith for the both of us.

CHAPTER 1

April 1, 1878

Lanky frame settled into the battered chair, a glass of bourbon within easy reach, and an enigmatic smile upon his lips, the well dressed sporting man appeared a distracted participant in life as it swirled about him. In reality, nothing was further from the truth. Playing the part of the disinterested onlooker and doing it well was a ploy which worked to good advantage when a man made his living, or most of it, from reading the thoughts and actions of those with whom he interacted. For John Henry, *Doc* Holliday, gentleman gambler, the ability to appear less than focused served him very well indeed. While sending clouds of cigarette smoke heavenward, tippling from a bottomless bottle of the finest bourbon, cracking witty asides, or quoting from the great poets, Holliday distracted those with whom he gambled while he stayed sharp and focused beneath his facade. Little escaped his attention.

Deputy Marshal Wyatt Earp pushed in through the heavy

doors of the Long Branch. A gust of frigid air enveloped the solemn figure like a shroud before being released onto those unfortunates closest to the door. Earp stood for a moment, his sharp gaze sweeping the smoky haze of the crowded room before settling on Holliday. Doc noticed him as well, acknowledging his presence with an almost imperceptible nod.

Before the deputy, muscling his way through the crush of Saturday night revelers, reached his table, Holliday folded. Stuffing bills and coins into various coat pockets, he slipped a delicate ruby ring onto his pinky.

"Kate will enjoy this bauble if she sees fit to take leave of Wichita and return to this fair city."

Doc tipped his hat to those gamblers still at the table, "Good evening to you, gentlemen. It appears the law requires my presence."

Almost as an afterthought, Holliday plucked the full glass of whiskey from the table and tossed the shot back. "A waste of fine bourbon is a sin indeed."

Without so much as word of greeting, Earp grabbed Holliday by the arm, steering him as away from the crowd as was possible considering the packed house. At the farthest end of the bar, he relinquished his hold on the gambler. Doc straightened his rumpled coat and adjusted his cravat. Words of droll, albeit sarcastic, rebuke at the less than civil treatment accorded him by the local law died on John Holliday's lips, the agonized expression on the deputy's face a potent silencer. Close up, the haze of tobacco smoke less thick, the yellow glare of the overhead chandelier revealed more than just a seriousness of purpose on the lawman's face. It revealed horror and grief.

"My God, Wyatt, what's happened?"

The deputy swallowed hard, once, before clearing his

throat. One hand rested on the edge of the mahogany bar, the fingers tapping nervously. He looked away from Holliday, staring hard into the mirror before him.

"A young woman died tonight, murdered. She was with child." There was a pause, long enough for Holliday to ask the man to "go on, please."

Earp nodded, continuing to stare into the mirror. "Across the tracks on Locust Street, the first shack on the corner. The husband found the body though how he recognized her as his wife I can't guess." He lowered his chin to his chest, taking a moment to compose himself before continuing.

"I smelled it from outside, the blood, thick, like the stink from a slaughterhouse, and Holliday?" With effort the lawman raised his chin and gazed at the gambler's thin face reflected back at him in the mirror.

"Go on," Doc urged.

"Make no mistake, it *was* a slaughterhouse." Here the narrative ended as the deputy fought to control his emotions, wiping one hand back across his mouth as if to wash away the lingering taste of the blood.

"Bartender, two whiskeys here," Holliday ordered, but Earp shook his head. Doc corrected his mistake. "Make that one large whiskey and a coffee, black."

The deputy accepted the steaming brew, sipping while Doc nursed the bourbon, for once not slamming it down so fast, but savoring the taste of it upon his tongue. "The killer remains on the loose, I imagine."

"Killers, four of 'em. They wandered into the Alhambra. Guess they didn't know, maybe they didn't care, her blood was on their clothes. By the time somebody got round to sending for the law, they sobered up enough to realize the situation. They lit outta town headed for the territories."

"What is it you want of me?" Doc asked. He'd known

Earp just long enough to realize what the taciturn lawman *didn't* say was often more telling than what he did.

Earp's attention shifted from the coffee he held between both hands to Holliday, his gaze steady. "You're known to be good with a gun and pretty much fearless. All I want to know is if you're willing to prove both."

"Before I answer that, I'd like to say something."

Wyatt nodded.

"Although you know little of John Holliday aside from hearsay and innuendo, it appears you are willing to take a chance on me. Your faith is not taken lightly, I assure you. Therefore, I *am* willing to prove both."

Somewhat embarrassed by the stretch of silence following his statement and tired of toying with the whiskey he still held, Doc tossed the liquor back, blotting a drop or two from his moustache against a shirt cuff. It had little effect on the queasy feeling in the pit of his belly, and he signaled to the bartender for a refill which he disposed of quickly. He welcomed the hot burn of it. The queasy feeling vanished.

"What about the other members of the Dodge City constabulary? Might they take offense at an interloper stepping on their toes, so to speak? After all, marshal, I am no lawman."

"Charlie Bassett is off refereeing a range argument. Bat and Ed Masterson are over to Hays City on county business. That leaves me and Charlie Trask, and Trask is down with the measles. So long as he stays in the office he's all right, but as for going out in this weather." Earp angled his head toward the steamy window where a drover worked with his neckerchief to open a spot that allowed him to peer, squint-eyed, out at the storm. Snow, driven to horizontal by a vicious north wind, made the lawman's point.

"I'm certain no offense will be taken, Holliday," Earp added.

Doc extended his hand. "To seal the deal, marshal." The handshake between them was warm and solid.

Wyatt did not bother with thanks, but got straight to the point. "Meet me at the Dodge House Livery at dawn."

Occupied in loading supplies onto the horses tethered in front of the livery, Earp seemed taken aback by Holliday's wraith like appearance from out of a whirlwind of blowing snow. The surprise on the other man's face allowed Holliday a wicked, if quick, moment of satisfaction. It wasn't often he took Wyatt by surprise. "It's just me, marshal," he added for effect.

Earp nodded, his earlier surprise already past. He stopped Doc before Holliday could so much as check the cinch on his saddle. It was now the gambler's turn to be surprised. "Raise your right hand," Earp instructed.

Holliday did so, but not before first removing his glove.

"Do you, John Holliday, solemnly swear to uphold the laws of the city of Dodge and the state of Kansas to the best of your abilities?"

"I swear."

"You're now a deputy marshal. Put your glove back on and let's get goin'. Oh, before I forget, pin this to your coat." Earp handed Holliday a deputy's badge.

Doc stared dull-eyed at the badge of office and then, figuring he'd better pin it on before his fingers froze, he did so with a pride he had not thought possible. Already the numbing cold made shoving the pin through the heavy sheepskin and fastening it difficult.

Although the wind died down later, the unseasonable cold held and the hours in the saddle passed too slow. Wyatt's question came from out of the blue, jolting Doc from some rather more pleasant thoughts of warm saloons, pretty girls, and straight flushes. "Why did you come along, really?"

Doc took out a cigar and lit it with clumsy fingers. Inhaling, he felt the usual calming influence tobacco always provided. "Because you asked me," he said. Noticing his companion's wrinkled brow and the scowl playing around the lips beneath the thick mustache, Holliday elaborated.

"I was bored. An adventure sounded like just the ticket. I don't mind your company, though at times you are dour to the point of exasperation. However, you are honest and sincere to a fault, qualities I find admirable. You listen well. I like to talk. Simply put, we are perfect foils for each other."

Earp's scowl deepened. "Not to bring killers to justice, Holliday? This is just a lark to you?"

Doc shrugged. "I want justice for that murdered girl as much as you, but there are other motives for a man's actions. And, marshal, I do not believe this expedition will be anything even remotely resembling a lark." Finished with the cigar though the cigar itself was far from finished, Doc flipped the remainder away.

The pair crossed over into the Indian Territories late in the afternoon, having yet to stop for a meal or rest. They dismounted and continued at a brisk walk, allowing their horses a much needed break.

"Not that I am versed in the laws of the state of Kansas," Doc asked, "but do we have any actual jurisdiction in the territories?"

Plodding along, reins in hand and eyes focused forward, Earp replied, "We're two civilians intent on bringing killers to justice. Does that bother you?"

Doc lit yet another one of his endless cigars. "Not in the least. Besides, it's a bit late for that question now, don't you think?"

Sunset came upon them with little introduction, so it was a piece of good fortune when their trail led them to a small sod hut, a reminder of earlier times when the earthen structure most likely housed itinerant buffalo hunters. It provided shelter from the vicious changeability of the plains' weather, and little else, with its low door, no windows, and no fireplace to speak of aside from a hollowed out pit in the dirt floor holding the sad remains of a fire long ago burned out.

There was little in the way of wood to burn around the soddy, barely enough to make coffee and fry up some bacon for dinner, and none to spare for a fire against the creeping chill of night. The men slept in their heavy coats and covered themselves with wool blankets. Accommodations were far from luxurious, but comfortable enough in a make do situation.

Doc hunkered down for a long night. Sleep was slow to come and for the second time in less than a day, his companion surprised him by beginning a conversation.

"We've known each other for some months and I've never had reason to ask this before." Wyatt cleared his throat as if what was coming next was a mighty uncomfortable subject for him to broach.

Doc waited with interest for Earp to continue.

"By what name should I call you? We're apt to be in this for some time and callin' you Holliday lends itself to boredom."

For some reason, Wyatt's question amused Doc, and he smiled into the darkness. Few people asked him by what name he would like to be called. Most just made up their minds without bothering with formalities or pleasantries, yet here was this roughshod frontiersman being more gentlemanly than most gentlemen.

"My family calls me John Henry, but I consider that a pet name, more the name of a boy. Some call me John and others Doctor Holliday. A few just call me sonofabitch. And then there's Doc. You, sir, since you were kind enough to ask my preference, may choose for yourself." Holliday fumbled a hand out from within the many folds of his blanket. "Cigar?" He felt the stogie lifted from his fingers.

"Thanks, Doc."

"So it's settled then, I take it?" Holliday lit up.

"You have any brothers or sisters?"

Doc took several moments to answer. Family was something he tried not to think about too much or too often, the pain of separation a dreadful ache in a lonely man's heart. "I had a sister," he began. "She died before I was born."

He continued uninterrupted and for that he was grateful, for if Wyatt stopped him to question or to comment about his mother's death when John was still a boy, about the schism which developed between him and his father after Major Holliday's precipitant remarriage, about the brutal aftermath of war on a conquered people, he wasn't certain he could have continued with any sense of detachment. Finished at last, he lay staring with dry, burning eyes into the surrounding blackness, grateful for its cover. Wyatt's low offered, "Goodnight, Doc," went unanswered.

Finishing off yet another smoke, Doc flipped the butt into a far corner, pulled the blanket closer, and tried to sleep. Through the open doorway he heard the sound of the plains. Mostly it was the wind, rushing, always rushing, as if in a terrible hurry to get somewhere fast. At this time of year there was no rustling of high prairie grass, but a soulless wail that swept across the bare landscape, sometimes accompanied by the mournful song of a coyote calling for its mate. In this lonely world, John Holliday felt right at home. Sleep did finally come, but it was restless.

Morning broke noticeably warmer, the bone-chilling cold of the previous day only a memory. The lawmen started out with no hot coffee and no breakfast to speak of aside from a bit of leathery beef jerky.

"Good thing I've always taken care of my teeth. Eating this is like masticating a boot sole." Holliday tore off another stringy strip, grinding away with purpose. Forgoing water, he pulled a full bottle of whiskey from the depths of his saddlebag

"Something to wash down breakfast, marshal?"

Holliday extended the bottle to Wyatt who looked at him with a disapproving expression and a firm shake of the head. "I loaded the supplies and that bottle wasn't among 'em."

"No need to apologize, marshal. You can't be called upon to remember everything." Holliday peeled away the paper and uncorked the bottle, taking one long pull, then another. The whiskey burned going down, but warmed his stomach and made it at least feel full. It also served to warm the slender body. Replacing the cork, Doc stowed the bottle back among his things and changed the subject.

"So, preacher, aside from there being four of these killers, what else do you know?" Doc did not fail to notice Earp's furrowed brow at the term *preacher,* though Wyatt said nothing.

"I'm thinkin' they'll steer clear of Fort Smith, too much law there."

"Wyatt, that leaves a great deal of territory they won't steer clear of."

"I know, but when I was checkin' on one of 'em, J B Dixon by name, I saw a pattern. Him and his gang rode a loop last year, up from Guthrie in the territories, north to Deadwood in the Dakotas, across into Iowa, back over to Nebraska, and down into Kansas. Back then they seemed more interested in small potatoes: thieving, horse stealing, and robbin' miners of their pokes. This year it's rape and murder, seven killings in the past ten months. I'll just bet they're gonna follow the loop back around."

"And that would bring them to where after this?"

"I'd say Fort Gibson."

"A guess then?"

"Let's just say an educated one, unless you have a better idea?"

"Fort Gibson it is." Holliday pondered several moments. "Why hasn't anyone caught them yet, I wonder?"

"That's the part scares me. Can't be nobody didn't care enough to run 'em down. Maybe they're so greasy they slipped away back into a hole somewhere, or could be they're just that good nobody wanted to try. You worried, Doc?"

Holliday met his companion's question and inquiring gaze with typical directness. "I would be a fool if I said no."

CHAPTER 2

Winter's last blast gave way to the first moisture laden breezes of spring and the promise of better weather to come. Doc delighted in the warmer temperatures. Shrugging out of his sheepskin jacket, he folded the garment across the saddle in front of him.

Wyatt had long since shed his. "Take a while for you to warm up, does it, Doc? Sort of like a lizard needin' a hot rock?"

Holliday stretched his arms toward the distant sun, raising his face to meet the welcoming rays. "Damn straight, marshal. In Georgia cold weather is fleeting, like a pretty girl's smile. It doesn't hang on as it does out here." His voice took on a dreamy tone. "Back home the magnolias are in bloom, lilacs, roses, wisteria. The scent is intoxicating. All you have here," he glanced around, and a look of disdain settled onto his face, "is dust and scrub brush and too much of both."

"If you like Georgia so much, then why leave? Runnin' from something? The law maybe?"

Holliday turned in the saddle to face Earp, his expression anything but friendly. Anger churned hot in his gut, anger he found difficult to control. An invisible line had been crossed.

"Why I left my home is no concern of yours, marshal. It has no bearing whatsoever on the business at hand. Suffice to say, if I could return to Georgia, I would gladly do so. I might not have brothers or even a mother, but what family I have, I hold most dear. Rest assured, if or when I deem it necessary you know of my past, I will inform you. That is at my discretion, not yours." Doc delivered the tirade in a low, rather menacing tone which appeared to have the desired effect. The lawman seemed chagrined. Perhaps he meant no offense after all. Doc hoped that to be the case. "Do we have an understanding?"

"We have."

As quickly as Holliday's anger flared it ebbed just as fast. *"Good.* I'm glad that's past," he said. Tugging a pair of cigars from his vest pocket he handed one across to his companion. "Smoke, marshal?"

With the sun threatening to dip below the horizon, the men were pleased when a small ranch came into view. "Maybe we can fill our canteens there," Wyatt said. "Looks like a right enough place to me. Nicest spread we've come across so far."

"Indeed and perhaps, if the lady of the house is kind, we can prevail upon her for a bite of supper." Doc sighed. It seemed forever since he'd sat down for a meal at a table, eaten from china plates, or drunk coffee from anything but a heat conducting tin cup. He ran his tongue over the last blister raised on his lip from just such a torture device.

Wyatt rode up close. "You miss the homey comforts, Doc?"

Holliday couldn't tell by his companion's expression if Earp mocked him or not. He settled on not. "You read me like a book, sir. I do. You might say roughing it has never been my strong suit."

"I've done a lot of roughing it, sleeping out cold, wet or both, eating half cooked game and poor coffee, and all I have to say is it never gets any easier." Wyatt pulled his hat down low and urged his horse into a trot, calling back over his shoulder, "Let's see if the lady of the house might find it in her heart to set two extra places at the dinner table."

Doc needed no encouragement to follow.

They did not expect the sight which greeted them. Between the house and barn, a man toiled over a shallow grave, his work with the shovel slow going. Every other spade full or so he stopped to blot his eyes against a filthy shirt cuff. Near him stood two boys, one about six years old, the other perhaps ten, the younger sobbing, the older standing stiff and silent.

Doc and Wyatt rode up to the house and tied their horses to the hitching post. On the narrow porch and covered by a blood soaked quilt were what appeared to be two bodies. While Wyatt checked, Doc walked over to where the farmer labored. Oddly enough, no one paid any attention to his approach and he waited in silence, hat in hand, for Earp.

In the nearby corral stood a sorry looking gray gelding, its condition in vivid contrast to its well tended surroundings. Healed scars as well as new wounds made by sharp-roweled spurs scored the animal's flanks, and the horse hung its head in misery, too dull even to swat the flies which worried its open sores. Lifeless eyes watched the proceedings with little interest.

At Wyatt's approach Doc turned, Earp leaning in close to whisper his findings, "A boy of about twelve and his mother, hacked to death." He paused, taking a deep breath, the pain reflected in his eyes more revealing than words, "just like in Dodge, exactly like in Dodge."

"We're on the right track then," Doc answered.

"We're on the right track," Wyatt replied.

The marshals took over the grave digging from the exhausted farmer. In darkness they finished and in darkness the bodies of a woman and her son were put into the ground. Like the young mother in Dodge, they would find no peace until their killers found justice.

"I didn't want it like this, under these circumstances, I mean." Doc topped off the coffee in Wyatt's cup with fresh. The cup wasn't fine china, but plain earthenware and the plates they ate upon the same. "I'd rather sleep every night out of doors in pouring rain and drink swamp water than...." Pulling out a chair he slumped into it, elbows resting on the table, head buried in trembling hands. Behind him, in one of the tiny bedrooms off the kitchen came the sound of muffled heartbreak.

"Make no mistake, we'll get 'em, Doc. We'll get 'em."

Holliday felt the gentle pressure of fingers against his shoulder, but didn't look up or reply. Wyatt said it all and said it best.

Hours on horseback meant nothing to Doc. He'd gotten used to the pounding of bone and muscle against saddle, and the creaking of leather against leather became familiar and almost comforting. For two days he and Wyatt followed the killers' trail. Four men on horseback, one riding a big bay mare taken from the farmer whose wife and son they'd killed, his own lamed animal left in exchange. One good thing and one only came from the horror, a new clue to finding the murderers.

The farmer, having once had a fine horse stolen from him, wanted no repeat of the deed. From that day onward, he incised a V into each shoe of every horse he owned. It was this trail the Kansas lawmen followed when earth and conditions allowed.

For more than an hour Wyatt and Doc searched the parched ground, both down off their mounts, eyes narrowed, attention focused, hoping, praying to pick up the lost track.

"Well that tears it." Wyatt kicked at a chunk of rock, taking his frustrations out on the inanimate object.

"I assume this means you haven't discovered anything of merit?" Holliday rose to his feet, stretching.

"Not a thing. We came so close."

Holliday lit up a smoke, holding one out to Wyatt. Earp stalked over and took it, his anger at what he perceived as failure obvious to anyone with half an eye. He accepted a light from Doc's burning cigar. For several moments they smoked in silence while the tobacco worked its calming magic on both.

Doc flicked a stubborn ash from the end of his cheroot. "We still aren't out of the race, marshal. What about your original guess as to the killers' whereabouts? Fort Gibson, wasn't it?" Taking great pains to form his lips just so, Doc blew several smoke rings in a row, each one closer to perfect than the one before. If Wyatt was impressed, he didn't acknowledge it. He did, however, acknowledge Doc's question.

"We lost their tracks five miles after the Fort Gibson cutoff. I really don't think...." Dropping the cigar at his feet, Earp crushed it into the ground with a boot heel, "But why not? Why, if they thought they might be followed, why not circle back?" A smile, or at least what appeared to be an effort on the lawman's part to produce a smile, played around Wyatt's eyes. "Fort Gibson it is. Thanks, Doc."

Holliday barely avoided being cuffed on the back by his reenergized partner by swinging up into the saddle and turning his mount south. "Fort Gibson it is, and the last man there buys lunch."

Putting spurs to mount, Doc kicked his horse into a run leaving Wyatt no choice but to follow. The man could ride, that was certain. Holliday flew across the open terrain, lean body hugging the saddle, offering the wind little to resist. His light weight gave him an added edge when it came to Earp overtaking him, or at least catching up. So it was that Doc arrived in Fort Gibson some time before Wyatt, horse lathered, rider exhilarated.

Dismounting, Doc slapped the Stetson against his pants raising a cloud of dust. He attempted, with limited success, to brush the same from his shirt, at last just slapping at it. The released cloud made him cough and it was several minutes before he could stop, eyes watering, nose running. Taking out a linen handkerchief, he solved the runny nose problem, tucking the used kerchief into a trouser pocket.

While Holliday extricated himself from the dust dilemma, a man stepped onto the boardwalk. Catching movement in the plate glass window of the haberdashers in front of him, Doc looked up. Since the man was a stranger to him, he went back to his own business of tying his mount to the hitching post. Preoccupied with the chore, Doc still managed to keep the man's movements under close scrutiny in the window's reflection.

Although the stranger wore clothing typical of the sporting set, it was the uniform of a gambler down on his luck: frayed cuffs poked out from beneath a frock coat worn shiny, while a silk cravat stained with spots of undetermined origin pointed to its use as a napkin.

The man appeared middle-aged and possessed of average height. In fact, most things about him were average. A bowler hat sat at a somewhat rakish angle upon his head, and he was in sorry need of a haircut. Even his reddish moustache needed a good trimming, the ragged tips curled down almost into his mouth.

The gun belt at his waist sported a Colt revolver in a plain holster, nickel-plated with bone grips. No matter how low in his luck the gambler slipped, he appeared to keep the badge of his profession, his fine pistol, in good repair.

Standing on the boardwalk not ten feet from Holliday, the gambler called out to Doc in a gruff tone, the words meant to insult, "You, boy."

Holliday was not looking for trouble, but then trouble had no difficulty in finding him. He'd try tact. "I left boyhood some years back, sir, so you are mistaken. Perhaps you've taken me for someone else?"

There was no need to turn around just yet. Holliday could see fine in the glass. What he saw, besides the stranger, was his own reflection: hat hanging down behind his back on stampede strings, wavy hair wind blown, tall and lean and dressed like a typical cowhand. In all fairness to the down-on-his-luck gambler, Doc figured he did appear somewhat younger than his twenty-six years. The look was not one he often cultivated, that of the cosmopolitan man-about-town. He thought he might just give this fellow the benefit of the doubt and felt quite proud of himself for coming to such a conclusion, for all of a second and a half.

The gambler's voice came again, louder this time and annoying. "Boy, I know you, boy, and I ain't mistaken as to who you are."

The benefit of the doubt flew out the window along with Doc's good intentions. Something was eating away at this fellow, and he seemed bound to have his day. "Well, I am not acquainted with you, sir. That leaves me at a disadvantage."

As Doc turned to face his accuser, the stranger became aware Holliday was armed with pistols at both hip and shoulder. His pale eyes bugged out at the sight, and he swallowed with difficulty around the lump forming in his throat. His ruddy complexion paled, yet to his credit he seemed determined to finish what he'd started.

"You killed my brother in Fort Griffin. You're Doc Holliday."

A knot of curious people gathered. No one blinked at the name. Holliday was an unknown commodity in these parts.

"I *am* John Holliday, but I killed no one in Fort Griffin."

The man stepped a bit closer, wagging a finger at Doc for emphasis. "You tryin' to tell me you don't recall Ed Bailey?"

Doc did recall and the memories were less than pleasant, "Ed Bailey, of course. He cheated at cards and attempted to draw on me when I called him on it. I was faster, and he was run out of town. I will admit to humiliating the man. He deserved that and more. However, I did not injure him in any way other than his pride. I would've said his dignity, but he was not possessed of that quality. If you heard otherwise, you were lied to." Out of the corner of his eye, Doc noticed Wyatt rein in down the block, dismount, and then squat down, poking at the dirt. Maybe he'd found something pertaining to the killers. But right now there were other things to occupy Doc's attention, and he blocked out all save the ranting man standing before him.

"It's you who's lyin'. My brother's dead and you killed him."

Without waiting for Holliday's response, Bailey went for his pistol. Falling on difficult times proved no detriment to his speed. The man was fast. No one on the street moved. A single shot rang out. Bailey spun around, his Colt flying from nerveless fingers as Doc's bullet slammed into his forearm, through flesh, muscle, and tendon and out, burying itself in the boardwalk several feet beyond.

Holliday's speed led a bystander to comment on it to the tall man standing mute at his shoulder. "That was some shot. I didn't even see that fella draw." A whistle of appreciation followed.

But Wyatt *did see* and rumor and innuendo paled at reality. Holliday never raised his voice, never broke a sweat. Even now he appeared cool and calm, almost disinterested, as he holstered his weapon. He could have killed Bailey as easily as not, yet chose only to wound him, an impressive example of skill coupled with self-control.

Pushing through the crowd and eager to get close to the shooter was the town sheriff, a freckle-faced youth of about twenty in whose hand a .44 caliber pistol trembled. The untried youngster was coming up against one of the great unknowns, a shooter of obvious talent. Was the man behind the gun good or bad?

"Put up yer hands," he ordered.

"It was self-defense, sheriff," Holliday offered as the lawman motioned one of the locals over to disarm him.

"Sure was, Ephraim, self-defense, plain and simple. Anybody else'll tell ya the same." The local lifted both Colts, the nickel-plated .45 and the walnut gripped .36. Doc hoped to get them back, as they were serviceable weapons, though the loss of the plainer pistol would be felt the most. As a gift from his Uncle John upon his graduation from dental college, it was irreplaceable.

Turning aside, the local spit into the street, wiping his lips on his shirt cuff. "Finest exhibition I seen in some time." He grinned up into Holliday's face, exposing yellow stained teeth.

Doc hid his disgust. "Don't forget my knife," he pointed

out. Lifting the narrow blade from the sheath at his belt, he reversed it with ease and passed it handle-first to the sheriff's helper who in turn handed all over to the lawman.

Earp stepped up next to Holliday and introduced himself. "My name is Wyatt Earp. I'm a marshal from Dodge City. This man is my deputy, and it *was* self-defense." Wyatt was ignored.

"Gotta take it before the judge," the sheriff wagged his pistol at Holliday. "Let's go."

Wyatt shrugged. Doc was not encouraged.

The courthouse was a one story, frame building with a false front. Not much to look at from the outside, still not much on the inside either, but it served its purpose. The judge appeared on time, and the hearing commenced.

Sheriff Ephraim Johnston stepped forward, hat in hand. "This here fella discharged his pistol on the city streets, your honor, wounded a man in the arm, fella named Bailey."

The judge, a smallish man in his fifties, peered down at Holliday from a high perch behind a massive desk. Doc's first impression of the man was that he resembled an owl as the judge's large eyes blinked at him from behind thick-lensed spectacles. He also wondered if the owl's reputation as a harbinger of bad luck would come into play here. He hoped that would not be the case.

His honor wasted no time getting the ball rolling. "First off I need a name, son, and an occupation."

"Your honor, my name is John H. Holliday. My occupation is dentist. At this time I am also acting as a deputy marshal for the city of Dodge."

The judge squinted down over the lenses of his spectacles at the young man standing before him. "*Doctor* Holliday is it? Do you realize doctor, or is it marshal, that you have no jurisdiction here?"

Before Holliday could speak, Wyatt interrupted, "If I may answer, your honor?"

"When I hear who you are and what your business is, then I will decide if you may speak in my courtroom."

"My name is Wyatt Earp, and I'm a deputy marshal out of Dodge City, and yes, sir, we realize we have no legal jurisdiction in the territories."

Oh, good, preacher, very good so far, Doc thought, raising his eyes heavenward. *More help from you and I'll be locked up till I'm old and gray. I should live so long.*

"All right then, since you are both well aware you lack any sort of jurisdiction," *here it comes*, Holliday imagined the worst, "what made you, doctor, draw your weapon and fire it at another man on the streets of my town?"

"He drew on me first. I had no choice but to defend myself."

The judge looked skeptical. "So this Bailey just picked you outta the crowd and threatened to shoot you?"

"No, sir, Mr. Bailey accused me of killing his brother in Fort Griffin, Texas some months back. I did not kill Ed Bailey. I barely knew the man. A telegram to that town will prove me out."

"Sheriff Johnston, did this Bailey fellow draw first? Is this a case of self-defense?"

"I didn't see it myself, your honor, but word on the street is this here Doctor Holliday was just defendin' himself."

"Have you ever killed a man, Doctor Holliday?" The judge squinted down at Doc as if hoping to read the truth from an expression, a twitch, a look. When Holliday answered, "No, sir, I have never killed a man," His honor seemed satisfied, though a few rather tense moments ticked by before he got down to the business of passing judgment.

"I could wire Fort Griffin to confirm your story, doctor,

and I still might just do that, but I believe you're telling me the truth so, Doctor John Holliday, I fine you ten dollars for discharging a weapon within city limits. A repeat offense will find you doing thirty days. Pay me and case dismissed." At that, the magistrate slammed down the gavel.

Doc handed the judge up a ten dollar bill, and considered himself a lucky man.

"What are you two doing so far from Dodge?" The magistrate scribbled out a receipt which Holliday folded and slipped into his waistcoat pocket.

"We're tracking four killers. They murdered a girl in Dodge and another woman some two days' ride from here." Wyatt replied.

"And you believe they're in Fort Gibson?" The judge stepped down from behind his desk, removed his robe, and draped it over the polished railing.

"I'd say they *were* here. I found a set of tracks matching one of their horses outside the mercantile. They headed east out of town."

Doc felt a weight lift from his shoulders at the news. For so many reasons he wanted to bring those men to justice and now to find out there was still a chance.

"They only kill women, these fellows?" The judge asked.

"Unless someone gets in the way," Doc added. "They murdered a witness, the victim's twelve year old son."

"Scum's what they are. It would please me no end to get those men in my court. I'd see justice done, I can tell you." The judge sighed, but brushed aside business for a more pleasurable pursuit. "I was about to get a bite over to the cafe before the sheriff called me in. Join me, boys?"

"The offer is temping, sir, but we need to get back on the trail. Perhaps next time?" Doc figured he spoke for himself and for Wyatt, but Earp had other plans.

"I think we can take the time to get a decent feed,

Doc. If I could send a supply list over to the mercantile, they can fill it while we eat." Earp turned to Holliday. "What do you think?"

Surprised, Doc agreed. "I am with you, marshal. Let's break our fast."

The three men strode uptown to the restaurant where a table was set and the group seated. Holliday's stomach grumbled, causing Doc more than a little embarrassment. Luckily the food arrived.

Doc shoveled in steak, potatoes, beans and bread, washing it all down with large cups of coffee. When he finished, settling back in the chair with a contented smile upon his face and a warm full feeling in his stomach, he realized Wyatt was watching him. Earp appeared bemused, as if he'd never seen Holliday eat before.

"The food was quite good, didn't you think?" Doc asked, blotting away one last stray crumb from his lips.

"I'd say so," Wyatt agreed. "Especially since the last meal we had in any sort of restaurant was tortillas and frijoles with the frijoles hard as rock and so spiced with chilies, the whole mess was nigh on to inedible."

Doc smiled, turning his attention to the judge. "But even worse, the coffee was thick as mud and laced with chicory, much to Marshal Earp's disgust. This food is a great improvement and, your honor," Holliday reached out, pushing the judge's silver coins back towards him, "luncheon is on the marshal."

The judge grinned. Wyatt's expression was not quite as pleasant as he counted coins out onto the table. When Doc reminded him not to forget the tip, Earp's eyes took on an icy expression and Holliday swore he noticed Wyatt's lips move beneath the brushy mustache, a curse perhaps?

"Good luck to you boys," the judge said over handshakes,

"You'll need it. All you can get or make."

Out on the boardwalk, Doc stretched. He felt good, very good indeed. His belly was full, the recurrent cough had yet to plague him, and the situation with Bailey turned out all right after all.

"If you're ready, Doc, let's grab our supplies and head out. We can make some decent time before dark."

Holliday nodded. "Indeed, sir. Let's ride."

CHAPTER 3

The road was an actual road in that it was a wide spot between clumps of sagebrush and little more. Being hard packed made travel easy, but tracking nigh on to impossible. Once again they lost the killers' tracks. Each time a fork branched off, Wyatt and Doc were down off their mounts casting about like bloodhounds on the scent. For the better part of a day, the search continued in vain until at last Earp let out a yelp of discovery. "Here. They broke off the road here."

Holliday hunkered down, checking the place Wyatt pointed out. They exchanged brief, tired smiles with Doc adding, "Tracks look fresh. They must've gotten more sleep than us. We can't be too far behind."

If indeed the killers were as close as reckoned, stealth and vigilance were crucial. Soon the sweeping, open plains gave way to lush, rolling hills dotted with trees of significant size, trees large enough to provide cover to a shooter.

Darkness fell, but the lawmen pushed on. A chill came

up, forcing Holliday to rummage through his saddlebags in search of a light coat he shrugged into, grateful for its warmth. Wyatt seemed comfortable in shirtsleeves.

At first it was only a slight tickle in the back of his throat, slight, but persistent. Soon the tickle turned into a wheeze Doc could not—as much as he tried and he tried mightily—to ignore. Then, just to clear the thickness in his chest Doc coughed. Once it gained a foothold, the cough often turned pernicious and unshakeable. It took Wyatt no time at all to notice.

"Catching cold?"

"Don't know. Maybe." His illness was his alone, a private and personal hell, not to be discussed. Luckily, this time the cough died off. Riding in to a nest of vipers was one thing, telegraphing the visit quite another.

The pair rode on in silence, aware of what might lie in wait for them. The hunters could become the hunted. Doc reined in his horse, pointing off into the distance. A pale glimmer of light blinked off and on, off and on like a small beacon, a tiny lighthouse in a sea of dark undulating hillocks.

The two continued on another half mile or so before dismounting and tying their horses to a tree. Removing their spurs and leaving them behind, they took rifles from scabbards as well as extra ammo. They crept toward the light, the flickering illumination mesmerizing. *It's drawing us in*, Doc thought, *like moths to a flame*.

Closing in on the light source, the lawmen noticed it issued from a half-shuttered window in what was left of a squatter's shack. A decent sized bush outside the window moved with the breeze, defusing the light, making it appear to flicker.

Four horses stood out front, tethered to a makeshift hitching post. In the blackness there was no certain way to tell if these animals belonged to the killers or just some wayward pilgrims. This was not a time to jump to conclusions.

Loud voices issued from the dilapidated structure and among them the unmistakable voice of a woman. Wyatt and Doc exchanged glances. The woman did not sound in distress, at the moment. This changed things. Another life might be at stake. Delay was no longer optional.

Wyatt signaled Doc to go around the back. Doc nodded, moving with great care through overgrown grass and bracken and soon disappeared around the corner. Perhaps two boards in and just about eyeball height, appeared a knothole which Holliday used to good advantage. Peeking through offered a panoramic view of the hut's interior and of those within.

There was indeed a woman in the company of two men. All three appeared filthy, clothing stained, hair unkempt.

The woman looked like a trollop, though she dressed as a man. Dark pants were tucked into knee high boots. A striped shirt hung well off her shoulders and her hair was cut short like a boy's.

One of the men, his black hair sticking straight up from his scalp like wet feathers, clasped the woman to him, struggling to kiss her as she protested. Was this coquettishness on her part, or was she distressed at the unwanted advances. "Aw, come on, give us a little kiss," he coaxed.

Again the woman struggled to free herself. A backhanded slap against his cheek seemed only to spur his advances. "Knock it off, Dix."

Dix. Is this the J.B. Dixon of whom Wyatt spoke? Doc thought, *yes.* He prayed Earp also heard.

The second man looked different from the first in every conceivable way. Short and rotund, the fellow's hair was as fair as the other's was dark, while his eyes were the milky blue of opaque marbles. As he walked, the Texas style spurs he wore jingled. The mistreated horse at the murdered woman's farm had been mutilated by just that type of spur.

More parts of the puzzle coming together, more bits of the whole, Holliday thought.

There being four horses, at least one man appeared to be missing. The woman might have ridden double with one of them. Doc felt a sudden rush of apprehension. *Where was the other?*

Almost as soon as the question sprang to mind, Holliday felt the sharp jab of a pistol barrel in his back. "Drop the rifle." The fetid breath near his cheek was almost bad enough to cut through Doc's anger as he tossed the Winchester aside. How had he allowed himself to be taken so damned easily? The first time Wyatt needed him and he failed. Holliday's captor removed Doc's pistols as well as his knife and thrust the now unarmed man through the back door. Doc hit the dirt floor hard.

"See what I found?" The speaker was the third man of the group, broad shouldered with a shaven head and brushy mustache, and if Doc was seeing right, yellow eyes. A wide sombrero hung down his back. Like the others he stank of bad teeth, unwashed body, whiskey and death.

Grabbing the already disarmed Holliday by his jacket, Doc's captor dragged him upright, twisting one arm behind his back. Holliday swore beneath his breath eliciting laughter from the men, but interest from the woman.

She pushed away from her admirer, her curiosity piqued by the new man. Seemed her previous behavior had been of a teasing nature.

"Name's Pearl, Pearl McLaughlin. What's yours, honey?" she purred, closing in on the imprisoned Holliday.

Doc struggled, appalled by the woman, by her mousy hair alive with vermin and her innocent appearing eyes whose depth lacked any sort of human warmth.

"Don't hurt him too bad, Horton. I might have some use for him," Pearl said.

Horton grabbed a handful of hair and jerked Doc's head back. At the same instant, he applied pressure to the pinned arm, half lifting the slim man off his feet, offering Pearl free access, and forcing Doc to grit his teeth at the pain.

Pearl touched Holliday's face, running a broken-nailed finger across his lips, standing on tiptoe to look at him full on. "Mighty purty," she giggled, attempting to kiss the struggling man on the mouth.

Even as Doc fought to free himself, his mind raced. Pearl was no prisoner, but one of the killers. It was not four men. It was three men and a woman.

"Aw, come on, Pearl. What you need him for, huh?" A jealous reaction, Horton whined.

Pearl ignored her cohort, focusing all her attention on Holliday as she gazed into his eyes. Perhaps hoping to see interest there, but she was disappointed. The handsome stranger's icy glare held nothing but contempt.

Pearl drew back a hand and slapped him with as much strength as her hurt feelings could muster and that was plenty. Holliday's head snapped back and a bead of blood formed on his bottom lip.

Pearl's seductive purr changed to a grating, edgy growl, "what you doin' here anyways, purty boy?"

Doc ignored the question, his attention diverted to the tiny window visible over her head, the black rectangle from behind whose dark cloak he hoped Wyatt watched. Doc knew to act soon might be his only option, *if* he planned on living much longer.

"I know what he's doin' here, Pearl. He's a lawman. You a lawman, pretty boy, huh? Or maybe he's one of them bounty hunters lookin' to get himself a big reward." Laughing, Horton jerked up hard on the prisoner's pinned arm.

Again Pearl leaned in close to her victim, taunting him.

"You might end up gettin' somethin' awright, but I wouldn't count on no reward, purty boy. You're right nice on the eyes, but you don't know how to treat no lady. Don't worry none about that, though, 'cause ole Pearl is a prime teacher, ain't I boys?"

"Sure are Pearly. That's right," the men bobbed their heads in unison. It appeared not only was Pearl a member of the gang, but their unopposed leader.

Little in the cluttered, dim room offered Doc much in the way of hope. The man holding him was well armed, and the other two were no less heeled. On a table near one of the kerosene lanterns lay an amazing assemblage of edged weapons of every sort and style, just the type to wreak carnage on a human body. Not a pretty picture.

Doc formulated a plan. At the time of Holliday's capture, Horton had tucked both Doc's pistols into his belt. All Holliday had to do was get a hand on one of his weapons, much easier thought than accomplished, and he had to trust Wyatt to come in on things at the right moment. Not giving himself time to come to his senses, Doc acted.

The woman hovered near, her rather obvious interest in him overwhelming her previous anger. *It might work. It might just work*, Doc thought. Swallowing revulsion like a bitter pill, he took on the persona of interested suitor. Gazing into her eyes, those cold, soulless eyes, Doc's own warmed and softened. In his most charming southern drawl, he sought to buy time. "I just stumbled onto your place and thought I might come in out of the cold. Tell your flunky here to release me, and I'll prove it to you, Pearl."

"Leave loose a him. Let's hear what he's got ta say." Pearl yanked Holliday by the coat, jerking him toward her and away from his captor.

As soon as he felt himself free, Doc pushed the woman back and spun around, yanking both pistols from Horton's belt and firing the .45 into the man's belly. Horton died writhing on the dirt floor, Doc's slug blowing a hole clear through him.

Wyatt fired through the window, his shots finding their mark in the second man's chest, killing him instantly. In the confusion that followed, Dixon leaped over the bodies of his dead cohorts and ran out the back door, leaving Doc to deal with Pearl. The woman wasted no time bolting out the front for the horses. Pulling a rifle from the saddle of the nearest animal, she turned and fired at the advancing Holliday. Silhouetted against the backlit shack, he made a perfect target.

Even knowing the extent of the murders she'd committed and the heartless cruelty exhibited in those acts, John Holliday remained cognizant of the fact that Pearl McLaughlin was still a woman. That awareness initiated a moral dilemma which in turn caused a split second of indecision. Doc hesitated, allowing Pearl to get off the first shot. It was a mistake he would seldom, if ever, allow himself again.

Her bullet tore through the side of his loose fitting jacket, but his shot was true. Pearl shrieked once, dropped the rifle and clawed at her throat. Blood spurted from between her fingers. Like an automaton, she walked forward several steps, body rigid, fingers clutching at the spewing wound. Pearl sank down almost at Doc's feet, her dead eyes staring up at him. John Holliday felt numb.

His attention was drawn away from the scene when several shots rang out, echoing back at him in the dark. They seemed to come from two different locations, but it was difficult to gauge their origin with any exactitude.

Holliday holstered his pistols, bent down and grabbed Pearl's rifle, checking to be sure it was well loaded. Circling, he listened for more shots. None were forthcoming. Already pale bands of gray and pink lightened the eastern sky. He called out for Earp, his voice reverberating back at him. Hollow silence answered.

The topography of the land was much different in the light, much changed from what it had been just miles back. Some thousand yards beyond the shack was an abrupt drop off.

Glancing over the edge, Holliday could not see the bottom as daylight had yet to penetrate that far. Shadows filled the void. He turned away, calling again, but wary. The last killer remained at large.

Searching for Wyatt proved fruitless, and Holliday despaired of finding the marshal alive. As a last resort he fired off three shots, aware the sound carried much further than his voice. A returning shot answered, then two more in quick succession. They issued from the drop off.

Holliday ran toward the cliff, out of breath when he arrived. Full daylight offered a clear view as to what had occurred there. Someone had slipped down the steep embankment in the dark, probably unaware the drop even existed. "Wyatt? Wyatt?"

This time there was a reply, albeit a weak one. "Here. We're both here."

Doc tossed the rifle aside. Choosing the path he considered of least resistance, he slipped and slid his way to the bottom, hoping he wasn't raining rocks onto Wyatt's head. Part of the trip was made on his backside, but at least he never lost his balance, quite a feat in itself as the decline was more abrupt than it appeared from the top.

Doc came upon Dixon first, Dixon's head twisted upon his neck at an impossible angle. Quite dead. Wyatt lay about twenty feet farther on, and although he looked bad, Holliday's relief at seeing him alive knew no bounds. It seemed Earp's relief was just as great. As Doc knelt at his side, Wyatt held a hand out to him and a smile brightened the bloody countenance.

Doc took the hand and returned the smile. "You look like hell."

"Cracked my head good when I fell," Wyatt mumbled. "The blood blinded me. If Dixon hadn't a broken his damned fool neck…"

"No more talking. Let me look at that." With great care Holliday examined the gash in Earp's scalp above his right eye. Like most wounds of that nature it had bled profusely and continued to bleed.

Holliday untied the bandanna from his own neck, folded it and applied pressure to the gash. After long moments the bleeding stopped. "Anything hurt besides your head?"

"No, but that's enough, believe me."

"I want to sit you up so I can check your back and ribs. We'll do it slow and easy. Let me do the work and if anything hurts, let out a yell."

Earp did not cry out in pain, but when Doc laid him back against the ground, the hand he'd used to support Wyatt's head was slick with blood, a revelation Holliday met with an expletive.

"What's a matter?" Earp's words were slurred.

"You've got a wound in the back of your head, and it's bleeding pretty bad. I'm going to roll your over onto your stomach."

Holliday took out one of his many white linen handkerchiefs and attempted to staunch the blood so he could get some idea of the extent of the injury. Like the other gash, it was lengthy. However, this went far deeper and a flap of scalp hung loose. Blood soaked Wyatt's shirt collar.

Doc removed his coat and folded it, placing the makeshift pillow beneath Wyatt's cheek. "I'm going up to get the horses and my bag. Do *not* move. I'll be back soon."

As Doc passed Dixon's body, his gaze went automatically to the corpse. Blood oozed from the nose and mouth, and the open staring eyes were already glazed over. If the killer's neck hadn't broken in the fall, Wyatt would've been a sitting duck.

Holliday looked around for the best place, the safest place to bring the horses down. From where he stood, it was clear the only choice lay fifty or so yards farther down the gully, the angle there being much less steep. Scrambling up was easy.

Time being of the essence, Doc trotted back to where the horses were tethered. Picking up the discarded spurs, he stored them in Earp's saddlebag and swung up into the saddle. Holding the bridle of the riderless animal in one hand, he kicked his own horse into a trot.

The ride down the embankment was hairier than Doc anticipated, with the riderless horse almost losing his footing on the loose rocks. The animal recovered, but not before almost wrenching Holliday from the saddle.

Kneeling at Wyatt's side, Doc laid a hand on the injured man's back, feeling deep even respirations, a good sign. "Wyatt? Come on now, Wyatt," he urged, hoping Earp would respond.

"I need to take some stitches in your scalp. The bleeding hasn't stopped, and the wound won't heal well without them."

"Whatever you say," Wyatt murmured.

Doc exchanged one of the bedrolls for the coat beneath Earp's head. Opening his saddlebags, he removed a flat leather case. Inside, each nestled in its own hollowed out section, rested the silver instruments of the dental profession. From the various instruments he chose a curved needle and a blunt-nosed scissors. Rummaging through one of the case's many pockets he also located silk suture material.

Another search through his saddlebags produced several bar towels. Using one of the towels dampened with spirits from the whiskey bottle, Doc eased the flap of Wyatt's scalp back into place, patting the edges of the gash together. This produced a response from Earp, a sharp intake of breath and a graphic expletive.

"Sorry." Doc poured whiskey onto the palm of one hand and rubbed the liquor between his hands in a washing motion, drying them on the used towel. He wanted nothing he had touched, or that had touched him, especially in the killers' hovel, to communicate itself in any way to the patient.

Using the scissors, Doc cut the hair away from the deep wound. He lifted imbedded hairs from the injury one strand at a time. There appeared no extraneous matter in the wound, no dirt or gravel.

"You have to lie still now, Wyatt. This'll hurt, but I'll be as fast and easy as I can."

Holliday patted Wyatt's shoulder once in commiseration. The only time the patient moved or complained was at the initial stitch, an involuntary twitch.

True to his word, Holliday worked fast, taking tiny perfect stitches, drawing together the jagged torn edges of the wound while blotting away blood. For the dentist, this was much easier than stitching inside a patient's mouth where space was a premium. When he was through, the wound was visible, a mere line of perfectly executed sutures with the bleeding under control. Taking a clean towel, Doc again dampened a corner with whiskey and blotted the injury. Wyatt stirred, but did not complain.

"All finished. Now I just need to bandage it." Holliday used the last of the towels to tear into strips. One he used as a pad, another secured the bandage around Earp's head.

Holliday eased the marshal over onto his back and checked the injury above his forehead. The bleeding had stopped so all that was required was a good cleaning. Rinsing out one of used towels in canteen water, Doc cleansed the wound and finished by wiping as much drying blood as possible from Wyatt's face.

"Thought you were a dentist," Earp mumbled. "Act more like a real doctor."

Holliday offered water, which Wyatt accepted, drinking until Doc figured he'd had enough for the moment. "You can have more later. Too much at once will make you sick." Laying aside the marshal's canteen, Doc reached for his own, taking several long, much needed, swallows.

"About that MD business," Doc sat on the ground next to his patient and gazed off into the distance. Somewhere, far to the east, was his beloved Georgia. Closing his eyes, Doc found it quite easy to visualize home as he had last seen it.

"My uncle, John Holliday, was a surgeon, and for a while I believed that to be my calling. I followed him on rounds, assisted him at surgeries. He operated on me when I was barely two months old. If you look close enough you can see the scar."

Wyatt stared at Doc's face, straining to see any visible mark where Holliday pointed. The flaxen moustache obscured most of it, but a tiny line snaked from upper lip to nostril.

"Cleft palate," Holliday explained. "Uncle John saved my life, he and an associate of his, but it was John who steered me toward dentistry. Told me it was the more scientific branch of medicine, more advanced in techniques, anesthesiology and such, fewer charlatans, as well. Harder to fake putting a crown in someone's mouth, I would assume, than telling them 'here, take this pill and see me in the morning.'"

Doc continued on for some time until he noticed he'd lost his audience. Wyatt had drifted to sleep. "Just one of the reasons I don't like to bore folks with my life story."

Wyatt mumbled something unintelligible. Doc patted his shoulder. "Sleep if you want, marshal. I'll be close if you need me."

Leaving his patient's side, Doc opened out his bedroll near the corpse. Moving Dixon's body onto the blanket proved an exercise in technique. The dead man's head lolled on its broken neck. The body and its extremities, not yet into rigor mortis, moved and flopped about at Holliday's every attempt to shift or lift it.

Adding insult to injury, the corpse stunk to high heaven from being unwashed; it was doubtful decomposition would make it smell much worse, different perhaps, but not worse. Flies hummed and buzzed about, already interested in what they knew to be a dead thing.

Securing the blanket around the corpse with a piece of rope around legs, torso and neck, Doc slumped to the ground, exhausted. One down, three to go. The bodies needed to be transported to Fort Smith and soon. They would not last long in the warming spring climate.

Struggling to his feet, Doc walked over to Wyatt. Finding a spot close enough to keep one eye on his patient, he tossed aside several marble sized rocks and sprawled out on the bare ground. Not comfortable, but with folded arms for a pillow it was easy enough to drift off in the sun.

"Perhaps in my previous life I was a lizard," he mused aloud. He could think of more unpleasant ancestors.

Holliday came awake, one hand clutched to his chest as he panted for breath. Without warning the cough was upon him, deep, wet and painful, doubling Doc over with the force of it. Lasting only moments, it was loud enough and frightening enough to bring Wyatt—woozy and holding his head as if to keep it upright on his shoulders—to Doc's side.

"What's the matter? You sick?" Wyatt touched Holliday's sleeve.

Doc jerked away. "No. No, sorry, Wyatt. Guess it was just a dream, a nightmare. I couldn't breathe. I was suffocating and there was blood," Doc kneaded a singular spot on his chest as if it hurt, "so much blood," he whispered, his face creased in anguish.

"Were you hit?" Fearing the worst, Wyatt eased Holliday's hand away from his ribs. There was no wound, no blood. "For a minute," Earp closed his eyes and willed himself calm. "Dreams can seem damned real."

When Wyatt handed Doc a canteen, Holliday refused it, reaching instead for his own and drinking plenty. Slowly he calmed down and his breathing eased. "It *was* just a dream," he admitted.

Earp nodded. "That's all it was."

Doc wiped sweat from his hands down his shirtfront, lingering for a second over the spot where the imaginary pain had existed. To his chagrin, there *was* a sore spot between his ribs. He let the knowledge pass without mention, throwing the discussion and emphasis back onto his patient. "How's your head?"

Earp touched close to the bandaged area, but not too close. "Sore, but can't say I have much of a headache and I'm not seein' two of you."

"Well, some things are blessings in disguise," Doc replied. "Think you can sit your horse? I don't know about you, marshal, but the thought of spending the night in this place is not a prospect I relish."

"I can ride." Once on his feet Wyatt swayed, holding both arms out for balance. At Doc's concerned look he commented, "It'll take more than bein' dizzy to keep me in this place."

Although he allowed Wyatt to help him hoist Dixon's body across his horse, Doc insisted on doing whatever else it took to secure the corpse. Wyatt followed on his own mount as Holliday led the pack animal up the incline. By the time they reached the top, Doc's breathing grew labored and he was out of breath, panting, but made light of it when Wyatt glanced his way.

"I am spending too much time sitting on my ass in saloons."

Wyatt nodded, turning his horse toward the shack. Doc trailed some yards behind, every step a struggle as if his boots were mired in sticky clay. The returning pain jabbed between his ribs, penetrating deep into his chest. Doc doubled over in agony. When the pain eased off enough for him to stand upright, he noticed Wyatt loping away. He hadn't seen the episode. There would be no questions. Good. Pain eased into bearable discomfort and Doc made his way to the cabin.

By the time Doc arrived, Wyatt had finished rolling the woman's body into a blanket and was in the process of securing it with lengths of rope, much to Holliday's relief. To look at her again... Shaking the image from his mind, he focused on Earp. "Wyatt, take it easy. I don't want you passing out on me."

Earp brushed aside the concern. "I'm fine and the sooner we get this done the sooner we can get the hell out of this damned hole. Or did you change your mind about spending the night here?" Wyatt reached up, scratching at an itch beneath the bandaging.

Holliday resisted the urge to swat the offending hand away. "Bite your tongue. I've got the willies just standin' outside. You win, Wyatt, but if you feel lightheaded do us both a favor and faint out here."

"Done," Earp concurred. "Now let's finish this up."

Together, the lawmen secured the bodies onto the remaining horses. Doc chose to ride the stolen animal on the grounds it somehow had less to do with the killers, coupled with the fact it was a better mount. He wished he'd thought to change saddles before strapping Dixon's body to his horse. His saddle was well padded since he was not, and well broken in besides.

The worst part of the afternoon was not handling the bodies, but going through the items stolen from the murder victims and the trophies taken as souvenirs. Among the cache were costly items, gold jewelry, ear bobs, pocket watches and the like, as well as trash: pot metal bracelets, rings with colored glass stones, ropes of fake pearls. The killers either didn't know the difference or didn't care.

However, certain items were of a more personal nature to the victims. While digging through the deep pocket of a saddlebag smelling of mildew and worse, Holliday discovered something he wish he hadn't, hair of various colors, lengths and textures, scalps, one of striking beauty, a braid two feet long and of the loveliest red/gold color, the plait tied at the bottom with a piece of bloodied ribbon. Dropping the disgusting trophies, Doc just made it outside.

Wyatt followed some minutes later, having wrapped the sad remains in a piece of blanket along with his own discovery, more of the same. Waiting at a discreet distance for Holliday to finish, Wyatt helped the shaky dentist to his feet. "See if you can't find a shovel or something to dig with. We'll bury these."

Doc disappeared around the back of the shack. He returned with a small hand trowel, but it was enough to get the job done.

The two walked some ways from the cabin to a pretty spot beneath a spreading elm. Holliday got to digging, working up a decent sweat by the time he finished. The hole was a good two feet deep and as wide. With respect, they laid the remains to rest, covering them with dirt and a layer of heavy stones to discourage scavengers.

"I feel like we should say some words, but I don't have any," Wyatt murmured.

Holliday bowed his head. "I don't remember much of what my mother read to me from the Bible, but this was her favorite: *The Lord is my shepherd. I shall not want. He maketh me to lie down in green pastures. He leadeth me beside the still waters. He restoreth my soul.*"

Nothing else they found touched either man as hard, and it was a somber pair who walked to their horses after the job was done. Found objects were stored in saddlebags and as the two stood staring at the shack, Wyatt took out fixins' and rolled a smoke, lighting it. He looked over at Doc, the lit match in his hand.

"Indeed, sir," Holliday agreed.

Within moments the shack was ablaze, a leaping tongue of flame devouring everything within, purifying, cleansing away the stench, the horror and the pain, cauterizing what had been an ugly open wound. The flames were visible for miles. They were still visible to the men when they camped for the night.

The horses bearing the bodies were tied up some ways from camp which caused Wyatt no little concern over wolves and coyotes bothering the corpses. Doc, however, was flippant.

"Hell, Wyatt, if the coyotes want 'em, let them have at it. Everything's got a right to eat."

At Earp's disapproving look, Doc shrugged. "Tell me that scum deserves any better, and I will recant my statement."

Wyatt said nothing.

Holliday lit a cigarette, blowing a misshapen smoke ring skyward while he rummaged around in his saddlebags.

Pulling out the whiskey, he offered it first to Wyatt, who declined.

"Suit yourself, marshal." Doc took a quick sip and then another. He was hungry. They'd left most of their food behind to make space in the saddlebags for the property they were returning.

Wyatt seemed okay with jerky, hardtack, and coffee. Wyatt always seemed okay if he had coffee, but Holliday would have enjoyed a meal. The disease eating away at him had yet to steal his appetite. In fact, it caused him to burn up much more food than he could consume. Always slender, he was now slim almost to the extreme.

His physician back in Georgia told him it was the consumptive fever. "Like feeding a furnace that always needs stoking. You'll lose your appetite some time. When that happens, you'll know the disease is progressing."

So, for the young dentist, hunger was a good sign, but it did not keep his stomach from growling or make him any happier about his present circumstance, the lack of dinner.

At least the whiskey burn made him *feel* full, and it helped the sharp, little annoying pains that had not quite disappeared from between his ribs. No great shakes as a drinker, it took very little to affect him, a few decent shots and he was bleary-eyed, but at least he wasn't hungry and his chest didn't hurt.

Doc watched Wyatt for some time before sleep overtook him. If Earp's head hurt, he wasn't complaining, though Doc figured the stitched area had to be tender. At last Wyatt turned onto his side, drifting to sleep without delay and leaving Doc alone to stare up at the stars. *So many stars blinking on and off in the black velvet backdrop of a cloudless sky, such peacefulness, so very deceiving.*

Holliday woke well before dawn, the dream one of the worst he could recall. The memory would fade in time, he hoped, but for now it was fresh and real and horrifying. He found himself perspiring, breathing hard and downright shaky as he sat up and tried to clear his head. To his embarrassment, Wyatt was awake and watching, the only thing visible the whites of the other man's eyes, surreal in the near total darkness.

Without comment, Wyatt, too, sat up, searching through his pockets for the makings of a quirly. He rolled one and lit it, passing it to Holliday, the red tip a tiny beacon in the night as Doc inhaled.

Rolling another, Earp drew the acrid smoke into his lungs, a cloud of white circling his head before being carried off by a freshening breeze. For several minutes the two sat without speaking, Wyatt finally breaking the tense silence.

"I never killed a man before," he confessed, the flat, Illinois accent accentuating the tone of his depression. "Sure wasn't like I thought it would be." Several more moments of silence crept along. "I thought I'd feel like the king of the world, almost like God dealin' out justice with my six-shooter, but it wasn't like that at all. I felt, I sorta felt like…"

Doc finished the sentence in a broken whisper, "like a murderer."

"Like a murderer. A man died and it was my doing, but it couldn't a been any other way." Not a statement of fact, it was more like Earp hoped for affirmation.

Holliday provided the assurance. "No, it couldn't have been any other way, Wyatt. I'm glad they won't kill again. And I'm glad you and I are still alive to have this discussion. I just wish we could've left the killing part to the courts, but that would be the easy way out, wouldn't it? Let someone else shoulder the burden. Let someone else dream the bad dreams. Let someone else carry the memories."

Doc ground out his cigarette and buried his face in his

arms. "A man died and it was my doing," he quoted Earp into the muffled cover. "But a woman died and it was *my* doing," he added.

"It couldn't a been any other way," Wyatt repeated.

CHAPTER 4

Stopping long enough to rest and water the horses, the two lawmen made excellent time to Fort Smith, arriving tired, dirty, and hungry, as the sun hung poised just above the horizon.

"I don't believe I've ever seen so lovely a sight," Doc mused as he reined in next to Wyatt and lit himself a smoke. Below the short rise, the bustling town bespoke many things meaningful to Holliday, a soft bed, a good meal and the promise of numerous gambling establishments.

Wyatt snorted. "You use that *lovely* term kinda loose, don't 'cha, Doc? If I recall you said that very same thing about the painting hangin' over Nellie Price's bar at the Lady Gay. What's it called, Venus Rising or some such?"

Holliday raised an eyebrow, turning his slow gaze toward his companion. "Did I indeed? I don't recall."

Earp shook his head in mock disgust. "Funny how you *don't seem to recall* only what you don't want to. Everything else comes quick to mind." With that, Wyatt headed his horse, trailed by the pack animals, down the rise.

Doc tossed aside his smoke and followed.

At their first stop in Fort Smith, the undertaker, Earp pinned a piece of paper to each of the corpses for identification purposes. While going through the killers' belongings, the lawmen found numerous newspaper clippings and wanted posters the four had thoughtfully kept, chronicling their lives of crime, many complete with physical descriptions and even a drawn likeness or two. J. B. Dixon joined, respectively, Kim Horton, Frank McMillan and Pearl McLaughlin.

The undertaker, a rather portly man whose rolled up sleeves exposed thick muscular forearms, was not what was usually expected in a man of his profession. He was neither dressed in black nor lacking a sense of humor.

"Kinda ripe, aren't they?" He joked. "But I am right glad to see 'em. Rotten trash got just what they deserved. Woman killers." He spat out a lengthy strand of tobacco juice. "Let me shake the hands of the men that brought 'em in." His grip was warm and firm as he shook the hands of both. "Good job. Fine job."

"I'll be back with a voucher for payment of services," Wyatt said. If he seemed putout over the undertaker's rather jovial demeanor, he kept it, Earp-like, to himself.

Doc was more than relieved to turn the bodies over to someone else, and more thankful yet with Wyatt's next statement. "Let's put the horses up and check in with the territorial marshal. Then our time's our own."

At the marshal's office, Wyatt did most of the talking, rather a reversal of roles, with Doc confirming the information. Both signed the affidavit prepared by the lawman.

Marshal Anderson gave the pair a visual going over. "Get a decent meal and some sleep. You look like you could use it. I'll take the vouchers over to the undertaker for ya."

Shuffling through the papers strewn across his desk, he chose one out of the pile. "There's a reward for the four of 'em, five hundred a piece. I'll advise the powers that be to send it to Dodge City. Should be there by the time you get back."

Unspeaking, Doc and Wyatt walked side by side the short block to the hotel, red dust sifted from their clothing at each heavy step. Spurs jingled and leather creaked. They appeared rough hewn, trail hands or perhaps frontiersmen. For one this was a façade, a temporary life lived for only weeks. For his companion it was the slipping back into a way of life left behind. Either way, the look fitted each man to perfection.

Holliday noticed as Earp walked he rubbed at his neck, rotating his head in an attempt to relieve the stiffness there and the pain that had to be plaguing him from the head injury. He stopped Wyatt with a hand on his arm, "Get us a couple rooms. I'm going to find a physician."

Wyatt started to argue that he didn't need a doctor, but he was too tired to fight, much easier to just do as he was told.

Holliday stopped at the mercantile, purchased a handful of cigars, and asked directions to the doctor's office.

"Down two blocks, turn right. Upstairs."

The office was easy to find and the doctor, a spare man with thinning hair, a brushy mustache, and sober expression, was in. "Sit down there, young man, and tell me what ails you, though if you give me a moment, I'll bet I can tell you."

Doc bit back an angry reply at the physician's inference that *he* was the patient. "Your services are required for my friend who has a head injury. If you could accompany me to the hotel?"

"I can." Grabbing up his black bag, the doctor followed, barely able to keep up with the tall man's stride.

Stopping at the front desk, Doc got the key to his own room and the number of Wyatt's.

"You're in 207, Doctor Holliday. Marshal Earp is next door, 209."

Holliday climbed these steps with difficulty. His chest pained him and the short flight of stairs winded him.

Knocking on Wyatt's door, he opened it before the other man could answer. Earp was at the washstand drying his face on a towel. He had removed the bandaging from his head and tossed the dirty, stained material onto a small table.

"Sit down here and let's have a look, marshal." The doctor indicated a straight-backed chair. "Turn up that light will you?"

Holliday complied.

"Hand me some cotton soaked in disinfectant. The bottle's in my bag. It's the brown one with the cork stopper." Taking the cotton wool from Doc, the physician dabbed none too gently at the gash, loosening clotted blood and cleaning the injury.

At every rough daub, Wyatt cringed. After a minute or two, he swore under his breath. The physician ignored the obvious signs of discomfort, turning his attention to Holliday. "So, doctor, is this your work?"

Leaning against the doorjamb, hat in hand and nearly out on his feet, Holliday nodded, replying softly, "Yes, it is."

"I take it the term 'doctor' I heard mentioned by the hotel clerk is not just an affectation on your part? This is excellent stitching. Best I've ever seen and the wound's clean, no infection. Tell me, Doctor Holliday, from what medical school did you graduate?"

"Pennsylvania College of Dental Surgery," Holliday replied, rather enjoying the look of surprise on the old physician's face.

"Dental school, eh? Young to be graduated and practicing, aren't you?"

"Looks are often deceiving, doctor." Holliday soon tired of what he considered prying by the old physician. Perhaps it was mere curiosity, but it gave Doc a headache sure to rival Wyatt's.

Realizing the dentist was not in a talkative mood, the old fellow got back to the business at hand. "Don't believe I'll rebandage that. The wound needs to dry out. I'll be back day after tomorrow to remove the stitches, unless of course your original surgeon would like to provide that service?"

Holliday acquiesced. "No, by all means, sir, you do the honors."

The physician turned back to his patient and the minor injury above Wyatt's right eye. It required a quick cleaning, the bruising around the cut worse than the cut itself. "Bad headache, seeing double?"

"Not seein' double and the headache is just sorta there, worse when I'm tired and that's been most of the past couple days."

"Get plenty of rest, the both of you. Looks like you could use a good feed, too. Sleep, and then eat. Doctor's orders."

Packing up his bag the physician turned to leave, taking Holliday by the arm and steering him out the door. Doc did not have a chance to say anything to Wyatt, but Earp had already settled his aching body on the bed and closed his eyes.

The two doctors walked the few steps to Holliday's room. "How much do I owe for your house call?" Doc reached into his pocket pulling out several folded bills.

"Nothing, nothing at all, Doctor Holliday. Call it a professional courtesy. However, colleague to colleague, you could answer a question."

Holliday was trapped. He knew what the old man was getting to, probing into his private life. Resigned, but resentful, he replied, "Ask your question."

In the dim light of the narrow hotel hallway the old man looked over the younger. Doc knew what he saw, what his physician's eyes noticed. Beneath the tanned and wind-burned complexion lurked a tinge of unhealthy gray, and then there were the dark circles beneath the eyes and the pain Holliday could not hide from the other medical man.

"Is it tuberculosis?"

Holliday pivoted, turning his back on the other man. Unlocking the door to the room, he stepped through. "Yes." He couldn't make out the doctor's reply although it had to be some well meant words of sympathy or worse, pity.

On the other side of the door, John Holliday sank to the floor, burying his face in both hands. Silent sobs wracked his body. The illness was back with a vengeance. He'd almost been able to forget he carried with him the specter of death, the dark legacy of a mother who adored her only son. He had almost forgotten, but it was not to be. Overcome with exhaustion, he slept where he lay, curled on the bare floor.

A knock roused him just past daybreak. It was Wyatt. "Come on, Holliday. Get your sorry butt outta that bed and let's get breakfast. I'm starved."

The banging continued until Doc answered. "Gimme a minute won't you? I need to wash my face."

Stiff and sore, Doc got up and made the few steps to the washstand, stretching as he walked.

Peering into the mirror while he poured water out into the basin, he found his reflection appalling: bloodshot eyes the likes of which he'd seen after a round-the-clock poker game played in an ill-ventilated saloon, a blotchy complexion and a shock of pale hair in total disarray. Scrubbing at his face with the rough toweling, he pressed the damp cloth against his burning eyes.

Outside the door, Wyatt grew impatient. "Let's go,

Holliday. There's a steak callin' my name. Let's go. I don't care how pretty you are."

Giving up any attempt at looking human, Doc threw the towel down, finger-combed the unkempt hair, grabbed his hat and opened the door.

Earp lounged up against the jamb, and although he did not react in any way to Doc's appearance, Holliday decided to beat him to the punch anyway, just in case the subject came up. "I need a proper barbering, a shave and a haircut," he commented as they walked next door to the restaurant.

Earp eyed the other man up and down. "A bath wouldn't hurt either one of us either, a bath and a change a clothes."

"Indeed, sir. I've forgotten what a gentleman looked like." As Earp passed him to enter the eatery, Holliday added, "Or smelled like."

Wyatt pasted him with a dirty look, but grinned nevertheless. "You can't get my goat this morning, Doc. Things went too good for us. Four murderers brought to a just end and neither of us too much the worse for wear."

After tucking away a breakfast of monumental proportions, the two went their separate ways. First stop for Doc was the mercantile where he purchased an entire set of new clothes, a cowboy rig, since there were still many days left on the dusty road back to Dodge. Among the items were a band-collared shirt, wool vest and pants, new underclothing, several pair of socks, a paisley bandanna and half a dozen handkerchiefs.

The next stop was the tonsorial parlor for a hot bath, shave, and haircut. Laying back in the padded leather chair, cracked more from use than age, the barber fussing over him hoping for a large tip, John Holliday found himself in a state nearing nirvana. Eyes closed, but right hand beneath the linen throw resting on the butt of the .45 in the shoulder holster, Holliday was as relaxed as he could get without being asleep.

Relaxed and thoughtful, he allowed his mind to wander. Maybe the consumption was not the cause of the chest pain. Maybe he'd banged up a rib somehow. There was little discomfort at the moment and no trouble breathing.

Making up excuses was easy, believing them was another matter, but by the time the barber worked his magic, Doc was convinced he had pretty much imagined the consumptive symptoms.

The stranger staring back at him from the mirror was clear eyed and full of youthful ambitions. When a man is young a day, an hour, can make all the difference in his outlook. John Holliday was still of an age when that was true, of an age and a time in his life when fate had not dealt quite so many hands against him. One true blessing comes with youth, and it is optimism.

Doc sauntered down Fort Smith's main street, taking in the sights, tipping his hat to passersby and deciding which of the many saloons would best suit his needs. Settling on the most raucous and crowded establishment, The Shanghai Cabbage, Holliday decided to first return to the hotel.

The door swung open on soundless hinges. On the bed lay Wyatt, sprawled out across the generous mattress in a semblance of perfect contentment, dressed as was Doc in new clothes, and snoring. Holliday tiptoed near enough to take a good look at his former patient. Although one eye was swollen considerably and quite black and blue from the lawman's tumble down the hillside, his breathing seemed regular and his color normal. Doc rested the back of his hand across Earp's forehead. *No fever, that's good*, he thought. He stood for a moment pondering on whether or not to leave Wyatt a note as to his whereabouts, finally settling on not. Wyatt would find him, of that he had no doubt. Holliday backed out of the room and pulled the door shut behind him.

Doc went into the poker game at The Shanghai Cabbage an underdog and an unknown. In the guise of a cowboy he retained certain anonymity, not marked outright as a sporting man as he would have been dressed in his usual garb of the professional gambler.

The other players pegged him as an inexperienced drover with a paycheck to squander and a few hours in which to do so. To their chagrin, they found they were mistaken. Several gamblers were downright annoyed that a ringer seemed to have caused them such a smooth parting from their money. Annoyance soon gave way to more jovial feelings when Holliday offered to continue play until the men had a chance to recoup some of their losses.

A tumbler of whiskey sat within easy reach, untouched, and a huge stack of chips, each color piled neatly into its own little tower, made it obvious Holliday was on a tear, noticing neither thirst nor hunger. He did, however, notice a presence standing back and to the left of his chair. "What's on your mind, marshal?"

All eyes at the table now focused on Wyatt, all save those of Holliday, upon whose lips a sly smile appeared. Not one to waste a golden moment, Holliday called, raking in another pot.

"Supper's on my mind, and I was wonderin' if you cared to join me?" Wyatt leaned his hands on the back of Doc's chair and peered over his head at the loot accumulated in front of the dentist. "Maybe 'join me' wasn't what I meant to say. Maybe what I meant to say was you're buyin, aren't you, Doc?"

Stuffing bills and coins into his various pockets, Holliday rose from his seat. "Glad to join you, Wyatt and delighted to pay. However, fair *is* fair. I expect you to leave the tip."

To the concerned men sitting around the poker table hoping to win back some of their cash, he offered words of comfort. "I will return in an hour or so gentlemen, and I would be pleased if you'd all join me for another go."

Worried expressions gave way to smiles and nods all around. Hope did indeed spring eternal.

A nondescript barfly, watching the action at the poker table, was quick to point out some information to those men drinking beside him. "See that fella, the one jes' got up from playin' cards, tall and slim?"

The men seemed disinterested. After all, they hadn't lost money to the cowboy.

"I jes' got in from Fort Gibson in the territories. That young fella killed a man in a gunfight right on the main street and I was there. Saw the whole thing I did. Fastest man I ever seed and I seed 'em all."

Of a sudden, men tripped over each other to buy the storyteller drinks. With each whiskey consumed, the barfly spun a more embroidered tale. Doc Holliday was well on his way to a checkered past, one he did not deserve, but which would mark his life and follow him to the grave.

By the time Doc and Wyatt returned from supper, half the saloon patrons knew of Holliday's deadly history, embellished to the point where he had not only murdered Bailey in Fort Gibson, but his brother Ed in Texas, eviscerating him in fact. He had also, he purported, shot dead several buffalo hunters in the territories because their stench offended him, and for good measure, dealt death to a fellow cardsharp in Dodge City.

The body count included no mention of the few people Doc had ever killed, two of the four murderers he and Wyatt brought to justice. That would have been the only nonfictitious statement to come from the barfly's mouth. But then truth did not matter in the rumor mill started by a drunken drifter.

When Holliday returned, oblivious to what had transpired in his absence, with a belly full of good food and an itch to continue his favorite pastime, not one man would oblige him with a game and all seemed nervous and edgy in his presence, smiling too much while refusing to meet his gaze or answer a simple question.

Since they had nothing much else to do and the evening was yet young, the two lawmen decided to have a couple beers and watch whatever action was available.

A Faro game began and several of poker, but not one of Holliday's previous players made any move to include him. "Seems a chill wind blew through here while we were gone, Wyatt," Doc said

"Appears so. How 'bout another beer, Doc?" Wyatt's attempt to cheer up the dentist fell on deaf ears, Holliday's attention diverted by a bevy of young women descending the staircase from the rooms above, each decked out in a different color dress, each outfit showing a tease of cleavage and a hint of well-turned ankle.

"They have the appearance of a bouquet of lovely spring blossoms, do they not, marshal?"

"No loyalties to Kate?" Wyatt asked, bemused.

Doc laughed, "As if she's being chaste in my absence, Wyatt. What do you think she does on those little sojourns to Wichita or Hays City? And what about you, preacher? Don't tell me you aren't tempted or do you consider yourself a married man, forsaking all others etcetera, etcetera?" Holliday drained the remainder of his beer, blotting a bit of foam from his mustache with the corner of a handkerchief drawn from an inside pocket. Leaning chin in hand, he awaited an answer.

Wyatt was adamant, "No, I'm not tempted. Not in the least. And I do consider myself a married man."

Holliday smirked. "I believe you are blowing smoke, preacher. However, I am sure the time will come when this subject will once again rear its ugly head. And you can be certain I shall remind you of the words spoken here tonight."

Before Earp had a chance to respond, Doc's attention narrowed to a comely girl, dark tresses unbound across creamy shoulders, brown eyes enhanced by long black lashes, which she used to good effect on the smitten Holliday.

Tall and slender, she was just the sort Doc seemed to favor. Kate had much the same look herself aside from the eyes. Where this girl's retained at least a hint of innocence, Kate's held all the world's wisdom she had accumulated, and that was plenty.

"Come over here, darlin'," Doc beckoned. He rose to meet the young lady, taking her hand in his and bringing it to his lips for a gentleman's brush. Surprised, the whore actually blushed. "And what's your name?" Holliday inquired.

"Iris," she stammered. "My name's Iris."

"Charmin', simply charmin'," Doc drawled.

Earp rolled his eyes skyward. This was not lost on Holliday who poured on the charm and the Georgia drawl. "Don't bother to keep my seat warm, Wyatt. I shall be otherwise occupied." Taking the girl's arm, he led her to the stairway.

Doc returned before the girl. Indeed, she did not show up for another half hour and then came directly to Holliday's table, whispering something into his ear.

Smiling and nodding, he explained to Earp, "I promised I'd play a tune just for her." He angled his head toward the piano gathering dust in the corner.

"Sure, Doc. *Chopstick's* right up your alley?" Wyatt asked.

"Would you care to accompany us, marshal? Perchance I can do better than *Chopsticks*."

Wyatt grabbed his hat, handed Doc his Stetson, and

picked up his beer. This was an opportunity not to be missed. "Let's do it then."

Holliday made a great show of dusting off the seat with one of his handkerchiefs, indicating that the young lady should sit beside him on the bench. Running the scales, he made a wry face as he noticed several off key notes.

Wyatt waited for the show to start, trying not to tap his foot in impatience as Doc fiddled around looking for music, any excuse, it seemed, to waste time and put off the inevitable need to play. The final flourish was a great show at knuckle-cracking.

"Seems I must make do without music, however, I believe I remember a piece or two from my youth," Holliday grinned. At his side, the girl gazed adoringly up at him.

The music, a piece by Beethoven, was slow and melancholy with Doc ringing every emotion from the notes, not playing by ear, but from the heart. At the conclusion, the majority of saloon patrons applauded the performance, albeit somewhat timid as if not knowing what to make of this *shootist's* other, gentler, talent. Doc seemed touched by the response, rising part way from the bench to acknowledge the applause with a slight bow.

"Play more, won't you, Johnny?" the girl pleaded, her hand on Doc's arm, tears in her eyes. "I've never heard anything so pretty," she fawned.

Doc looked up at Wyatt who stood silent next to the piano. Holliday did not know what he expected from Earp, but it was not silence. It appeared Wyatt Earp was stunned by what he still did not know about John Holliday.

Wyatt finally offered teasing encouragement, "by all means, Johnny, do play some more."

Holliday chose Mozart. The music was light and airy, full of laughter and joy and when he struck the final note the room burst into deafening applause, for the moment at least talent overwhelming gossip. Coins rained down onto the performer, his companion, and the piano like hail on a stormy summer day, the customers keen to show their approval of the rare, yet well done, entertainment.

The girl was delirious, whirling about, picking money from the floor, laughing in delight as she found not only silver, but the occasional gold piece among the offerings. Each coin made a satisfying clink as it was dropped into a beer glass among its cronies.

"Well, *Johnny*," Wyatt commented, "If you can't make a living as a gambler, you can always fall back to the stage."

Holliday smiled. "Bite your tongue, marshal. However, I shall keep that in mind."

Doc continued to play until he tired of being on exhibit. No one wanted him to stop, but he was fatigued, his fingers and back cramping due to the unaccustomed workout.

"Maybe tomorrow evening," he pacified those who were upset by his decision to stop for the night.

Iris clung to his arm, basking in the glow of envious giggles and stares from the other *ladies*. Doc gave her the coin-filled beer glass.

"Come on up, Johnny? It's not so late as all that," she whispered to him as he picked his hat up off the piano and stretched out achy arms and stiff back.

"Not tonight, darlin', tomorrow perhaps?" Again he took her hand in his and brought it to his lips. "Goodnight, now."

Iris found herself enveloped among the girls, all talking at once, begging to hear everything about the handsome cowboy who played the piano so well and acted the part of the southern gentleman.

By next morning, the gossip concerning Holliday had spread all over town. Even the physician saw fit to comment as he removed Doc's well placed stitches from

Wyatt's scalp. "Quite the reputation you've got going for yourself, Doctor Holliday."

"I have no idea to what you are referring," Doc said, yawning behind one hand, the long evening spent at the piano catching up with him.

The old physician glanced up from his work. "Don't you know what folks are saying about you?"

"That he's a fine piano player and quite the ladies' man?" Earp quipped between gritted teeth as the physician tugged at a stubborn suture.

"No, but for his sake I'd rather that be the case." Finished, the doctor dropped the used tweezers onto the tray on the table and looked at Holliday. "There's talk you're a killer, fast on the draw, cruel, and you hide it behind a badge."

Holliday's jaw dropped, and Wyatt jumped to his feet. "That's a damned lie."

The physician reached out, resting a gnarled hand on Wyatt's arm. "I think I know that. I also know one drunk spreading rumors is more apt to be listened to than a sober man armed with the truth."

Doc and Wyatt exchanged looks, as much as asking each other, "Now, what are we going to do about this?"

Holliday, his voice low, his expression grim, paraphrased. "I think he doth protest too much," explaining to Earp when Wyatt expressed confusion, "The more I protest my innocence, the more people will believe I am guilty."

"So we just say nothing and let it go?" Wyatt was angry and fast becoming angrier. "I say put a stop to it now, before it gets out of hand. This'll plague you…"

Doc shook his head. "No, Wyatt. What's said is said. We ignore it and hope it goes away. You *can* let it be, can't you?"

"I can. But I hope it's not gonna be something we both live to regret." Wyatt stalked over to the window to gaze down into the street below. "Dammit," He whispered. "Damn 'em all."

The rest of the time spent in Fort Smith passed without consequence, although paranoid or not, John Holliday felt himself the object of curiosity, fear or both. Staring eyes drilled holes in his back, and every move, every word spoken became fodder for talk.

True to his word, he returned to the saloon and played the piano for his paramour of the previous evening, but it was no good. Everything appeared changed. Was it his imagination that when people applauded it was out of fear of retribution, not appreciation of the music, as was the case twenty-four hours before?

In bed with Iris, even there he felt the change. She feared him as if he'd been anything but gentle and appreciative of her. She tried too hard to please him, even offering to degrade herself. That angered him, which in turn frightened her.

On the bed with the sheet to cover her nakedness, she cowered at the headboard, trembling like a bird baited by a cat, breast rising and falling in quick respirations as she waited for him to pounce. Blind to Holliday's hurt and confusion, the girl saw what her mind told her lurked beneath the cultured surface. She heard only what others said of him.

Bewildered and upset, John Holliday dressed, tossing a five dollar gold piece onto the bed. Perhaps Wyatt was correct when he said the rumors needed to be quelled and fast, but if so, how?

He wasn't surprised to find Wyatt leaning over the railing mere feet from the whore's room. In pretense, Earp appeared to be keeping an eye on the action in the bar below, but Doc understood Wyatt's true motive. He was watching Holliday's back, so to speak.

At Doc's footsteps, Earp turned around. "Leave in the morning?"

Doc nodded, "Can't be soon enough for me."

At breakfast the usually ravenous Holliday picked at his food. He felt haggard, old beyond his years, drained. Looking up from the plate, Doc noticed Wyatt's concerned expression. He smiled, attempting to pass it off with the wave of a hand. "I'll be right as rain as soon as this town is a memory."

"Sure, sure, Doc." Wyatt did not sound convinced.

From the comfort of his favorite chair on the boardwalk in front of his office, Marshal Anderson puffed on the first pipe of the morning and watched the town wake for the day. He'd observed the pair for some time as they rode up the long street from the livery at the south end of town, and when they got near, he motioned them over. "What they're sayin' about you, Holliday, tell me it's not true."

Doc looked down from his seat on the tall horse, pulled the brim of his Stetson low and questioned in a dull voice, "Does it matter now, marshal?"

"To me it does," Anderson replied.

"You know the only lives I've ever taken."

"Figured as much." The marshal rose from his chair. Reaching up, he shook first Doc's hand, then Wyatt's. "Take care, boys. We can use all the lawmen like you we can get in these parts. And watch your backs."

"You do the same, marshal." Kicking his horse into a fast trot, Wyatt led the way out of Fort Smith and toward home.

For Doc, the day wore on forever. He'd hoped the more miles put between him and Fort Smith the more himself he would become. Instead, as the hours passed, he shrank more into a shell. By nightfall and the making of camp, he was silent and morose.

Wyatt had long since given up attempting to lure the

dentist into any sort of conversation and for that, Doc was glad. He had enough to occupy his thoughts, not the least of which was the recurrent stabbing pain between his ribs. Night couldn't come fast enough for him. At least in the dark he wouldn't have to see Wyatt's furtive, guilty glances in his direction, although the lawman's intense gaze penetrated the dark, a knife through hot wax.

Dawn broke with an unsurpassed show of colors. Reds, pinks, corals and blues radiated down from the sky like fingers from heaven. From his bedroll, Doc watched Wyatt. Sitting on a short knoll, Earp basked in the new day, his face raised to the light as if gathering strength for what might come. For the first time since Doc had known him, Wyatt appeared at ease, relaxed. Doc was loath to disturb him. Instead he sat up and lit a cigar. Wyatt appeared not quite as preoccupied by the glory of the sunrise as Holliday imagined, as he turned at the slight sounds.

"Up for breakfast?" He asked, rising from the ground and stretching. "I've got coffee on the boil."

"Coffee sounds wonderful, 'though I believe I will pass on breakfast this morning," Doc replied.

Wyatt frowned, but said nothing. Squatting down at the fire, he poured out two cups of the hot black brew, passing one over to Holliday. Into the heavy cast iron skillet he sliced off several thick rashers of bacon. Soon the air filled with the delicious, smoky scent of frying pork.

Instead of making him hungry, the smell turned Doc's stomach. Rising to his feet, he took himself some ways away from the fire and upwind. His chest felt heavy and he coughed, muffling the sound against his sleeve. To his relief, the cough did not worsen nor did it recur, and the chest pain vanished. Giving Wyatt enough time to eat his breakfast at leisure, Doc returned to the campsite, his heart lighter than it had been in some days and his outlook brighter.

The day passed much more pleasantly with Doc once again talking. Though not quite up to snuff, Holliday was quick to make a joke or tell a good story, at one point even making Wyatt laugh, that quite a feat in itself.

Doc ate some of the midday meal, but seemed more interested in drinking anything liquid, matching Wyatt cup for cup when it came to coffee.

By nightfall and camp, Doc was well into his second canteen, which prompted Wyatt to chide him. "Doc, I ain't seen a water source since we left Fort Smith. You'd best be taking it easy with yours. You're liable to run out before we find a spot to refill."

Holliday stopped drinking, capped his canteen. "I hadn't thought, Wyatt. I shall be more conservative."

Doc seemed disinterested in the evening meal. Taking the food from Wyatt's hand with a perfunctory, "thank you," he held the tin plate across his knees as he stared off into the fire, picking at the contents, but eating nothing. In a few moments, he put the plate aside, got to his feet and walked away from the fire. The pain in his chest had returned and he wanted to deal with the hurt and any possible consequences alone.

Rolling and lighting a cigarette, knowing it wasn't the wisest of choices when your chest already felt like it was being squeezed in a vise, he drew the smoke into his lungs. But tobacco had a calming influence on him, and he needed calming. Difficulty breathing frightened him, and whenever he attempted a deep breath, his chest felt like it had knives being driven into it.

The last drag on the cigarette triggered a cough. Once started, it refused to let up. Pulling a handkerchief from his pocket, Doc covered his mouth, attempting to muffle the sound, knowing it was fruitless. The coughing continued, tearing his chest apart. Taking the kerchief from his mouth, he was shocked by red against the starched white. There had never been blood before.

The cough took him again and he doubled over with the force of it. Now he couldn't catch a full breath, and with all he had left, he called for Wyatt. The cigarette dropped from his fingers, and he fell to his knees and hands, shaking, sweating, terrified.

But Earp was already there, frozen to the ground, struck dumb and helpless by the sight of Holliday, down on all fours, head hanging, sweat dripping from his chin, body trembling, breathing wet and labored.

Raising his head with great effort, Doc looked at Earp, speechless, eyes begging for help. Wyatt stared back, stricken, unmoving and looking like all he wanted to do was run. Doc knew brave men, men like Wyatt Earp who stood up against incredible odds, yet whose courage persevered. He also knew that every brave man feared something. Perhaps Wyatt feared what he could not see and could not fight.

In all honesty, the blood on Doc's lips and the liquid, strangled breathing was enough to frighten even the most hardened man. Illness raging unchecked was insidious, creeping and often invisible, leaving death in its wake as any bullet might.

Doc grew more frightened by the moment, breaths coming faster and shorter as he gulped what little air he could into starved lungs. He felt he was passing out, yet remained conscious. Hearing, sight, those senses were yet unimpaired, but the rest of his body was no longer within his control. His arms felt like rubber, his strength lost. He hit the ground hard, and blackness enveloped him. It was a blessing. Being unconscious allowed the body to act without the influence of panic. Lungs expanded and contracted. No matter how short and shallow the breath, air was air.

Doc regained consciousness feeling the world swimming about him, the metallic taste of blood thick in his mouth. He felt like retching. His head buzzed with fever, and it still hurt to breathe. He prayed the coughing wouldn't begin again. He thought it just might kill him. Nothing prepared him for this, the next step in his illness. Perhaps the physicians *had* warned him. Perhaps the future was just too ghastly to contemplate for a young man with the world at his feet and a lifetime to dream.

He needed some water. Opening his eyes, he noticed Wyatt close, sitting, silent and watching with the same stricken expression while still not making a move to help. Doc wanted to ask for a drink, but considered it useless even had he been able to get the words out.

The cough took him again, tearing through his body and leaving chaos in its wake, the chaos of pain exacerbated by terror, the combination unbearable. Holliday doubled up, arms wrapping his chest, whimpering in agony like a hurt child and rocking, rocking, rocking.

He had no concept of the passage of time. Hours or mere moments? He lay still now, rung out, exhausted and breathing with incredible difficulty. A tentative touch against his arm alerted him to Wyatt's presence. *Thank heaven*, he thought. *Thank heaven.*

He felt himself drawn into a sitting position, braced against Earp's chest. The upright position did indeed aid the ability to get air into his starved lungs, and he relaxed back against Wyatt, the cough quieted.

With one hand, Wyatt reached for the canteen, pulled the cork with his teeth, and placed the container to Doc's lips. Attempting to drink and breathe at the same time was difficult at best requiring several moments for Holliday to obtain enough water to slake his thirst. Finished, he faded back against Wyatt, pressing a hand against his chest to ease the sharp, nagging pain.

"Hurt bad?"

Doc nodded.

Easing Holliday back onto a saddle he dragged over as a support, Wyatt searched through the saddlebags, coming up with Doc's whiskey. Uncorking the bottle he offered Holliday a drink.

The smell of whiskey, even fine bourbon, put Doc off. He never did favor it, although he found the taste to be quite acceptable. Once past the bouquet, the whiskey went down well, beyond the raw throat abused by coughing and into the empty stomach. Results quickly materialized. The chest pain lessened along with the anxiety. Doc stopped kneading the painful area over his ribs and his expression grew sleepy, almost languid.

"Better?" Wyatt asked.

Holliday nodded, closing his eyes.

That night, neither man got much rest. Holliday lay caught up in his illness. His fever elevated by the hour, his breathing more difficult and labored as he coughed without letup. Wyatt snatched bits and pieces of sleep when exhaustion momentarily pushed worry aside.

Morning brought some difference in the dentist, none of it good. The fever worsened, burning his cheeks bright red, eyes swimming and bloodshot. Even with the bright campfire burning and blankets tucked up to his chin, the ill man shivered.

Earp shook the last canteen. It was less than half full, and Doc wasn't getting all he needed, his lips were cracked and on the verge of bleeding. The desperate need for water brought Wyatt to a decision.

Kneeling next to Holliday, Wyatt related his plan. "I need to be gone for a while, a couple hours at most. We need water and I have to find it. The river should be around here close by. The canteen's here when you need a drink. I'll be back soon." Taking the half-filled container, Wyatt laid it next to Doc, snug up tight where its presence could be felt.

Doc had no idea Wyatt had left. He'd heard Wyatt's voice, yet had not understood a single word. In his illness, the words were garbled sounds without form or substance, a maelstrom of rushing wind. He was lost, his world relegated to fever, pain, and the constant fight for a decent breath.

Watching the fire dip, swirl and dance to the winds' eddies kept him occupied as much as he could be outside the sickness. Fever-blurred vision gave the flames an eerie beauty. They fascinated the confused mind, giving the sick man something to focus on besides the fight to live.

Earp returned some hours later, empty-handed, his worry increased. He failed to find the river. Making matters worse, a rapidly forming storm advanced from the southwest, a line of black roiling clouds stretching from horizon to horizon, split through by vertical bolts of lightning.

Being caught out in that, a storm of such magnitude with no shelter, would spell certain death for Holliday and perhaps Wyatt as well. It was the type of storm that spawned tornados. Coming from the Midwest, Earp witnessed enough of those killers to know when to run and when to hide. Now was the time to do both.

Wyatt's first action was to offer Holliday water. Doc wanted more, protesting when Earp recapped the container. "Later, you can have more later. We gotta move out. There's a storm comin' and we can't be caught out in it. I'll gather the gear and saddle the horses."

Holliday watched Wyatt's face as he spoke, needing to understand what was being said, but unable to make much sense of the jumbled nonsense. His desperation was obvious to Earp who soothed, "Never mind, Doc, it's all right. I'll come get you when I'm ready."

It took no time at all for the marshal to stow gear and put out the fire. Moving Doc over to lean up against a large rock, he saddled the horses, packing his own tired mount with their belongings, and attaching a lead line to the other horse. Doc's fresh animal would carry both men. In his condition, there was no possible way Holliday could ride unaided.

Doc sat the saddle in front of Earp, slumped over. Wyatt circled him with both arms, one holding Holliday, the other the reins. Nudging the horse in the ribs, he urged the animal forward at a fast walk.

It was a rough go with the storm advancing at an alarming rate, Doc wavering between conscious and unconscious, and the horse tiring of carrying both men. Wyatt swung down from the saddle meaning to walk a while, but Doc slipped sideways, unable to hold himself upright, and Earp was hard put to keep him from tumbling to the ground. He remounted.

The wind coming up off the storm blew with a purpose, as if to make the mens' flight impossible. Blowing dust turned the horses skittish, blinding Earp as he tried to keep to the trail. It grew chilly, and Doc got to shivering again. Though late afternoon, the storm-blackened sky gave all the impression of full on night.

Just when they needed a miracle, they got one. Materializing out of the gloom, a dot of light flickered against a dark, threatening backdrop.

Holliday, shaken from his stupor by an enthusiastic Wyatt, raised his head from his chest squinting through grit filled eyes to a spot the marshal pointed out. "We're gonna make it, Doc." Wyatt shouted against the storm's roar. "We're gonna make it. Just hold on."

All that kept Doc in the saddle was Wyatt's firm grip

about his waist. Doc felt boneless, like a child's rag doll, bumping and jolting to the eccentricity of the horse's gait. At last the journey appeared to be at an end, the rocking step of the horse blessedly stilled. With great effort, Doc raised his head into the gale, hard put to make heads or tails of Wyatt's shouted words.

"We're lawmen out of Dodge City, Wyatt Earp and John Holliday. John's sick. If we could shelter in your barn?"

There was a pause and then a light was thrust into Doc's face, a light so bright he felt the heat of it against his already burning skin. He turned his face away, blinking, and sought to raise an arm to cover his eyes against the intrusion, but he lacked the strength to do so. In a moment the light vanished, though not entirely. It glowed from a distance like a gaslight through fog.

"Barn's for livestock. Bring him into the house." This voice belonged to a woman, or was it only Holliday's imagination?

"He's mighty sick, ma'am, might be typhoid." That was Wyatt's voice. *Typhoid? Perhaps that explains Wyatt's reticence, why he didn't want to come near me.*

"Bring him in and be quick about it. Then you can tend to your horses."

When next he came to consciousness, it was to a vision he could not have imagined. Her face was unlike any he had ever seen: young, but not young, beautiful, but tragic. He was in awe of her, and speechless in her presence even had he the strength *to* speak. As she bent low over him, he was aware of the scent of her, clean from the soap she'd used to wash her hair and homey from the clinging scent of bread she'd baked that morning. There shone from her green eyes a tenderness he had known too seldom in his young life. Her cool touch against fever-warmed skin soothed and calmed him as only one other ever had.

The word came out a dry whisper, "Who?"

"My name is Cleva Moss. You're at my ranch. Some water first and then rest." She held a glass to his lips and he drank, stopping to breathe between sips. "Rest now," she said, "Sleep."

But sleep and all thoughts of sleep were overwhelmed by a sudden and terrifying feeling in his chest. It was as if he were drowning, strangling in his own blood. He panicked and reached out to her. He was pulled upright, held firm in her arms, his head resting against her shoulder. Relief was instant if not total. Fighting the panic, Doc willed himself calmer. Her hand rubbing his back in a slow circular motion, the soft words of comfort whispered against his hair, were a great help.

Wyatt walked in, dropping a saddle to the floor. There was a moment of silence, save for Holliday's labored breathing and the storm raging outside. Earp's question, directed at the lady, was asked as if he were shocked. "Aren't you afraid of the sickness?"

Cleva Moss shook her head, her hand still rubbing Doc's back in that soothing, gentle way. "No, I'm not." She answered. "Are you?"

Again a rather long pause before Earp's answer: "Yes," he said. "Yes, I'm afraid."

He bent down, arranging the saddle on the pallet the woman had prepared on the floor. A fire burned in the nearby grate while the storm howled outside. Rain beat a staccato rhythm against the shingled roof and wind banged unhinged shutters and unlatched gates.

Cleva laid Doc back against the saddle. His breathing seemed easier, but as she settled him back, he moaned. Reaching out, she rested the back of her hand against his hot forehead. It was a mother's instinctive touch, and one that Holliday appreciated, even in illness.

Morning broke, and with it, Doc's fever. Opening his eyes, he wasn't surprised to see the lady, Mrs. Moss, seated at his side in a small, straight-backed chair. Although she appeared asleep, she roused at Doc's not quite muffled cough.

"Some water?"

Doc nodded.

She lifted his head and put the glass to his lips. He drained it and lay back against the pillow, spent. It was then he realized he was no longer on the floor but in an actual bed. He must have looked rather surprised for the lady came to his aid.

"Marshal Earp carried you in early this morning. I figured you'd be more comfortable in a real bed. And your illness, it isn't typhoid. Typhoid shows itself with small red blotches across the body. You've got nary a one." She laid a hand on his shoulder and smiled, as if the knowledge should put him at ease.

Holliday remembered back to the conversation he'd overhead and the mention of typhoid, a heinous illness to be sure, yet when compared to what really ailed him. Well, he would prefer typhoid over consumption. At least the former had a beginning and an end, and if you fought hard enough and long enough, the chances of survival, though not great, were at least there. Consumption, that was another matter altogether. No amount of fighting or praying had any effect. It was a death sentence, without the possibility of commutation. Doc turned his head away from the lady, but she was perceptive, he'd give her that.

"You knew it wasn't typhoid."

Doc did not answer.

"You know what it is, though."

He cringed at her directness.

"You knew all along, but you didn't tell your friend."

The hand on his shoulder squeezed. "It's all right," she said. "Your reasons for keeping this to yourself are yours alone."

Doc turned back toward her. It was then, in the brightening light, in his new clear vision, he noticed her beauty. The beauty he'd been so taken with the night before was flawed. A scar, its livid, purple color attesting to its still healing status, snaked down her face from temple to chin. He caught his breath at the sight. Her hand flew to her face, to the abomination. This time it was she who turned her face away.

"I-I," he stammered, but the words would not come. How could he tell her she was still lovely, still all the things he had thought of her at first sight. And why would she believe him, a stranger and a liar? Yes, he was a liar, perhaps by omission, but a liar nevertheless.

Still ill, somewhat feverish, Holliday passed into sleep fraught with dreams and nightmares. He woke to the lady fussing over him, straightening the pillow beneath his head, and wondered if she ever slept or took any time for herself. He longed to apologize, sought to find the words, but then, as she busied herself with his comfort, Cleva's plait fell loose from its moorings at the nape of her neck. Her waist-length braid, of the most singular red/gold color, dropped down over her shoulder and within Doc's easy grasp. He reached out, touching it, feeling in it the delicate softness, the womanness of it. He noticed the end of it was tied round with a bit of white ribbon.

A horror enveloped him. He was back in the killers' cabin, back among the objects he'd discovered, he and Wyatt, the hair, the scalps. Just then a door slammed. It was Wyatt entering the kitchen, his arms laden with kindling, but Doc had no idea the presence was benign.

Pushing Cleva Moss aside, he grabbed for the pistol that hung in its holster from the back of the small chair. Leaping from bed, he shoved the woman into the corner, a place where he might better protect her against the threatening evil. Standing between her and what might come, crouched low, he thumbed back the .45's hammer and he waited.

Wyatt walked in, not expecting the sight that met his gaze. "What in hell's goin' on here? Doc?"

Holliday, deep into his waking nightmare, did not recognize Earp. Indeed he did not recognize the place he found himself. To his clouded mind, he was back *there*, once again facing the enemy, but this time all that stood between them and yet another innocent victim was John Holliday.

"John." Her hand was on his arm, her voice insistent in his ear. "John. Don't. It's Marshal Earp. It's your friend. John."

He mistook her pleas as petitions for help. Trembling from weakness, he tightened his finger on the trigger. He had to fire before it was too late. He took as steady an aim as was possible.

"Doc, Doc, it's me. It's Wyatt. Put down the gun." Wyatt held his arms out, palms up to show he held no weapons. Holliday hesitated, torn by what he perceived as real in his tortured mind and by the trust he placed in Earp. "Doc," the voice came again, so calm, coaxing, "put the gun down now. It's just me, Wyatt."

Doc allowed his gun hand to drop. Slow and easy he let the hammer down. His knees buckled.

Worried faces stared down at him, worried and confused. Too exhausted to explain, Doc reached out, once again taking Cleva Moss's shining plait in his hand. This he held out to Wyatt. Between the men no other explanation was needed.

Wyatt nodded his understanding, and Doc allowed the braid to drop away.

"Missus Moss, ma'am, we need to talk." Wyatt left the door between the rooms ajar, allowing Holliday to hear that which passed between Cleva and Wyatt. The marshal told her how they had tracked the killers, how they had brought them to justice, and what he and Doc had found secreted away in their filthy hideout.

Cleva's words flowed without hesitation as if once she paused she might not be able to continue. "They came while my husband was away, the three men and that woman," she began. "It was just my daughter, Lorena, and me. They used us in the most vile ways. When I awoke days later, I found my daughter already laid in the ground without even a mother's touch to tend her poor, broken body. I never knew those savages had done that to my Lorrie, taken her hair, her beautiful hair. I lived, but barely, scarred as you see me now. My husband, not being a strong man, took things hard. He tried, but the grief was too much for him to bear, that and the guilt. Had he only been home, he thought, though I doubt that would have mattered. I found him one morning. He'd hung himself out in the barn." Here Cleva's narrative ended as she broke down sobbing. Doc turned his hot face into the pillow and grieved with her.

There were sounds of Wyatt offering rather awkward comfort, and then Cleva's voice once more. This time there was no sorrow. In fact, she sounded elated. In a moment there was the scraping back of kitchen chairs, and Cleva appeared framed in the doorway of Doc's bedroom. Her step was quick as she came to sit beside him, and although her eyes were red from crying, there was a smile upon her lips. She took Doc's hand in both of hers.

"Thank you," she said. "Thank you for what you did, for bringing those murderers to a just end, and for what you, you and Wyatt did for my little girl and those other poor souls. Perhaps some day you and Wyatt might bring me to the place where you laid that part of my Lorrie to rest? I'd like to see it. Wyatt says it's a peaceful spot, a pretty spot. Would you, John?"

"It would be an honor, ma'am," Holliday whispered.

Leaning forward she brushed the tousled hair from his forehead and kissed him there and once on each cheek. Her smile was warm and unguarded. "Before, you were protecting me, weren't you, from them?"

"I thought so," John replied. "I hoped so."

The next days remained a blur to Doc. His single outburst cost him. His strength failed to return, and he lay in bed, listless and disinterested, taking in little or no nourishment. At first Wyatt attempted to lure him up with the temptation of a game of chance or any other pastime he figured Holliday might enjoy, but to no avail. In time Earp gave up. From dawn to dusk the sound of hammering, sawing or nailing told Doc how Wyatt spent his hours. The ranch, without a man these long months to keep up with repairs, was in dire need of help. Wyatt was doing his part to put the place in good order.

Cleva took to sitting at Doc's bedside mending, sewing, or doing crochet. Her presence was a welcome comfort, though even she could not tempt him from his bed. Sometimes she read to him from her small library of classics. He enjoyed the sound of her voice, lilting and expressive, and more than once fell asleep under her spell. He also got to know the lady quite well, and the better he knew her, the more he liked Cleva Moss.

Once he woke to find her watching him with undisguised interest. She did not turn her gaze away, nor did she appear the least bit uncomfortable that she had been caught so. Instead she smiled and reaching out, brushed a lock of pale wavy hair off his forehead, the better to judge the heat of his fever with the back of her hand.

"You remind me of my son, very much so," she confided. "His name was Shelby. He would've been about your age had he lived past his tenth birthday.

"He was fair with a scattering of freckles across a straight nose, tall and slender, too, like a reed in the wind. Had he lived to grow into a man like you, John, I could not have been happier."

Doc was touched by her words, but hurried to put her straight. "I am not the kind of man any mother should desire her child to emulate, ma'am. I often find myself in the company of ne're-do-wells, gunslingers, and other miscreants. I myself often make my living as a sporting man, a gambler. I'm sure your son would have been a much better man than me, though it pleases me that you seem to think so well of John Holliday." He fumbled with the blanket that covered him, preoccupied with a loose thread.

Cleva placed her hand beneath his chin and bade him look up at her. "Wyatt Earp believes you are a good and decent man, John. Would you make a liar of him?" Her smile teased him for an answer.

Doc knew he was beaten. "No, ma'am. I would never do such an injustice to a friend. It appears I must indeed be a good and decent man…in spite of myself."

Although the following day dawned sunny and warm, Doc kept to his bed. He felt drained and wished he might explain how bad he felt to Cleva and Wyatt. Today, even the thought of putting forth enough effort to speak seemed more than he could manage. Had he a mirror in which to look, he knew he would see his reflection fading away by the moment.

Pounds he could ill afford dropped from his frame at an alarming rate.

Some days after the drawn gun incident, Wyatt stood alongside Doc's bed, hands on hips, looking down at the ill man while shaking his head in a rather sorry manner. It took a moment for Doc, in his dilapidated condition, to realize Earp was up to something. He looked too smug. Whether Wyatt was smug or not, planning something or not, Doc was too ill to prevent it.

"Come on, Holliday. It's a beautiful day. Sun's shining, birds are singing, the breeze is warm and the grass is green. Let's go." Earp tossed back the covers, bent down and picked up the sick man, calling out to Cleva, "Ma'am if you'd grab a blanket, I'd be obliged."

Passing the lady with a nod, Wyatt pushed through the screened door and out where he deposited Doc in Cleva's rocker, took the blanket she offered, and made a great show of tucking it in and around the frail body while clucking, mother hen like, "There. How's that? Warm enough?"

Doc looked up at the marshal, certain the man had lost his mind, more certain still when Earp smiled a big, silly, out of character, ear-to-ear grin.

"I'd rather not be out here, if it's all the same to you," Holliday offered, but to no avail. Outside he was and there he stayed until Wyatt believed he'd soaked up enough fresh air and sunshine.

That first day proved the worst. Being outdoors did not interest the ill dentist. All he desired was sleep. By the second day he perked up, due in part to a pair of new foals cavorting in the paddock, just kicking up their heels and enjoying life to the fullest. Watching the exuberant youngsters at play kept the chair-bound Holliday entertained.

The following afternoon, Cleva served lunch out on the

small porch. Earp washed in the basin outside, drying his face on a towel before pulling up a stool and digging in to stew and biscuits. Hard physical labor seemed to appeal to him. He looked happy and at ease, more so than Doc ever remembered seeing him.

Holliday picked at his food, his appetite not yet up to snuff. Cleva worried aloud, but Wyatt told her not to bother. "Stubborn's all he is. Probably won't eat because we think he should. Ignore him, ma'am. Tomorrow you'll see a difference."

Doc glowered. "Talk like I'm not sitting right here listening," he pouted.

For whatever reason, the next day proved Earp correct. Doc ate everything on his plate, delighting Cleva by asking for seconds. Her face flushed with relief, she turned smiling to Wyatt who winked, mouthing, "I told you so."

"I saw that, marshal. Remember, I *am* sitting right here." Doc forked another bite of potato into his mouth.

Holliday was just getting comfortable in the front porch rocker, a light blanket tucked about him, drinking his second cup of breakfast coffee, when Earp walked up leading his saddled stallion. "I need to send a wire to Dodge and figured to pick up some supplies for the ranch. According to Cleva, I should be able to make the ride to the nearest town and back in seven hours, at most."

"Since you'll be away, marshal, would you be kind enough to get me my revolver, the .45?"

Wyatt returned in a moment, handing Doc the pistol. "Expecting trouble?"

Doc checked the cylinder. Satisfied it held five rounds, he tucked the pistol beneath the blanket and smiled, "Not at all, but it pays to be safe."

Cleva poked her head out from the opened window behind Holliday's chair. "Take care, Wyatt. Don't worry about us. We'll be fine."

"I know you will, ma'am." Stepping up into the saddle, Earp tipped his hat to the pair and kicked the black into a mile eating trot.

Morning and early afternoon were uneventful. Doc rested and read aloud from one of several books in Cleva's well thumbed collection, Shakespeare's A *Midsummer Night's Dream*.

The lady came out onto the porch wiping flour coated hands onto her apron. Already the scent of baking bread wafted out through window and door. "The way you read, with such meaning, I feel like I've never heard those words before. But as much as I enjoy the sound of your voice, you've been at it for over two hours now, and it's time you put aside the book and rested." At Doc's look of dismay, she chided him in a gentle voice, "There's always tomorrow."

Wanting to please her, Doc leaned back and closed his eyes. He *was* weary. A nap would feel good. Dozing led to deeper sleep, and he was unaware of the stranger riding up the road until the trespasser was already within the yard. Holliday snapped awake, his fingers finding the .45 beneath the blanket.

"Well, I was told a widow woman lived here all by her lonesome. Didn't hear nothin' bout her havin' a grown son around the place. Or if she's a looker, might be she got herself a young husband." Brash and smug, the stranger's smile was as phony as a three dollar bill.

"Whatever you heard, you were mistaken. State your business, or be on your way." Doc's sixth sense kicked in.

The man snuck up way too soundless for a person on legal business, and he had the audacity to make a rude remark concerning Mrs. Moss. Being sneaky was one thing, but Holliday would tolerate no disrespectful behavior when it came to a lady like Cleva.

"That ain't a very nice way for you to be talkin' to a man who's interested in makin' this spread his own." The stranger peered at Holliday from beneath long, greasy bangs, and when he grinned again, Doc noticed his teeth were brown from neglect and tobacco. But if anything pointed out the lack of a man's character, it was in the way he treated his horse. The buckskin he sat hadn't had a decent feed in months, every rib showed through a bald-patch coat, mane and tail were matted, and the marks of quirt and spur were evident from the animal's neck to its hindquarters.

From where Doc sat, the stink of the man's clothing and body turned his stomach. "This place is not for sale. Just turn around and leave."

"Who said anything 'bout buyin' it? I'm just gonna take it, and by the looks a you, there ain't a thing you can do about it. Sick are ya? Don't think you could get outta that chair by yerself if ya had to." This time the stranger did not bother smiling.

"I don't need to get out of this chair." Holliday jerked the blanket aside revealing the shiny nickel-plated .45, cocked.

"From this distance I could just cut your reins. Or, I could put a bullet into your head or your heart. Or you could turn around and leave. It's your choice, and if you happen to see one of my brothers, you can't miss them, big men, sandy haired, tell 'em John said it was all right for you to pass on by. But if you happen on the one ridin' the black, steer him a wide berth. He is possessed of a foul temper and prone to shoot first, no questions asked."

"Ooooh, I'm shakin' in my boots." The stranger jiggled his body in a parody of a man suffering from St. Vitas' Dance. Putting spurs to hide, he forced his sorry mount closer to the porch.

Without further warning, Holliday fired a round from the .45, slicing the man's rein at a spot between the animal's head and neck, a thick, white, smoke cloud obscuring the shooter.

The horse reared in terror, pitching the rider who grappled with the cut lead, trying to get the animal under control. Now the stranger's trembling was real.

"Guess I was mistaken 'bout this place. I'll be leavin' now." Turning his mount, he kicked the unfortunate beast into a run. Scaring a widow off her place was one thing. Tangling with a widow and her brood of grown sons, with at least one of those sons a crack shot, was another matter all together.

Holliday breathed a sigh of relief. Easing the hammer down on the .45, he was shocked to hear the sound repeated from the small window at his back.

Cleva came out onto the porch, holding a big Walker Colt. "It was my husband's. It was Joe's," she explained. Reaching up, Doc relieved her of the pistol, resting the weapon in his lap. Taking her cold, trembling hands in his, he gently warmed them.

It wasn't long before Wyatt rode in through the ranch gates heading for the barn. It was pretty obvious from the haste in which he unsaddled and cared for his horse before heading up to the house that something was amiss. Earp's rather sour expression just clinched the deal for Doc. Wyatt-like, Earp came to the point, a point Holliday expected.

"What in blazes was that all about? Some muleskinner on a fleabit nag, if ever I saw one, rambling on about John said this, and I was to let him pass and all. What happened?"

"Did you play along, Wyatt?" Holliday asked, feigning nonchalance.

"I did, but I sure didn't know it to be a game."

Cleva interrupted. "That man thought he could just waltz in here and take my place. John showed him otherwise. That's pretty much it."

"I heard a shot." Wyatt pasted Holliday with one of his steeliest expressions, and the dentist knew a real explanation was in order.

"It's as Mrs. Moss said. That trash wanted this ranch. He figured it to be easy pickins' what with Cleva bein' alone and all. Men on the place weren't in his reckoning. I asked him to leave. When he resisted, I cut his rein. That really *is* all of it."

Wyatt sighed. "Well I sure can't say I'm surprised it's come to this. What does surprise me is that it didn't happen sooner."

Earp shifted the weighty saddlebags up onto his shoulder and gazed off to a point somewhere past the house, past the low rolling hills, silent for a moment, lost in thought. In a moment he looked up at Cleva. "Could we get some coffee, ma'am? We need to talk, the three of us."

"Certainly, Wyatt."

Before stepping into the house to build the requested pot of coffee, Cleva relieved John of both pistols. He patted her hand once and smiled. She nodded.

From the rocking chair, Doc heard Wyatt unloading supplies onto the kitchen table. In a moment he returned, walking right past Doc to sit on the porch stairs where he rolled and lit a cigarette. It was as if he'd forgotten Holliday was even there, until Doc interrupted the shared silence with an observation.

"I am no mind reader, but then it doesn't take one to know you're troubled."

Not bothering to turn around, Wyatt answered

between draws on his smoke, "I am. We'll talk when the coffee's ready."

Over coffee and fresh bread slathered with jam, the three sat inside at the small table, each uncomfortable.

Clearing his throat, Wyatt began. "Mrs. Moss, Cleva, it's my belief you should get out of here. Sell this place. Either move closer to what's civilized, or move into a town. This is no place for a woman alone. Not even a woman with your courage. It's just not right. What happened today proves it. Sell this place. Leave and do it now."

Wyatt drained his coffee cup. Cleva refilled it in silence.

Doc was far from happy with Wyatt's rationale, though he did agree with part of it. "I understand what you're saying, Wyatt. I do, but it's not your place to say. Mrs. Moss should not be forced to leave a home she loves, to be driven out by fears whether real or imagined. She's been through enough. It should be her decision, not yours and not mine."

Holliday stared down into his coffee. With a deep sigh, he continued. "I was forced by circumstances to leave a home I loved. I will regret leaving all my days."

He looked up and at Wyatt. "Once you asked me why I left Georgia if I missed it so? Now I'll tell you. I have consumption, tuberculosis, TB, whatever you choose to call it. Right out of dental college, just as I started a new life and a new practice, I got sick. Doctors told me if I stayed in Georgia with its damp climate, I'd die inside a year.

"There was no choice for me, Wyatt. I had to leave my home. Cleva doesn't. There are other options for her. We just have to help her find them."

Reaching out to Holliday, Cleva lay a rough hand over his with a quick squeeze. "At least now I know how come Wyatt calls you Doc." She smiled.

Wyatt interrupted. "I'm sorry for what happened to you,

what's happening to you, but it doesn't make one bit of difference in deciding what's to be done here. This place isn't safe for decent men or decent women.

"Look what's already happened to you, Cleva. Lord, how can you even think of staying here?" Wyatt jumped to his feet, pacing the small room like a caged animal, desperate to make his point clear. Stopping in front of Cleva's chair he crouched down, his face inches from hers. "You have to leave. There is no choice."

Cleva pulled back from the verbal assault. However well meant, it was still an assault. Doc leaped to the lady's defense. Quick to his feet, he knocked his chair over in the process and slammed both palms down onto the table, rattling the cups in their saucers and causing cream in the small pitcher to slosh over. His voice raised in anger, Doc confronted Wyatt.

"You don't seem to understand, marshal. You're so used to telling people what to do and how to do it, you don't understand that people, regular law abiding citizens, have a right to decide their own lives. What you have, Wyatt, is the 'I'm God and you're not' syndrome so many lawmen acquire. Not everyone in this world needs you to tell them how to live, where to live, or why to live, Marshal Earp."

Wyatt turned livid with anger. Storming out the front door, he stomped to the corral, saddled his horse, and raced off down the road without so much as a backward glance.

"I thought we were just going to talk," Cleva said.

Doc's smile was tired, but sincere, as he sought to explain things from his perspective. "Wyatt is an emotional man, whether or not he's aware of it. When he feels passionate about something, he acts first. Oh, he thinks about it right enough, but sort of as an afterthought.

"I'm still not sure why he deputized me back in Dodge. I'm no lawman. I'm a dentist and a gambler and rumored to be good with a gun. He didn't know for sure whether the gun business had any truth to it at all. He does now, and I think his choosing me was right, but back then he was caught up in the emotion, the moment.

"He's caught up in things here and now as well. He cares, Cleva. Maybe he cares too much for his own good and draws everybody in right along with him. Black and white, no holds barred, get it done and do it now. That's Wyatt."

Holliday righted his chair and sank his weary body onto it. "He means well. I know that. I also know I was too hard on him, that *I'm God* speech.'" Doc shook his head, but Cleva smiled at him.

"Things will turn out all right. You'll see."

Doc had little appetite for dinner, and both he and Cleva retired to bed early. He attempted to lose himself in a novel, but to no avail. The pain returned, that damned annoying twinge between his ribs, and as much as he tried to ignore it, the pain grew more and more defiant of his resolve, worsening by the moment.

Eyes wide with fear, breaths coming short and fast, jaws clamped tight to keep silent, he kneaded a spot on the right side of his chest in hopes the action might mitigate the pain, even a fraction, anything.

In the doorway appeared Wyatt, a lamp held high. He disappeared, returning with two pillows tucked beneath one arm. Setting the lamp upon the small dresser, he went to Doc, lifting him into a sitting position and tucking the extra pillows behind his head and back.

Reaching over to the table, Wyatt poured whiskey into the water glass. "This helped some before." Putting the glass into Doc's hands, he helped him drink. Many swallows later, the half filled glass was empty.

Holliday trembled with the hurt, but when Wyatt wanted to summon Cleva, Doc stopped him. "Better. It's getting better," he forced out from between clenched jaws. At first there were no signs of any such thing, but very slowly the tension on Doc's face eased, his eyelids fluttered closed, and the kneading of the painful area ceased. He relaxed into the pillows.

Whatever their differences of the night before, morning brought Doc and Wyatt together in peace. Wyatt woke so stiff it was all he could do to heave his protesting body up from the chair where he'd slept.

Doc, on the other hand, awoke feeling well, though he still needed a hand to climb out of the deep feather mattress. He remembered some of the previous night, waking in pain and seeing Wyatt's face floating within a cloud of yellow lamp light. He remembered the whiskey, too, if only from the disagreeable taste lingering in his mouth.

Cleva served up breakfast, which they ate in appreciative silence. Both men were ravenous this morning, both accepting seconds of ham, eggs, and biscuits when offered, and of course coffee.

"Good thing I brought in more supplies since we're doin' such a good job of eating up yours." Wyatt leaned over, again refilled his cup from the family-size coffeepot. Fragrant steam issued from its spout in a dreamy spiral.

"I'm happy to see it. Worries me when grown men don't eat enough," Cleva said.

"Come to any conclusions on your ride yesterday, marshal?" Doc leaned back in his chair, full of good food and better coffee, figuring why draw out the inevitable?

"I did, and I was just getting round to opening that discussion." Wyatt took out fixins' and rolled himself a cigarette, offering pouch and papers to Holliday who did likewise. "Don't go gettin' light headed on me, Doc, but I believe you were right yesterday when you said there were other ways to deal with the problem of Mrs. Moss livin' out here alone, aside from packing up and moving." A long drawn out pause followed while Wyatt enjoyed his smoke.

Doc wished Earp would either speak faster or get to the point. Patience was not a Holliday virtue. "And?" he prompted, exhaling smoke through his nose, realizing it was not a very gentlemanly thing to do at the breakfast table, and apologizing to Mrs. Moss for his rudeness. She accepted the apology with a smile.

"Do continue, Wyatt, please," Cleva prompted.

Wyatt crushed the cigarette out in the saucer of his coffee cup. Resting his forearms on the table, he leaned toward Cleva and spoke in earnest. "Ma'am, I think you could try hiring on a couple full time hands. Wouldn't need to pay 'em much hard money. Room and board and a bit to spend on Saturday night would do. I saw lots of men in Caldwell looking for work, a lot of 'em breeds and Indians, not that I consider that a problem so long as they have somebody to vouch for 'em. Might be you do, a neighboring rancher, some friend of your husband's maybe?"

"Splendid idea, marshal." Holliday reached over and clapped Wyatt on the shoulder. "Still waters do run deep."

Softly at first, then with a bit more decisiveness to her voice, Cleva spoke out. "Joe did have several good friends among the ranchers here about. We could ride over and have a talk with the closest. If that doesn't pan out and he can't give us any leads, then we could just try the next." She smiled and the room brightened all the more for it.

"You say who and when and I'll be ready to tag along. I'll leave everything up to you. I'm just along for the company." Wyatt looked over at Doc who nodded his approval.

Holliday discovered something about Earp which surprised, yet gladdened him. Wyatt proved far less narrow minded than Doc led himself to believe; intelligence and a willingness to compromise made for a most favorable combination of traits in a lawman, in any man.

Cleva rose from the table. "It's a long ride to the nearest ranch, the Dobbs' place. Let's say tomorrow morning right after breakfast? That gives me today to set the bread and get chores done."

"Let's do it then." Wyatt got to his feet and began gathering dirty dishes.

Holliday felt rather the third wheel. He would've enjoyed a ride, but doubted his ability to climb into the saddle, let alone go trotting off for who knew how many miles. It would've felt nice to be asked, though.

Spending the day in the chair on the porch, Doc busied himself with reading and watching Cleva and Wyatt at chores. The cough did not nag, and the fever was better, much better, he was certain of it. Resting a cool palm against his forehead, Cleva agreed. However, when he broached the subject of the next day's ride, the answer was a resounding, "No."

Just after daybreak the following morning, Cleva and Wyatt set off on their adventure, leaving John alone on the ranch to look after things, after him.

Feeling well and in good spirits, Doc decided to take some initiative. As soon as he could no longer see the dust from the departing horses, he dropped the lap blanket to the floor, rose from his rocker, went to the bedroom, and slipped into the shoulder rig, holstering the .45.

Then it was out to the corral to saddle the mare. That tired him more than he imagined, so he took a moment to lean up against the corral and smoke a cigarette. Finished, he swung up into the saddle, unlatched the gate and rode out.

Keeping the buildings in sight, Doc loped around the perimeter of the ranch. He felt human again, like a man and not an invalid.

The countryside was pleasant, with rolling hills in various hues of green interspersed with wild flowers. An occasional tree broke the landscape, providing depth and interest.

Glad he remembered to fill his canteen, he drained it before arriving back at the house. He'd been gone several hours and by the time he unsaddled the mare, rubbed her down and given her a ration of oats, he was starving and exhausted.

Food was first on the agenda. Cleva left a picnic of cold fried chicken from last evening's dinner and a large slice of strawberry pie which he wolfed down with warmed over coffee.

An after meal nap was next in order. Removing the shoulder holster, Doc decided to keep the .45, as before, on his lap beneath the coverlet.

When Doc woke he found Cleva and Wyatt standing over him looking displeased, as no smiles were in evidence, very much out of character for Cleva if not Wyatt.

"John, I hope you were doing nothing more than sitting on the steps here without a hat on," Cleva admonished.

Wyatt pointed out the dust coating Doc's boots. "Out riding?"

"There a law against that in these parts now, marshal?" Holliday shot back.

"There is when you're too sick to be out riding and riding alone, of all the foolish tricks," Wyatt replied.

"I am not too ill to be out riding, since I was out riding,

and it seems to have done me no harm at all." Holliday noticed Cleva slip into the house, returning with a mirror in hand.

She held the glass out to him. "No harm?"

Doc checked himself in the mirror, twirling his moustache up into rakish points and playing the self absorbed dandy to a less than amused audience. He noticed the slight sunburn on cheeks and nose, but chose not to mention it, "No harm whatsoever and for the record, I never considered a bit of sun warming one's complexion to be detrimental to the health."

"We'll see about that tomorrow when you're too bad off to get your sorry self outta bed." Wyatt feigned disgust, but appeared amused and almost relieved at Doc's antics.

Doc, quick to change the subject, one he was uncomfortable with, did just that, "So was your trip successful?" He continued to preen in the mirror for effect until Cleva withdrew it and herself into the house to start supper.

Wyatt sat on the steps and took his time rolling a quirly. "I believe so. Mr. Dobbs seems a nice enough man, easy to trust." He placed the finished smoke between his lips and lit it. Relaxed and at ease, he leaned into the post at his back and stretched out his legs.

Once again, Holliday wished he would get on with it, the not knowing giving him fits.

"Tomorrow he's sending over a couple hands for Mrs. Moss to check out, see if they'll fit in. He's let a half dozen or so men go. His heart's bad and he can't run the stock he used to, so he's cutting down on operations.

"He claims these two worked for him goin' on five years. They're sober and hard working and most of all, loyal. He placed a great value on the loyal part. Some do." Wyatt paused, flicking the cigarette ash onto the ground.

If Holliday got Earp's somewhat cloudy innuendo, he

made no mention, nor did his expression change, but it wasn't like the quick witted dentist to allow even a cloudy innuendo to slip by.

Wyatt continued, "Cleva needs the loyalty of decent hired hands. I'll accept nothing less in them and we won't be leavin' until I'm satisfied."

Doc leaned forward toward Wyatt, his voice low, "She means a great deal to you, doesn't she?"

"She does." Wyatt replied and then he did something Doc had never heard him do before. The quiet, reticent lawman waxed poetic. "She stirs me somehow. It's her courage I guess, but, too, the way she gave so much of herself to us, strangers who wandered into her life, hurting and needy. She is all woman and then some."

Holliday found himself impressed not just by Wyatt's soliloquy, but how he opened up to a friend. "I agree, marshal. We shall do right by her before we depart. We owe her that and more."

"Much more," Earp agreed and there was a warmth in his voice that touched Doc, that particular innuendo not lost on the dentist. The sentiment brought a ready smile to his lips. Although he'd almost died on the trip, Doc figured he'd lived a lot more. All things considered, he wouldn't have missed a single moment.

True to his word, Mr. Dwight Dobbs sent two hands over the next day, late morning. The men were Texicans, one about twenty and the other nearer forty, and they were brothers, not father and son as folks first believed when meeting them. They were Oliver and Joseph Mushgrove, and to their credit they never gave Cleva's scar so much as a second glance upon meeting her for the first time.

The younger brother appeared shy, not speaking unless spoken to, while the elder seemed a little more outgoing in that he volunteered more information than a terse one word answer to Cleva's questions.

Wyatt and Doc kept out of the interview, preferring to stand down by the corral and watch the proceedings and the two candidates while pretending not to. Appearing disinterested while catching every aside, every innuendo, was a Holliday forte. He saw nothing out of the way in the Mushgroves, telling Wyatt, "They just feel right to me." Earp agreed.

The brothers rode off the ranch, and Cleva walked over to give Doc and Wyatt the news. "I hired them on. They seem fine men, quiet, but steady." She shrugged. "I'm not sure if you'll understand this, but they just feel right."

Doc and Wyatt exchanged grins. "Speaking for the marshal and myself, ma'am, we do indeed understand," Doc said.

A week passed before Wyatt believed Doc ready to tolerate the long days yet ahead of them to Dodge City. Seven days also gave both men a chance to get to know Cleva's new hired hands. They were not disappointed in the brothers Mushgrove.

Parting was sad and bittersweet. Cleva cried, though it was obvious she tried her hardest to be strong. She kissed each young man once on either cheek and once on the lips, then found herself enveloped within strong arms in embraces she almost did not have the strength to break.

Doc had a hard time breaking their embrace. To the young man who had lost his own mother by age fifteen, it was almost like being torn from her arms again. At least this parting was not due to death, but time and circumstance. Nevertheless, leaving was a hurtful thing indeed.

Even the Mushgrove brothers were moved at the tender

farewells, so moved as to offer words of comfort to the lawmen as they stepped into their saddles, "Don't you worry none. She'll be safe with us here. Bet on that."

John Holliday, looking into the face of the elder Mushgrove, saw the truth there in the prematurely lined countenance, the deep-set blue eyes whose forthright gaze never wavered, and the straight firm line of a mouth. It lightened his heart and made the nagging guilt and grief he felt at leaving easier to take, for a bit.

The lawmen rode for some miles in companionable silence, the *companionable* a hard won and valuable commodity.

Holliday reined in, making a great show of patting down his pockets for tobacco and papers, but coming up empty. Wyatt noticed the predicament and rode in close, extended a hand. On the palm lay papers and a sack of Bull Durham. Rolling a quirly and placing it between his lips, Doc lit the smoke and inhaled in satisfaction, proceeding to tuck sack and papers into his vest pocket.

"No you don't." Wyatt held out his hand and Doc deposited the makings in the palm.

"Just wanted to save you some trouble when I need another," Holliday quipped.

"No trouble, Doc." Wyatt replaced the items in his shirt pocket.

"Do you think things have changed much in Dodge since we've been away?" Holliday asked, urging his mount back into a walk, Earp keeping slow pace alongside.

When Wyatt answered some half an hour later, Doc had almost forgotten he'd asked the question. "Things have changed in Dodge, I'd bet on it. But I reckon what's changed most is us."

"Would that be in a good way, Wyatt, or a bad way?"

"Both."

Holliday smiled, "Succinct as usual, marshal, and enigmatic. *That* hasn't changed."

"We've got days to go before we get back. Talkin' about change now might be..." Wyatt searched his vocabulary, brow furrowed, for the correct word.

"Presumptuous?"

"Presumptuous," Wyatt nodded. "A lot could happen yet."

"I agree, but I'd like to get back before either of us changes to such a degree that we don't recognize ourselves in the mirror." Doc kicked his horse into a trot. Turning in the saddle he yelled back, "Of course for some that might not be such a bad thing at all."

CHAPTER 5

Two days out of the Moss ranch found Doc and Wyatt halfway to Dodge. Nothing of consequence had happened so far, and for that both were glad. They'd passed any number of small squatter's cabins. From a distance, which they maintained, it was difficult to see who occupied the rundown abodes, but Wyatt offered a fair guess, "Trash, just trash." Holliday shrugged and the pair rode on.

The third day found them in a dusty, no name town which boasted a mercantile, a livery, and a saloon. Loafing about were any number of individuals of rather dubious character.

Dismounting, Doc mentioned to his companion how very odd he found it that no one bothered with cleanliness anymore. He mentioned this without thinking to do so in a whisper, just as an individual of unkempt appearance slouched past. All that seemed clean on the man was a small area ringing his eyes so that he had the look of a shaggy raccoon in tattered human guise. Holliday opened his mouth to add yet another observation to those already voiced, when Wyatt cautioned him.

"I'd watch my tone around here was I you, Doc."

"As you wish, marshal," Holliday replied, though he didn't think he'd been too boisterous in his remarks. And he hadn't been untruthful.

Wyatt preceded Doc up onto the boardwalk, such as it was, and into the mercantile. Glancing around, Holliday was quick to notice the thick dust layering every item, including crackers in a barrel and rock candy in an uncovered glass jar on the counter. He frowned and pointed this out to Earp.

"What do you want me to do about it, Doc?" There was more than a hint of impatience in his voice.

"Must we make our purchases in this, this hole? Can't we wait until the next town?" Holliday asked hopefully.

"Doc, the next town is Dodge and that's still two days' ride. We didn't take much in the way of provisions from Cleva's. We're already out of coffee."

"Oh, I see. Well, that explains everything. How could we go on without coffee?"

Doc's sarcasm was countered by Wyatt who impaled Holliday with a look dirty enough to match their surroundings and then some.

Holliday did not allow that to pass without comment. "I'll wait outside if you don't mind, Wyatt. And while you're at it you might ask the proprietor if he happens to have soap in stock." He passed a finger across the grimy glass countertop, holding it up towards Earp. "Though I doubt it," he added.

Earp picked a tin of peaches up off the counter and lobbed it at Holliday, just missing his head as Doc ducked sideways. The can sailed out the door and into the road where it came to rest at the feet of yet another disreputable appearing denizen of the no name town.

Holliday ambled out as well, taking up a stance near the hitching post where he figured to take in the town as he waited.

The man at whose feet Earp's misdirected projectile

landed was no mere man, but a giant. He was not just tall, but broad shouldered and barrel-chested. Doc gave the fellow a thorough visual going over, coming to the conclusion that this individual had to be the filthiest human being he'd ever had the misfortune to lay eyes upon, up to and including his earlier sighting.

Holliday shrank from the figure as it approached lest it brush against him, shuddering at the very thought of what might be transferred from the giant to his person, whether it be animal, vegetable, or mineral.

The bearded giant's facial hair was encrusted with old food and tobacco drippings. That bit of decoration continued down onto the fellow's torn shirt, the color of which could be described as *encrusted sweat*.

Trousers looking as if rolled in horse manure were held up by ragged braces with the whole package stinking to a high degree. Doc wrinkled his nose in disgust, his sensibilities offended as the man pushed past and into the mercantile, the tin of peaches clutched in one beefy paw.

But offense aside, Doc figured something interesting was about to happen, something he did not want to miss. He rolled a cigarette and lit it, inhaling, the smoke plume fanning out about his head. Leaning back against the rail, he watched the goings on inside the mercantile.

"What 'cha throw this at me for?" The giant directed his question at Wyatt who answered without looking up, so absorbed was he in counting out the dollar and several odd cents to the merchant for supplies, including the tin of peaches.

"Sorry, I didn't throw it at you. I was aiming at that loafer out there," Earp glanced at Holliday through the opened door, "the skinny one smoking the cigarette." Smiling, Doc touched the brim of his hat in acknowledgement.

Only then did Wyatt look at the man standing next to him. And by the expression on his face, a combination of shock and surprise with a bit of revulsion thrown in for good measure, one could see Earp felt the same way about the gentleman as did Doc.

The giant's personality proved as foul as his appearance, and he would not take Wyatt's word that Holliday was the can's intended target and not he.

"Why would I go out of my way to instigate a fight? I don't know you. I have no reason to get on your bad side." Earp picked up the sack of goods from the counter and walked past the giant outside where he could at least breathe a breath of fresh air. He filled his lungs.

"Making new friends, are we marshal?" Holliday teased with a grin. The grin disappeared as Earp's new acquaintance shoved Doc aside and headed straight for Wyatt.

The bag flew from Earp's hands, the sack of flour it contained bursting onto the ground looking for all the world like scattered snow. Wyatt's protest, uttered an instant before the giant's fist caught him, overlapped Doc's shouted warning.

Wyatt lay sprawled on the ground half way into the road, rubbing his sore jaw. That it was sore and not fractured was no doubt a minor miracle. Either that, or the big man couldn't land a blow to save his soul.

Holliday, watching from his position by the store looked on incredulous when Earp, still rubbing his jaw, smiled. It wasn't a true smile, but a sort of knowing grin. It was enough to make Doc bring his hand away from the gun at this hip. Holliday knew now without a doubt that whatever happened next would be very good indeed.

The giant stood over Wyatt, feet planted, fists raised as he waited for his victim to get vertical. Using the power of coiled leg muscles, Earp sprang up at his opponent as if propelled by an unseen force. Every bit of his one hundred seventy pounds was behind his fist when it caught the big fellow beneath the chin, snapping the shaggy head back, staggering the man. Several quick jabs and a powerful left/right to the midsection followed. As the giant doubled over in pain, Wyatt laid him out for good with a solid right to the nose. Blood gushed, and the big man toppled to the ground. He did not rise again, phoenix-like, but lay where he was, groaning and bleeding.

Wyatt walked over to where Doc stood, mouth open, cigarette stuck to his bottom lip and too close to burning the skin, as Holliday seemed oblivious to everything but what he had just witnessed. He came around just in time to flick the butt away, saving the lip a blister.

"My God, Wyatt. That was amazin'. I have never seen anything like that in my life."

Earp bent over the horse trough, swishing dead bugs out of the water before giving his hands a thorough wash.

Doc patted his friend on the shoulder, handing him a clean, white handkerchief. "The best display of fisticuffs I have ever been privileged to witness."

Earp smiled. "Thanks, Doc." He dabbed at the bead of blood oozing from a tiny cut along his jaw, then blotted his dripping face dry. He tucked the used kerchief into a vest pocket and turned to survey the damaged goods scattered about the ground.

"Guess I'll have to buy more flour." Earp kicked at the burst bag and then bent down to pick up what was left of his order. As he straightened, the storekeeper walked out. Eyes wide and glazed, mouth hanging open, the awestruck proprietor held out another sack of flour.

Doc fished in his pocket for payment, but the merchant shook his head, his rapt gaze never leaving Earp's face. "No charge. That was worth more than a bit a flour, mister," he said.

Wyatt took the offering, stuffed it into his saddlebags and mounted up.

Holliday swung into the saddle and offered an observation. "Well marshal, if you ever get tired of lawing, you can always take up prize fighting."

"I might do that, Doc. Someday I might just do that." Earp replied.

Evening and the making of camp did not bring Wyatt and Doc closer to agreeing on a subject they'd been bantering about all day, that subject being Holliday's need for boxing lessons.

Doc remained adamant. "Wyatt, the so called manly art of self-defense just isn't my style. Look at me." Holliday turned sideways to make his point, his silhouette narrow to extreme.

"You said it yourself back in town, skinny. You called me skinny, and you're right. For me to go up against someone using my bare hands would be foolish indeed. Why do you suppose I'm such a good shot? For protection, Wyatt, protection in this backward, vicious land. Most men could best me with fists. However, few can boast that ability with a pistol. I'm even quite proficient with a knife."

To make the latter point, since Wyatt had already witnessed said proficiency with a hand gun, Holliday pulled the knife from the sheath at his belt and cast about searching for an appropriate target. A flip of the wrist and he'd pinned a leaf to a tree ten feet away as it drifted down from an overhead branch.

Now it was Earp's turn to be impressed. "That was good, Doc, more than good. But it still doesn't change my thoughts on you learning how to defend yourself with your fists. Wasn't that man back there a lot bigger than me? A whole lot bigger?"

Doc retrieved his knife from the tree and replaced it in its leather sheath. "Yes, yes he was a whole lot bigger, and I do see your point, Wyatt." Holliday sighed in resignation.

Walking over to his bedroll, he shrugged out of his lightweight jacket, folded it, and placed it onto the blanket. Both pistols followed. Moving into a nearby clearing, he struck what he supposed was a typical boxer's stance, head up, back curved, what butt he did have sticking out, legs planted and fists at chest height.

Wyatt started to laugh, but choked it back. "I'm glad you're giving this a chance, Doc. I don't think you'll be sorry." Earp followed his student's example and tossed his pistol down next to Holliday's.

Doc shrugged. "'Sorry' remains to be seen, sir."

Earp ignored him and the lesson began. "First off, your position is all wrong. Stand relaxed and don't plant your feet like that. Makes it too easy for an opponent to knock you off of 'em. Sort of bend, like you've got springs for knees. Sort of bounce up and down." Earp demonstrated and Holliday mimicked.

"Protect your face with your fists." Again a demonstration and again, Doc imitating his teacher.

All was going well until Wyatt told Doc to try and hit him. "Go for the face."

Holliday looked skeptical, but Earp insisted. "Hit me right square in the breezer."

Doc remained skeptical.

"Just try it." This time it sounded more an order than a request. Doc tried and Earp sidestepped. Holliday, caught off balance, hit the ground hard, but didn't stay there for long, brushing aside Wyatt's concerns with a wave of the hand. He was quick to his feet and ready for another go.

Both men worked up a good sweat, but Earp remained leery of pushing his student too hard. "That's enough for tonight, Doc. No need to overdo it the first lesson." Wyatt wiped his sweaty face across a shirtsleeve.

Doc bounced up and down, fists perfectly placed as he taunted his teacher. "Am I being too hard on you, Wyatt? Tired out? Too old? Name your excuse."

Earp shook his head. "That'll be the day," he replied. "Okay, but remember, you asked for it."

As in all endeavors, Holliday proved an apt pupil, not even minding when Wyatt caught him a good one right on the chin. The punch was pulled, but still managed to drop Doc, sudden like, to the ground.

"God, I'm sorry, Doc." Wyatt looked mortified, but Holliday laughed it off, though he did accept a strong hand up. Blotting watering eyes back against a shirt cuff, he grinned. "Show me how to do that, Wyatt and I'll say we've been successful in our endeavors."

Two evenings of lessons, and Wyatt figured Doc had acquired at least a sporting chance to defend himself in a situation, if one ever arose. The Georgia gentleman's chief attributes as a boxer were his incredible speed and lightning reflexes. What served him well drawing a gun from a holster, served him just as well when throwing a punch. He also learned to use what body weight he did possess to full advantage.

As the two sat enjoying coffee on their last night on the trail, Doc asked Wyatt where he learned to box. "I assume you'd need to protect yourself against so many raucous siblings, but who taught you the finer points?"

Earp sat cross-legged, sipping the warm brew. "When I'd see a boxing match in town, in any one of the towns we moved through when I was a boy, I'd be there, right in front, watching every motion, absorbing it all. Guess I musta been a sponge. When I got most of my growth, I volunteered as a sparring partner. Learned a lot there, I can tell you. Later on I even boxed for money."

Wyatt helped himself to more coffee, holding the pot out towards Doc who shook his head no. Earp's gaze drew to the dark bruise on Doc's chin courtesy of his own less-than-expert pulled right hook.

Doc rubbed a hand over the spot. "It doesn't hurt, Wyatt, if that's what you're thinking."

"That's not what I'm thinking at all. I was thinking it was worth that bruise and more to give you an edge, any edge against what might be waiting out there." Wyatt inclined his head toward Dodge, but Doc believed the "out there" to be a general term.

"Even though I was on the receiving end of that lesson, I agree with you, Wyatt." Of a sudden Doc groaned aloud.

Wyatt leaned toward him, frowning. "You okay?"

An impish grin lit Holliday's features. "I was just thinking, Wyatt, how much I've come to agree with you. And that, my friend, is groan inducing, indeed."

CHAPTER 6

The two lawmen rode into Dodge City, and it was a different town from the one they left. The most grievous change was the loss of Bat Masterson's brother, Ed.

A fine lawman, Ed Masterson was easy going and genial and quicker to talk his way out of trouble than he was to draw a weapon. The trait served him well, up until the night of April 9. While in the Lady Gay Dance Hall, Ed sought to disarm a drunken rowdy named Jack Wagner. Handing the weapon over to Wagner's boss, a man named Walker, Masterson believed the altercation at an end.

However, Walker returned the pistol to the inebriated Wagner and together the pair waited in ambush for the lawman as he exited the Lady Gay.

Wagner accosted Ed, shooting him point blank in the stomach, setting Masterson's clothing on fire. The mortally wounded lawman returned fire with his own pistol, killing Wagner and hitting Walker three times, the latter recovering from his wounds eventually. Ed died in Bat's arms, leaving the younger Masterson hurt and bitter.

Bat's bitterness carried over into his job as sheriff of Ford County and to his dealings with not just lawbreakers, but those he usually received with friendship or at least civility. One of those to bear the brunt of the changes was John Holliday.

Upon returning to Dodge, the first thing Wyatt and Doc did was check in at the marshal's office. There were reports to file and stories to be told and retold. Earp and Holliday felt bad about Ed Masterson's death and both offered condolences to the still grieving Bat and his younger brother and fellow lawman, James.

As Holliday shook Bat's hand and told him how sorry he was, he felt a distinct chill. Masterson hardly managed to look him in the eye and seemed abrupt in his mannerisms. At first Doc chalked up the cool reception to the great loss Masterson had suffered, but an incident moments later solidified Holliday's first impression.

Praise was handed out to Wyatt and Doc on their well accomplished mission and the two took it in stride, though truth be told, Holliday felt heartened at being accepted by men he liked and respected, among them the Masterson brothers and Charlie Bassett. He enjoyed the camaraderie, that sense of inclusion within a tight brotherhood, the feeling of a family of sorts.

Bat broke the spell with a clipped and unnecessary remark. "Hand in your badge, Holliday."

Doc was surprised since this came out of nowhere. Besides he'd already returned the badge to Wyatt and told Masterson so.

"Yeah, well I've heard all about your shenanigans, Holliday. How you killed and covered it behind that badge. I heard and I'll tell you right now, that won't go around here. It just won't go."

Wyatt came to Doc's defense. "You're talkin' through your hat, Masterson. What killings? Between us we accounted for four. You know who they were and the circumstances. That was it. Done."

Bat stood behind his desk, dark brows furrowed over bright blue eyes, pointing an accusing finger at Holliday.

"He killed a man right on the streets of Fort Gibson. Shot him dead. Killed that man's brother over in Texas somewheres, too, and a couple more after the Fort Gibson fracas. And he did it behind a badge of office. This office. And I won't have it."

Holliday moved past the shock becoming angry, angry and hurt. "You listen, sheriff and listen well," he said, his voice low and rational for all the hurt and anger, "I killed no one in Texas. I killed no one in Fort Gibson, to which Wyatt can attest. I killed after that, yes, a woman named Pearl McLaughlin and a man by the name of Horton, both murderers and both in self-defense. That I did behind a badge and I'm not sorry. Don't make me sorry, Bat." Doc's rough breathing was the only sound in a room packed with half a dozen lawmen.

Wyatt walked over to stand next to Doc as if forming a united front against Masterson's unwarranted attack. "Every word he said is true, and if you don't believe John Holliday, then you don't believe me. So wire Fort Griffin and find out for yourself. While you're at it, wire Fort Gibson, too."

Wyatt reached into the pocket of his waistcoat and dropped a deputy's badge onto Bat's desk. "This is Holliday's. If you want mine, too, so be it." He made a motion to remove the shiny disc, but was stopped by his boss, Charlie Bassett.

"That's enough, Wyatt. I don't want your badge. I don't want Holliday's, either. He's welcome to keep it. Your record speaks for itself and so does Doc's. This office needs men such as yourselves."

The lawman rose from his seat by the door, repositioning himself on the edge of Masterson's desk. He picked up Holliday's badge and held it out to Doc, almost under Bat's nose. "Take it, doctor and welcome."

Even though Holliday wasn't looking at Masterson, he felt the other man's heated gaze upon him. It discomforted Doc and made him uneasy. He shook his head. "I thank you for the offer, Marshal Bassett, but I believe I'll pass. It was an experience I shall remember always. However, it is not one I desire to repeat."

Nodding to the others in the room, Doc turned and walked to the door, head held high. His hand was already on the knob when Wyatt stopped him.

"Meet you later for dinner at Delmonico's, around seven?"

Holliday smiled. The gesture was weary and so was he, but very grateful for Earp's gesture. "Certainly, marshal."

Being snubbed and humiliated by Bat Masterson might have bothered John Holliday more had he time to think about it. After all, Doc had believed Bat and him to at least be on the friendly side. They played cards together on occasion and always seemed to get on well. But as he took the stairs, two at a time, up to his rooms at the Dodge House, all that lay on his mind was Kate. Was she there? Would she be waiting for him? He and Wyatt were a couple days late in returning, and the woman had no patience whatsoever, one thing she and Doc did have in common.

She *was* there, resplendent in a red satin dress, exposing creamy bare shoulders to perfection, skin like cream, dark hair unbound and loose like the mane of some wild thing. Holliday was intoxicated by the sight of her, and when he folded her into his arms and buried his face in that hair, by the scent of her.

Of a sudden she pushed him away, but not in anger. There was teasing in her eyes and in that voice, all warm and sultry.

"That you, Doc, or some handsome young drover come to ravage me while my man's away?" Hands on hips, she circled the bemused Holliday as she appraised him, her eyes missing nothing.

Kate had a penchant for cowboys, young, good-looking, as hungry for a woman as for the decent hot meal they hadn't tasted in too long. She also had a fondness for money and here were both, set before her like a feast on a golden plate.

"I like it," she said, nodding her head. "I like what I see, tall and lean and wanting." Kate pressed her body close and reaching up, she ran a hand through Doc's windblown hair, mussing it even further, Holliday was glad he hadn't bothered to clean up or change into his regular clothing.

Their sex was raw and full of abandon with much fevered undressing and long passionate kisses. As they lay spent in each other's arms, Kate asked him point blank if he'd had another woman in her absence. Not one to lie, he told her the truth, yes, one, in Fort Smith.

She smoldered at that a while, but let it pass, "How can I hold one little fall against you, Doc honey, when I ain't been perfect myself?" She purred.

Holliday stroked her cheek, allowing his finger to trace the line of her throat. "How true, darlin'," he agreed. "But let's not talk of such things right now."

They made love again before falling asleep, more leisurely this time. Doc enjoyed taking his time, offering pleasure and being pleasured in return. Drifting off, he wondered dreamily if he'd be late for dinner at Delmonico's should he oversleep.

He was not, waking just in time to dress and hurry out to meet Wyatt. He left Kate slumbering in peace, a new gold and ruby ring snug on her finger.

Wyatt's reunion with his common-law wife was less than joyous as Doc soon discovered. Though Earp attempted to hide his disappointment, the hurt went too deep for that. He needed to talk and Doc was a good sounding post. To Holliday, his friend sounded almost bereft.

"Mattie, she has these headaches," Wyatt began, his voice a whisper lest anyone at the nearby tables overhear, "headaches so bad she needs something to ease the pain. And I don't blame her for that."

"Laudanum?" Doc asked.

Wyatt nodded. "But it's gone too far. She can't get back, not to what she was, or who." Wyatt looked at Doc and the softest of expressions came into his eyes. "There was a time…"

The expression faded. "She stayed in the hotel while I was away, never went out…ordered room service when she ate, never dressed, never cleaned the place up or even tried to hide the empty laudanum bottles. She's fallen a long ways, and I'm not sure I can even help her anymore, and Doc?"

"Yes, Wyatt."

"I'm not certain I really want to."

Holliday leaned forward. "Do you love her, Wyatt?"

Earp thought a moment, a long moment before answering. "I want to, God help me."

"It's not God you should be lookin' to for help in this, Wyatt. It's you and you must dig deep for the strength it will take, if indeed you love this woman."

Wyatt accepted the offer of a cigar from Holliday and a light. He drew deeply on the cheroot. Exhaling, he leaned back in his chair, his expression turning inward and wistful. "I found her in San Antonio, in a real high class place. Doc, she was so damned pretty, so sweet, all I wanted was to get her outta that place, outta that line a work and I did. Her given name is Celia, Celia Ann Blaylock. I'm the only one calls her Mattie. I gave her my name. Thought maybe she'd like bein' thought of as a respectable, married woman. I thought I could keep her from needin' the hop. Thought all she needed was me." Sadness caused his voice to quaver a little. "I was wrong."

Holliday pondered his reply, giving it much thought, the right words difficult to come by in such a situation, even to so well-versed a man. "You *were* wrong, Wyatt. You cannot change her. She must change herself. All you can do is be there for her if, and when, she does. Wyatt?"

"I'm listenin'," Earp replied.

"I'll be around, if ever you feel the need to, shall we say, share the burden?" Smiling, Doc held out his hand.

Earp grasped the hand and the two shook. "Thanks, Doc. Thanks for bein' here."

"I hope it will always be so, marshal," Doc replied, though he knew *always* for him was not forever.

CHAPTER 7

Whil dealing Faro in the Long Branch the next evening, Doc realized someone was watching him. That in itself was not out of the ordinary. Most nights saw a share of idlers, men standing around, drink in hand, watching the play, often two or three deep around his table. But this was different. These two made no move to come closer. They'd sauntered in earlier, Doc wasn't sure of the time, stationed themselves over at the bar, and started downing shots at leisure. Their attention focused on him and not on the play made the gambler uncomfortable, but that was all. For the most part it just made him curious.

Plainsmen, the nearer of the two was dressed in fringed buckskins. A bright strip of color ran down the outside seam of his trousers and a pair of fringed leather gloves dangled from his cartridge belt.

Medium brown hair with flecks of gray hung well past squared shoulders, and his face was weathered by years spent out of doors. A bushy mustache nearly obscured his mouth. On either hip he wore a pair of 1851 Colts, butts forward.

His companion favored dark pants tucked into high-topped boots which were in turn accentuated by Texas style spurs. He wore a bright-colored shirt embellished with an embroidered eagle in full flight across the bib front. His high crowned Stetson sported a constructed beaded hatband, turquoise in color, to match his shirt.

Like the man whose company he kept, he wore two pistols, also Colts, but Peacemakers with seven and a half inch barrels. A black mustache dusted with gray adorned his upper lip and his hair was short but much the same color as his handlebar. Alert brown eyes missed little, and the weather beaten face must have been a handsome one some years before, before the sun and wind changed it from the unmarked map of youth into the well-traveled one of early middle age. Doc was intrigued.

Intrigued yes, but also glad when Wyatt put in an appearance walking over to talk to Charlie Bassett before wending his way over to the Faro table. Needing a break anyway, Holliday gave his deal over to his replacement and drew Earp aside.

Wyatt ordered a coffee from the bartender, and Doc took a beer. "See those two down the bar a ways, the ones who appear as if they've just now returned from an expedition on the plains?" Wyatt followed Doc's gaze and picked the pair out from among the crowd. He nodded.

"Know either one?" Doc asked as he sipped his beer. The strangers continued to glance their way, not a bit unnerved to discover the observed were now the observers.

"I think, just think mind you, that I do know that fella, the taller one with the salt and pepper mustache. We crossed paths in Deadwood if I'm not mistaken, and if that's the same man, he's a force to be reckoned with, I can tell you that."

"That's quite a heartening statement, marshal." Doc suddenly felt the weight of his pistols when only moments ago their same mass was negligible.

"Do we make the first move or do we let them have that privilege? Though if they were interested in doing me harm the intelligent thing would've been to make a move *before* reinforcements arrived." Holliday finished his beer and lit up a smoke, taking a deep drag.

"Seems we don't have to worry about making that first move, Doc, since they're comin' over to us." Wyatt turned slightly to greet the men head on.

"Help you gents with anything?" He asked as the two reached their destination. Though their expressions were virtually unreadable, neither were they threatening.

"Hope so," the taller one replied before making introductions. "Name's Turkey Creek Jack Johnson. This is Texas Jack Vermillion. We're told you'd be the marshals who cleaned up that gang of woman killers over to the territories. That true?"

"We'd be them, yes. I'm Wyatt Earp and this is John Holliday, and I believe I know you, Mr. Johnson. Were you up Deadwood way maybe a year or so ago? Had quite an altercation with a couple a sharpies near a cemetery as I recollect. Killed 'em both and you without a scratch."

"That's so." Johnson broke into a grin, adding more lines to his already well criss-crossed face. "Thought I recognized you, too, Marshal Earp. How you been?" He grasped Wyatt's hand, shaking it with enthusiasm. "But you weren't a marshal then."

"No, just a speculator. Buy you two a drink?" Earp beckoned the bartender over.

"Sure and thanks." Texas Jack also smiled and of a sudden, Doc's guns felt much lighter.

"Whiskey," the frontiersmen ordered in unison.

"Let's find us a table where we can talk without bein' jostled." Not waiting to see if Earp and Holliday followed, Creek picked up his drink and plowed his way through to the rear of the Long Branch in search of an unused table. He picked a table at random, never mind that it was occupied, and using his considerable presence, cleared it without hearing a complaint.

"Since it appears they mean us no harm, what have we to lose?" Doc asked. "At least we can determine what they *do* want."

Wyatt shrugged. "Why not?" Picking up his coffee he indicated that Holliday should precede him.

"Beauty before age? Why not, indeed." Doc replied, leading the way.

Texas Jack broached a subject which appeared dear to his heart. Sadness was evident in his eyes and even in the way he held his body, slumped forward onto the table, sort of boneless, heartless. It was difficult for him to speak, but at last the words spilled out.

"I just wanted to meet the men who took care of them murderers. See, I was told you were fine gentlemen as well as good lawmen." Jack left off toying with the glass in his hands to look up at Wyatt and Doc, glancing from one to the other, holding each man's gaze in turn.

"My brother and his family live a couple days ride outside Fort Gibson. Them killers came one day and murdered my brother's oldest son, a boy twelve years old and his maw. She was a sweet gentle thing and the boy just like her. You come along too late to stop the killin', but was you who saw to it they got a Christian burial, and you sent them murderin' bastards to hell where they belong. I thank you for that. I thank you kindly, and I'll be always indebted to ya both."

Holliday spoke first, his voice soft, the memories fresh. "Helping your brother and his family was the least we could do for them. But in all fairness, your brother was the one responsible for us catching the killers."

"I don't quite get it," Jack said.

"Your brother shoes his own horses, doesn't he?" Wyatt asked.

Jack nodded. "Why sure."

"He cuts a V notch into each shoe so he can track the animal if it's stolen?"

Another nod.

"When the killers stopped at your brother's place, one of their horses came up lame. They took one of his mounts. Doc and I tracked those murderers thanks to the V notch he cut into that mare's shoes. Without that, I doubt we ever would've caught 'em. We owe your brother our thanks."

"I'd be mighty pleased to tell Hank that next time I see him. But I'm right proud to make the acquaintance of two men such as yerselves." Hearty handshakes followed.

After an hour or two of each man buying rounds, everyone was in a good mood. The evening ended with Jack and Creek asking Wyatt and Doc if they'd care to come down to the livery the next day to check out some stock they were interested in purchasing.

"Sounds fine to me. Make it around noon?" Wyatt got to his feet and stretched. "That all right with you, Doc?"

"I hardly ever put in an appearance among the living until at least two o'clock in the afternoon," Holliday said, but at his revelation, both Creek and Jack acquired hang dog, disappointed expressions. Holliday sighed. "But to look at good horse flesh, I will determine to rise bright and early tomorrow." He checked his gold pocket watch. "Make that *this* morning. I shall be there, gentlemen. Count on it. In the meantime, I think I'll buck the tiger. It's barely one and I've found my second wind. Join me?" Neither Johnson nor Vermillion seemed the least bit tired, either, and were eager for a go at the gaming tables.

Wyatt, on the other hand, looked worn out. Even an entire pot of strong coffee consumed earlier had not beaten back the fatigue. "Not me. Morning comes too soon. Goodnight to you all."

Settled in at the Faro table, Creek and Jack seated on either side of him, Doc watched Earp make his way to the exit. "What will tomorrow bring?" he asked no one in particular, not even aware anyone heard the question through the noise and commotion, but Creek Johnson heard and answered.

"Hell, John, good times." He clapped his new friend on the shoulder.

"I hope you are correct, Creek," Holliday replied. With a cigarette dangling from the corner of his lip, he shuffled the cards, fanned them out and shuffled again. "But call me Doc. Everyone does."

CHAPTER 8

Doc and Kate joined Wyatt and Mattie for breakfast at a little cafe they favored a couple blocks down from the Dodge House, just off of Front Street. It was a pleasant, homey place with chintz curtains pulled aside to allow the light to enter. Matching tablecloths adorned cozy tables just large enough to seat four. The food, though plain, was excellent, served in portions large enough to satisfy even Doc's renewed appetite.

"You're bright eyed and bushy tailed this morning, Doc," Wyatt observed over a fourth cup of coffee. Indeed Holliday was animated, talkative, and genial despite the late hours he kept, the perfect host for the small breakfast get-together.

"And why not? After all I did get an entire eight hours sleep," Doc replied, skewering a second helping of hickory smoked ham from the communal platter onto his fork.

"What time did you give it up last night, anyhow?" Wyatt asked. "Couldn't a been too much after I left you."

"It wasn't. Although Creek and Texas Jack must've closed the Long Branch. They were still hard at it when I left them around two-thirty."

At that moment the two in question meandered by the window, tipping their hats in polite greeting as they passed.

"Speak of the devil," Doc said.

"Oh, you're speaking of those men?" Mattie asked.

Wyatt nodded, "Creek Johnson and Texas Jack Vermillion. I know Creek from Deadwood. Why?"

Mattie touched the linen napkin to her lips. "Because, while I was out running errands…"

Wyatt gave Doc a rather soulful look which Holliday took to mean *Mattie went to the apothecary to pick up laudanum.* He wanted to tell Wyatt not to jump to conclusions, but of course he held his tongue and his counsel.

"While I was out running errands," Mattie continued, "I saw both those gentlemen down at the livery. It couldn't have been past eight this morning."

Doc frowned. "I can't say I trust men who gamble away half the night then rise with the chickens. It just isn't" he searched his extensive vocabulary for just the right word, settling on, "human."

The men bid their women adieu and made their way down to the livery and behind that to the corrals. Creek and Jack were already there watching a fine gray stud and two mares as they cavorted within the enclosure. Hearing the approach of footsteps, both turned, smiling as they recognized Doc and Wyatt.

"What 'cha think of this horseflesh, marshal? I want your real opinion now. Won't hurt my feelin's none you don't think well of 'em." Jack said.

Creek added, "let us know up front since money ain't changed hands yet."

Wyatt and Doc were careful to keep an eye on the stud who, in return, eyed the men with extreme suspicion. Protective of his mares, he was more than willing to throw his weight around. Ears laid flat against his chiseled head, eyes wide and showing the whites, he charged the fence in an attempt to keep the newcomers at bay. Cautious, Earp and Holliday stepped up onto the first board of the enclosure to get a better view. All three animals were beauties, sleek muscles rippling beneath shining coats, as well cared for as well bred.

Earp, having a keen appreciation of such things, was impressed and said so. "Don't think you could do much better here, boys." But upon hearing the asking price for the three, Wyatt whistled through his teeth. "Steep. Bet you could talk the owner down a bit. 'Course if you wait, someone else might just snap 'em up."

Next to him on the fence, Holliday took his attention from the stallion to give Earp a quick glance. "Like you, perhaps?"

"I wouldn't mind. I like that stud. Wouldn't mind havin' him for myself at all, no, not at all," Wyatt replied.

"What do you think, Doc?" Creek asked. "Your opinion is valued here, too. I heared you southern gentleman know good horseflesh when ya see it."

Holliday laughed. "Why Mr. Johnson, whoever told you I was a gentleman? However, I'd like to try out that mare before I give you my answer, the bay. Is she broken?" Not waiting for an answer, Doc stepped down from the fence and stripped off his gray frock coat, handing it up to Wyatt.

"And if she's not, you plannin' on riding her anyway?" Wyatt asked as he draped the garment over his arm.

"I am." Doc smiled that enigmatic little smile of his.

"Do you need sense talked into you? 'Cause if you try ridin' an unbroken horse you're liable to have what little you do have knocked right out."

Jack answered Doc's question with a bit of uncertainty. "We was told they was all broke, mostly"

Creek Johnson, on the other hand, was all for the idea. Before Jack finished his sentence, Johnson was in the corral throwing a loop over the bay's head. He tied her up close to the post and reached for the saddle draped over the gate.

Wyatt shook his head as Holliday climbed the corral rungs and dropped into the dirt circle. He asked Creek if he might borrow his gloves seeing as his hands were of great importance in his line of business, in both lines.

Johnson offered his spurs as well, and while Holliday admired them for their fancy rowels that chinked at the slightest movement, he declined. "Won't be needing them," he explained with a smile. Pulling on the gloves, he heard the marshal's final comment.

"You'll break your neck," Earp hissed.

Holliday paid him no heed, but settled his hat down, pulled the strings tight beneath his chin and climbed into the saddle. He hadn't ridden a bronc in years, not since Georgia, and his heart raced and his blood pounded in anticipation of that first leap.

Creek released the mare's head and she was off. *"Mostly broken"* had to be the understatement of the year.

She shot up into the air straight legged, coming down hard enough for Holliday to feel as if the end of his spine was impaled in the thin leather of the saddle. She whipped around in tight circles like a dog chasing its tail, then attempted to roll. Jerking hard on the reins, Doc managed to keep her head up and prevent the action, but as soon as he felt relief at averting one disaster, she roared off on a different tack.

From somewhere to his left, Holliday heard Creek yelling encouragement and instructions. "Don't let 'er sunfish on ya, Doc."

Her repertoire of tricks was amazing, and it took all Holliday's attention to ward off catastrophe. He began to think this idea had been asinine, indeed, when a funny thing happened. Suddenly the animal just sort of gave up, or perhaps she just gave in to a critter even more stubborn than she. Her antics started to lose their originality as she repeated the same ploys over and over.

Doc now had her pegged and yelled to Jack, "open that damned gate and get outta the way."

Man and horse sped through the opening and down the road out of Dodge in a cloud of dust and to the whoops and hollers of both friends and onlookers.

Many moments passed before horse and rider reappeared over the short knoll giving those citizens concerned for Holliday's welfare pause. But worry proved unnecessary as man and mount headed back in, both dusty, both exhilarated.

Holliday reined up in front of Wyatt. Stepping down, he accepted the compliments and handshakes with an ear-to-ear grin. The experience itself left him feeling alive, more alive than he had in ages.

"Well, Doc? What 'cha think of her?" Creek held the mare's head, rubbing a rough hand over her soft muzzle. She wasn't tame yet and made to nip his hand. Only fast reflexes kept him from a painful bite.

"By all means, Mr. Johnson, Mr. Vermillion, pay the asking price. The mare alone is worth that and more." Attempting to brush the dust from his clothing and failing, Holliday gave up, turning his attention elsewhere. "I'm parched. Let's wrap this up and head for the Long Branch. Beers are on me."

CHAPTER 9

Lying on his back staring at the ceiling in the dim yellow light of a single lamp was not John Holliday's idea of a pleasant evening. It wasn't his idea of anything other than a dead bore.

Coming in rather late himself, he half expected Kate to be waiting in their rooms, angry at him for tarrying so long with his barroom cronies. He hadn't seen her since leaving for his Faro dealing stint at four. She'd been primping in the mirror, and if he wasn't mistaken, that was a new scent she daubed behind those exquisite, shell-like ears of hers.

Lying in bed alone, with memories of Kate readying herself for some other man, worked Holliday up to the point where he could not rest, let alone sleep.

"Why do I allow her to worm her way into me like she does? It's not as if I love her." He slammed his fist down against the mattress. "It isn't that damned simple."

Rolling over onto his belly he buried his face into the pillow. "Damn it." It was her pillow and Kate's scent flooded his nostrils. He threw the offending object across the room where it landed among several bottles of drugs used in his dental profession, sending several toppling to the floor. The subsequent sound of shattering glass forced Doc from his bed. Stomping in bare feet over to the shelf, he grabbed up a waste receptacle and bent down to pick up the broken pieces, careful not to step in any of the shards. Straightening, he grabbed a white towel and dropped it over the remaining splashed liquid, meaning to clean it up in the morning.

Without warning the energy seemed to drain from his body and within seconds he felt completely fatigued. Just standing upright required effort. Walking back to bed was like plodding through wet sand, and all thoughts of faithless women faded from his mind as exhaustion took over.

Yet tired as he was, sleep eluded him. And in moments he knew why. The cough started slow enough, but built with incredible speed and ferocity. Within the hour, his chest felt as if it was being crushed in a vise, and even one single deep breath was a lost hope. Blood stained the handkerchief crumpled in his hands, smeared his mouth, and spattered out across his nightshirt and white sheets, driven by the force of the unrelenting cough. Pain and breathless terror robbed his speech, so that calling for help was impossible. But who was there to hear?

Kate breezed into the room, humming to herself as she locked the door. Dropping her reticule onto the chair she turned toward the bed. "What you still doin' up, Doc? Waitin' for me?"

The sight that greeted her sent Kate into short lived shock. First she flattened herself back against the door, and then she screamed.

Doc heard Kate's screams as through cotton wool, and

the heavy pounding against his door the same. So taken was he by cough and pain, nothing mattered but his futile attempts to deal with both.

Kate's screams faded as did the hammering of fist against wood. Wyatt's face shifted and wavered in front of Doc, and although Earp's lips moved, the words made no sense, distorted by Holliday's ragged struggles for breath and his panic.

Wyatt grabbed Doc by the shoulders and shook him, hard. "Look at me. Look at me and breathe, dammit, Doc."

Holliday fought to look, fought to obey, but when he couldn't grab a single decent breath, his panic threatened to rage out of control. Somewhere far away he heard Kate's sobs; closer was the sound of Wyatt's voice, gentle now, coaxing, not threatening. "Please, John. Look at me. Look at me and do as I do. Breathe, easy, slow and shallow. Breathe."

Panic ebbed and Doc followed Wyatt's lead. "Slow and shallow, short breaths. Breathe.

"That's it. That's better." Wyatt turned to Kate. "Get pillows or anything else we can use to prop up his head."

Earp didn't have to ask Kate twice. She jumped to his bidding. From the spare bed, she grabbed up the extra pillows and a quilt which she folded and added to the stack. Wyatt laid Doc back.

Though he was getting some air into his lungs, the pain on the right side of his chest, in that same damned spot between his ribs, stabbed deep with every breath, no matter how shallow. Doc groaned, doubling over against Wyatt.

Again Earp looked to Kate. "You got any whiskey around here?"

"No."

"Get some. Go downstairs to the bar. If nobody's there, take a bottle. I'll pay later. But go and hurry up."

With a rustle of taffeta she was gone, but to her credit she returned within moments, already tearing the paper from the neck of the bottle.

Wyatt held the whiskey to Doc's lips. The first swallow went down hard almost choking him, the second much easier. By the third, the pain was already easing off a bit. "More, drink it down slow."

By the time the half-filled glass was empty, and the water chaser that followed, the pain had turned almost bearable, and when Wyatt rested him back against the pillows, Doc closed his eyes in relief.

When he got round to opening them, dawn's first pale blush colored the morning sky. From a chair by the windows, Wyatt watched the spectacle unfold, turning at Doc's faint stirring to smile in greeting.

Kate, too, stood near the windows, but she had not been enjoying the sunrise. Arms folded across her breasts, she shot angry daggers at Earp. Something had happened while Doc slept to drive a wedge between his woman and his friend. Somehow that did not surprise Holliday.

"It wouldn't upset me none if you left now, marshal," Kate said.

Wyatt rose from the chair, stretched and ignoring Kate, walked over to Doc's bed. "Doctor McCarty's due back in town later today. I'll send him over."

Not quite trusting his voice, Doc shook his head.

Wyatt pulled over a chair and sat down, leaning close, "Why not?"

"I don't want anyone to know." To Holliday's chagrin, his voice sounded husky and breathless, a whisper, and a small tickle lingered at the back of his throat. Wyatt poured out a glass of water and helped Doc get it down.

Wyatt, emulating Doc, kept his voice low. "Tom's not

just anyone. He's a doctor. Don't they go by some oath, some promise to keep a patient's secret?"

"No physician, Wyatt. I've seen enough of them. And this secret is mine to keep."

Wyatt rested a hand on Doc's shoulder. "Whatever you want is okay by me. Rest now and be well."

Holliday's attempt at a smile, though tentative, still got across to Wyatt who smiled in return. He rose to leave. "And a good morning to you, Miss Elder."

Wyatt managed to pull the door closed behind him just as something heavy and solid smashed against the opposite side.

Kate ranted and raved, swearing in Hungarian and English, a most impressive display. Doc was only sorry he was too ill and exhausted to really enjoy it. She paced the small room, kicking at table legs, tossing small items to the floor. Doc half expected her to start rending her clothing and hair, but alas that did not come to pass.

Eventually she calmed down, plopping herself in the chair Wyatt vacated. "That damned nosy lawman. Asked me why I got in so late. Ain't like there's a curfew in this town. Why does he care if my man don't?"

Doc did care, but at this point and with his lack of strength, getting into a good row with Kate, although the end results might be pleasurable—they usually were—was out of the question.

"Said you was my man and you needed me and where the hell was I?" She turned to Doc, her large brown eyes liquid with tears, crocodile or otherwise Doc didn't know. Either way the effect was charming. "But I did come home, Doc honey, and it's 'cause a me you got help. Did that big hulk of a farm boy see that? No. He sees what he wants. He hates me."

Kate leaned low over Holliday exposing her impressive cleavage. It was a great maneuver; Doc always enjoyed it, but this was not the time, though it *was* the place. She stroked the damp hair off his forehead and planted a soft kiss.

"What's wrong with you, honey? I asked the marshal, but he said I should ask you. 'Course he didn't believe me when I told him I didn't know and that you'd never been so sick as this in all the months we been together." Kate smiled, fluttering those long, black eyelashes like a coquette.

Doc sighed. He didn't want to lie to her, but one of Kate's worst attributes was her inability to keep any sort of confidence. A few crème de menthes too many and the news would be all over town that Doc Holliday was consumptive, a lunger. No, in this case a lie might just be Doc's best bet.

"A touch of pneumonia, darlin', nothin' too serious. I should be back up to snuff in a few days."

Kate sighed, settled back in the chair, kicked off her shoes and proceeded to remove her silk stockings. "That's good, honey. That's real good."

Doc closed his eyes knowing that in a minute or so the bed would creak as Kate climbed in. She'd cuddle close next to him, all warm and soft and woman and he wouldn't be able to do one thing about it. He also knew *that* part of it wouldn't matter. Kate was nothing if not a take charge kind of girl.

CHAPTER 10

Holliday sat in a chair on the Dodge House portico, lounging while amusing himself by checking out the activity across the street at the train depot. Workers scurried about like so many ants at a picnic, hither and yon, attending to the needs of the Santa Fe's many and diverse patrons.

Doc leaned forward, pushing his hat back on his head and peering at the goings on, zeroing in on a familiar figure. Dressed demurely in a navy blue suit with long sleeves and a high ruffled neckline, Kate appeared either to be meeting someone or inquiring about a schedule. Either way, Holliday was curious, but just. What Kate did was her own business. The same held true for him.

Wyatt walked up, settling his lanky frame into the chair next to Doc's. "Feelin' chipper again, Doctor Holliday?"

Holliday relaxed back, tugging his hat into a more proper angle. He turned to face his friend, appraising Earp with a tilt of the head, "Indeed, in no small part thanks to you. Funny, you don't have the appearance of a knight in shining armor."

"Doc, you're babbling. Why can't you just come out and say what you mean?" Sometimes the dentist confused the lawman with his flowery speech and references to things of which Wyatt held little knowledge.

"You *did* come to my rescue, did you not or am I mistaken, misled perhaps concerning the events of a week ago last? I was a bit under the weather and my memories are hazy on the matter. And Kate is of little help. The part I do recall is her, how shall I put it, her less than kind opinion of how she was treated by you on the night in question."

"Oh." Wyatt pondered a moment as Holliday waited for him to continue.

"I helped best I could, Doc, but that woman. Kate exasperates me, and I can't understand what makes her tick. She's *with* you, but not. Why, besides the obvious reasons, do you put up with her? How much of a companion is she to you? Do you love her?"

"Now you place me in a quandary, marshal." Doc slumped back in his seat resting his elbows on the arms of the chair and lacing his fingers together. Coming from anyone else, the questions Earp posed would have been met with anger. From Wyatt they were questions neither couched in oblique innuendo nor asked to broker an argument. Doc wished he could answer them as simply, as succinctly, as they were asked. He plunged ahead.

"I do love her, sometimes. Other times I hate the very sight of her. The sound of her voice grates against my nerves like nails on a chalk board. The scent of her perfume turns my stomach, and the web of lies she weaves, which she believes I won't see through, that's what I despise most. Truthfully, Wyatt, she's there when I want her. She uses me and I know it. But I also use her. That sounds so calloused and jaded and, my God, I guess that's what I've become."

He stopped contemplating his steepled fingers to gaze at Wyatt. "She allows me to see myself for what I am. Perhaps that's why I hate her. She's the mirror of my soul." Doc shrugged. "I'm not sure anymore. Hate, love, aren't they opposite sides of the same coin?"

Wyatt nodded. "I've found that to be so. Seems you can't hate unless you've already loved."

Earp got that wistful, hurt expression Doc had been privy to once before, leading him to believe Wyatt knew exactly what he was talking about in this particular instance.

"But about Kate," Earp continued, "All I know is I don't like her, Doc, and I guess you know how she feels about me. But she's your woman and it's your life, so until you say different, I'll butt out."

"I am grateful you know when to 'butt' out, marshal. Believe it or not that is a dying grace. However," Doc pressed himself up from the chair, straightened his coat, tugged his Stetson down low and extended his hand. "I am grateful for your friendship, Wyatt."

Wyatt relinquished his seat, likewise straightened his attire, and shook the outstretched hand.

The moment over, Doc clapped Earp on the shoulder. "Had breakfast yet, marshal? I'm famished."

"No I haven't. You buyin'?"

"Who me?" Doc patted his pockets for effect. "I think not. After all, I've been out of work for a week. I'm flat."

Wyatt rolled his eyes, but acquiesced. "This time the food's on me, but *you* leave the tip."

"Ah, reversal of fortunes," Doc quipped with a grin. "Done."

Holliday noticed the two individuals on the boardwalk at Front and Second Streets as he exited the Dodge House. They weren't loafing but seemed to be up to something while making a great show of being casual about it. They were heeled, each carrying a brace of pistols in embellished holsters, and young. Maybe drovers fresh off the trail, they had that intense alert look about them, a look that said "I have come to see the elephant, and woe be it to any man who gets in the way." The pistols and holsters appeared new as did their clothing.

To Doc Holliday it appeared these young men were looking for trouble and as much as he wanted to believe that trouble did not involve him, there was no mistaking the fact that even now he was under their close scrutiny. Sidelong, furtive glances, heads together in whispered conspiracy, and the occasional snicker proved out that point.

Doc figured he had two options, the first being to turn around now and go back inside the hotel, thus avoiding trouble before it started. His second option was to continue with his day as planned. If trouble came a knocking, then so be it. Being a man unable to back down from any challenge, no matter how small or imagined, Doc chose the second option.

Walking slow, he made his way down the block and toward the young men, stopping to chat with his friend, town doctor Thomas McCarty. A few pleasant moments passed, and Doc continued on the path he had chosen before he'd noticed the cowboys noticing him. They would not sway him from his habit, his morning constitutional, though the hands of the clock stood at some two hours past noon.

Halfway down the block, Holliday stopped to roll and light a cigarette. He figured it gave him the look of nonchalance he desired. Doc did not want an altercation, but neither did he wish these youngsters to think him intimidated.

Approaching their position, his heartbeat increased,

and he felt more attuned to life around him, more aware and alive. The sun seemed brighter, the air fresher. He tossed aside his cigarette.

The cowboys allowed him to pass, parting to let him go by on the boardwalk. There was a split second when Doc believed he'd been premature in this thinking.

In a Texas drawl and loud enough for anyone within fifty feet to hear, the challenge was issued. "Yeah, that's him. That's Holliday, the woman killer."

With slow deliberation, Doc turned back to face the two. The speaker was indeed nothing but a boy looking to make a name for himself. To Holliday it was a nightmare realized.

The voice was adolescent, scratchy and out of synch with the near-adult body, "You up to goin' against a man, Holliday?" The youngster patted the Smith and Wesson on his right hip.

Holliday stood his ground, offering, in his soft Georgia drawl, sound, well meant advice. "Do yourself a favor, kid. Get a girl, have some laughs, get drunk, but don't do this. You have nothing to prove here."

Doc took a single step forward, right hand extended palm up, empty of a weapon. "You don't need to do this."

Indeed, the boy appeared to have second thoughts. He swallowed hard, his Adam's apple bobbing up and down. Sweat beaded his forehead and upper lip, tiny droplets collecting among the peach fuzz hairs of a fledgling mustache. He seemed almost willing to chalk this up as a big mistake. Until his friend stepped in.

"He jes' called you a kid, Jed. Ain't you gonna prove 'im wrong? You gonna let him call you sech in front a all these folks?"

Jed tore his attention from Holliday just long enough to take a good look around. A crowd had formed. All those people watching, judging.

In his boy's mind perhaps he felt his actions stealthy, that he wasn't telegraphing his every idea through eyes and expression and stance, that he wasn't being obvious. But Doc Holliday saw and marked it all. Even as the boy drew, it was already too late.

With the weapon only half lifted from the holster, Jed felt the searing pain of Holliday's bullet as it skittered across the top of his gun hand. He screamed and fell to his knees, the brand new shiny Smith and Wesson .44 again snug in its fine black leather sheath.

His friend, the instigator of the whole affair, stood dumb struck as Doc holstered his pistol and knelt by the boy he'd shot. Pulling a handkerchief from his pocket, Holliday wrapped the wounded hand and assisted the boy to his feet. Searching the crowd, he noticed Charlie Bassett pushing his way through and also Doctor McCarty who took quick charge of the youngster, guiding the stumbling boy past the excited throng and to his nearby office. "He'll be fine. He'll be just fine," he assured those pressing in close. "Just a flesh wound."

"Let's go, Doc." Charlie drew his pistol, like he'd need it, and disarmed Holliday. Doc felt his face drain of color. In silence he walked before Bassett realizing that somehow he'd played right into the hands of fate.

Entering his office, Charlie put aside his gun and handed Holliday back his weapons.

"You're damned lucky, Doc. So's that kid out there, both of 'em. I'm glad it was you they baited and not some damn hot head feelin' the need for another notch on his gun. I've been watchin' those two. Wanted to throw 'em in jail for their own sakes, but had no reason. Nothin' in the law says a kid can't sow some wild oats.

"You're lucky it was me came on the scene and not Bat. He woulda given you as much grief as he could. Now me, I want to thank you. That kid's alive 'cause you're not one to court trouble." Charlie sat in his chair and opened the desk drawer, sorting through the clutter of miscellaneous items before finding the one he sought.

"Reconsider, doctor, reconsider and take this back. I've been holdin' it for you." Bassett pushed the deputy's badge across the desk toward Holliday.

Something in Doc wanted to reach out and take it. Something else in him said no. "Thanks, Charlie, but I still have to pass. If I'm not under arrest or anything, I'll be leaving."

"Of course you're not under arrest, but be wary out there, Doc. The herds are comin' in and there'll be more young studs feelin' the need to prove themselves. Watch your back."

Doc nodded, "You do the same, Charlie."

Later, in the Long Branch as Holliday sat nursing his first whiskey of the day, Texas Jack Vermillion walked over. That he walked and not sauntered, as was usual for him, was telling in itself. "Can I sit, Doc? Need to talk to you a minute."

"By all means, Jack, pull up a chair. Join me in a whiskey?" Not waiting for Vermillion's answer, Doc righted another glass and poured it full to the top.

Jack downed the shot. "You watch yerself. There's talk around and ain't none of it good. And who's spreadin' it's a man who'll be listened to, not some drunk lookin' to freeload."

Doc refilled Jack's glass and urged him to continue.

Vermillion leaned closer to Holliday and whispered, "It's the sheriff, the fancy dresser, Bat Masterson. Was him last night talkin' loud enough to be heard." Jack paused looking uncomfortable with what he was about to confide.

"Go on, Jack, please," Doc urged.

"Masterson said you was a woman killer. Said you didn't have the balls to go up against no man. Said other such lies, too, that I ain't gonna repeat. I'da stopped that lyin' sonofabitch right then and there, but Creek told me no. He said it was better we jest listen and let you know what's bein' said. Masterson's too smart to tell stories like that around Wyatt or Charlie Bassett. He don't know about us and that's fine. But those boys, those two gave you trouble earlier?"

Doc nodded.

"They was here last night, outside, standing right at Masterson's elbow while he spouted them lies, soaking 'em up like thirsty men at a water hole. Bat set you up, Doc. You watch yer back and watch it good."

Wyatt's words came back to Holliday as if prophesied right out of the Bible: *This gossip will plague you all the days of your life.*

As Holliday went about packing his saddlebags, a lone figure appeared in the barn doorway. Doc glanced up, but said nothing. How Wyatt knew his plans puzzled him for a moment, but puzzled or not, he kept on packing.

"Where you goin', Doc?"

When Holliday didn't answer, Wyatt walked closer, walked up to the saddled mare and placed a hand on the animal's arched neck. "Where, Doc?"

Holliday felt the intensity of Earp's emotions. They radiated off the other man like a halo of kinetic energy. Like it or not, want to or not, Doc looked up and into Earp's eyes. "Hays City. There's quite a poker game goin' on there, or so I've heard."

"There's quite a poker game going on here in Dodge every night. What makes Hays City so appealing?"

Holliday stared past Wyatt at some imaginary spot on the barn wall, his sigh deep and full of melancholy. "I just want to get out of this place for a while. It's settling heavy on me, Wyatt, like I can't breathe anymore, and I need to breathe."

"It's Masterson, isn't it? Masterson and what happened with that kid the other day. Tell me it's not so, and I'll let you leave without another word."

Doc nodded. "It's him and the fact that you were right back in Fort Smith when you said we should put a stop to the rumors then and there. You were right, Wyatt, but I didn't know how the hell to stop it then, and I still don't know."

"So you're gonna run from it?"

"No, not run, just put some distance between me and the talk, just for a while, maybe a month or so."

"Doc, it won't do any good. The talk is already there. This is something you can't run from or hide from."

There was a long moment, a very long pause. Holliday's thoughts, once blurred and fuzzy, came slamming into focus. "I could kill Masterson," he said, his voice cold.

"You wouldn't do that," Wyatt stated without hesitation or doubt.

"No," Doc admitted. "However, Bat could kill me, and in the end that's the only way I'll ever find a lasting peace."

Wyatt's jaw dropped and he took an involuntary step backwards. "You can't really believe that."

"I don't truly believe Bat would kill me, outright. Perhaps goading someone else into doing the job is more his style. I don't know him well enough to see what's in his heart and I don't believe I want to. As for finding a lasting peace, not in this lifetime, Wyatt."

"Don't run, John. It won't help." There seemed a hint, a very faint hint of desperation in Wyatt's voice.

Doc stood silent, head bowed upon his breast as if in deepest thought or even prayer, and then methodically he began unsaddling his horse. Perhaps what he'd needed all along was someone to reach out, someone to make the effort. Sometimes that's all it took.

"You win, Wyatt. I won't run," Doc whispered, resigned to whatever fate held in store for him, yet not realizing in the moment that men's fates often intertwine.

CHAPTER 11

Fate indeed stepped in. If John Holliday kept to his plan of leaving Dodge for Hays City, history might have recorded a much different ending to the events which followed.

Dodge was rowdy, and hell was in full swing. Texas trail herds roared in leaving the town packed to overflowing with liquored up, exuberant cowboys, all armed to the teeth and feeling no pain. However, some did not think highly of the lawmen charged with keeping the peace. More than one found himself the victim of a buffaloing by Wyatt Earp, Bat or James Masterson, Charlie Bassett, or any number of other deputies. Bad hangovers and sore heads did not mix well.

Doc Holliday stepped out onto the boardwalk in need of a lungful of fresh air and room in which to stretch. Hours spent dealing Faro in the Long Branch amid a crush of sweaty unwashed drovers, no matter how profitable those hours, left him desiring no company other than his own, a difficult if not impossible ambition during so busy a time in the Queen of the Cow Towns.

Still in all, the night breeze was pleasant, and for the moment at least, the streets were deserted. The seeming emptiness of the thoroughfare bothered Doc a bit, but just for a moment. He shrugged it off as lucky chance. Leaning into the clapboard side of the Long Branch, Holliday faded into the shadows, the pale blue spiral of smoke from a lit quirly signaling his presence.

A silhouette appeared across the railroad tracks, one man alone, tall and broad shouldered. Doc watched the man's progress as long strides carried him near. No spurs heralded his approach; each footfall sounded a light crunch against the gravel rail bed, and when he stepped up onto the wooden boardwalk, a mere faint tap of boot heels marked his movement. A gust of wind blew the loose fitting coat open, revealing a long-barreled revolver holstered high on the right hip. Doc smiled.

Wyatt Earp stopped to peer into Doctor McCarty's darkened drugstore, jiggling the knob before moving on.

Holliday figured to wait until Wyatt got a bit nearer before stepping out to greet him. Crushing the butt of his cigarette out against the side of the building, he watched and waited.

Wyatt crossed Bridge Street, his face illuminated by the corner street light. Doc stepped forward, but catching movement out of the corner of his eye, he pressed back into the shadow and listened. Surely those were the sound of spurs and hushed voices coming from the alley just beyond the Long Branch, but not hushed enough. Doc heard the plan whispered in slurred voices and his hand went to the .45 holstered beneath his left arm. He drew the weapon, his thumb light on the hammer. At that moment, a bawdy song burst forth from inside the saloon, sung in inebriated glee and accompanied by the stomping of feet and clapping of hands. Doc glanced at Wyatt. Earp walked on unconcerned and unaware of any danger.

Holliday stepped into the light, breath quick and ragged, heart hammering.

"Wyatt! Look out!"

Four men rushed from the alleyway, guns drawn. Doc dropped into a crouch and thumbed back the Colt's hammer. In the melee that followed, he thought he heard the report of Wyatt's pistol from behind and to his right, but in the noise and confusion, he wasn't certain. The gunfight, if it could even be called such, was over in seconds.

Holstering his now empty pistol, Holliday drew his second weapon, covering the four downed shooters. Two appeared to be wounded and those wounds seemed slight. Their accomplices groveled on their bellies, all too sober now and aware of the trouble they'd brought upon themselves. They groaned and bawled like children, which added to the cacophony of noises issuing from their wounded companions. To Doc's great relief, he felt a hand on his shoulder and a familiar voice near his ear. "That was too damned close."

Doc glanced at his friend. In the yellow light of the street lamp and through the dispersing cloud of gun smoke, Wyatt's complexion appeared pale and washed out, his breathing no less labored than Holliday's own, yet a faint smile played across his lips. He nodded and Doc returned the nod and the smile without hesitation.

At the appearance of Charlie Bassett and James Masterson, Holliday was more than glad to turn the miscreants over into the care of the law. He accompanied Wyatt to the marshal's office and wrote out his statement. To his surprise and embarrassment, his hand trembled so that he could barely hold the pen. If Wyatt seated across the desk noticed, he made no mention. Doc sat back and waited for Earp to finish. Wyatt signed his name to the document with a flourish then looked up at Holliday.

"Cup of coffee, marshal?" Doc asked.

Wyatt held his hands out toward Doc. They shook. "I could use one."

"You and me both, my friend." Holliday placed both hands onto the desk top, the fingers fanned out. If his shakes were less obvious than Wyatt's, there wasn't a hair of difference between them.

As the two sat in the cafe drinking the dark brew, fingers laced around the thick mugs for warmth in hands turned cold, each was lost in thoughts of his own. Neither spoke. Wyatt ordered pie for them both and that's as far as the talking went. Each man seemed content with just the company of the other.

As they rose from the table to go their separate ways, Earp broke the comfortable silence. "I'm glad you didn't go to Hays."

"My thoughts exactly," Doc replied.

CHAPTER 12

Wyatt had been in the Long Branch earlier in the evening to keep tabs on the action and to accompany Holliday out for a bite of supper. But there were no herds up this week, and no cows meant no cowboys, so Earp called it a night and went home to his Mattie.

Bat Masterson, however, must have had nothing pressing at home to occupy his time, so he hovered about the Long Branch, his keen blue eyes staring holes into and through the back of Doc Holliday's head. This made Doc uncomfortable, but he'd be damned if he'd give Masterson the satisfaction of knowing that. Besides, Doc was having one hell of a winning streak. What action there was in the Long Branch centered on the gentleman gambler and his game.

Creek Johnson and Texas Jack Vermillion stood at the bar, watching the play and enjoying a few beers. They had yet to leave town, wanting to look at a few more horses to fill out their *remuda* before returning home to Arizona.

As Holliday raked in the pot, much to his glee and the

loser's chagrin, Masterson strode over to the table, making his presence known in a loud and blustering voice.

"Holliday, you know it's against the law to go heeled north of the tracks. Hand over those pistols. You want to wear a weapon, go on over to the south end and do it legal."

Doc did indeed know of the recent law passed forbidding the wearing of guns north of the train tracks. However, Marshal Bassett determined to look the other way when it came to Holliday and the new law. Ever since the gambling dentist stepped in and saved Wyatt's life, Charlie thought of him in the light of an unofficial deputy. Bat knew that, but chose to ignore it.

"Besides," Masterson leaned in close, a leering grin on his face, "I was just over that way and I swear that was your woman I saw at Handy's."

Doc felt his complexion flush. Handy's was the most disreputable saloon in the red light district and that was saying something. Kate was indeed there, no doubt enjoying herself a great deal, much to Holliday's wounded pride. It was so nice of Bat to rub salt into the wound.

"I am exempt from that law as you are well aware." Doc's tone remained calm though he seethed inside. He made no move to hand the weapons over.

Masterson slammed one hand down onto the table, rattling poker chips and sloshing beer over glass tops. "You might be as far as Bassett is concerned, but your privileged status don't go with me. Hand 'em over now, Holliday or spend the night in jail."

A slight commotion at the bar diverted Doc's attention. Texas Jack made a move toward the table as if to come to Doc's defense, but Creek grabbed him by the arm, shaking his head. Holliday didn't need to hear the words to know what was being said. "Don't go buttin' in, Jack. This is Doc's business."

He did, however, hear Jack's less than muttered curse directed at Masterson, "Big mouthed bastard."

Vermillion's comment elicited several snickers and not a few guffaws, which only seemed to goad Bat on to greater heights or depths. Indeed, it seemed the volume of his voice went up several decibels as he berated Doc in front of the bar patrons, enjoying himself at Holliday's expense.

Not wanting to make trouble and wanting Masterson to just go away and leave him in peace, Doc lifted the .45 from the holster and handed it over as well as the more compact and brand new Colt .41 double-action Thunderer. He felt naked.

"Why thank you, Mr. Holliday." Bat smiled as he dropped the pistols into his coat pocket.

"That is Doctor Holliday, Mr. Masterson," Doc corrected with dignity.

"Oh, excuse me, doctor. I'm goin' over to Handy's now. I'll be sure to give Kate your regards." Tipping his derby to the onlookers, Masterson departed.

Doc fumed, but did so in silence. At his elbow a whiskey glass appeared, filled to the brim. He looked up and into the weathered face of Texas Jack. "Have one on me, Doc."

Holliday smiled. It was good to have friends.

CHAPTER 13

Doc's verbal altercation with Bat Masterson left him with a foul taste in his mouth and an anger he couldn't quite put right burning in the pit of his stomach. On top of that, Kate's cuckolding of him with God knew who over at Handy's made for a less than perfect end to what might have been *the* perfect day. He'd won well over a thousand dollars, closer to two, and yet as he walked toward his suite of rooms at the Dodge House, what he felt was humiliated and betrayed and angry.

As he neared his destination, a woman's laugh permeated the gloom, a drunken woman's laugh, raw, robust and devil-may-care. That it was not Kate's laugh did not matter to Doc, but it gave him the impetus he needed. Turning on his heel he walked across Front Street, across the railroad tracks and into Dodge City's red light district.

If there lurked a worse den of iniquity anywhere in Kansas, it would have surprised Doc. Liquor, cheap women, opium, there was no end to the vices those so inclined might indulge in here. While the respectable businesses across the tracks had long since locked their doors for the night, bawdy music, fist fights and all manner of lewd and raucous behavior lingered here until the wee morning hours until even the worst imbiber had to find a place to sleep off the intoxication.

Street lights were not the norm in this part of Dodge and thick clouds scuttling across the full moon lent an odd eeriness to the place. Shadows came and went, dissolved by bright moonlight, appearing again at a cloud's whim.

It was to this place Doctor John Holliday went in search of his woman. It was also the place he found her.

Standing in the street, Doc perused Handy's Saloon from its red painted door to its porch fronted second story. Shutters hung askew on curtainless upstairs windows and backlit silhouettes of ladies and their gents showed Doc it was still business as usual even at so late an hour.

Taking a single deep breath, Doc forced himself toward the inevitable. But just as his foot touched the boardwalk, a voice called to him from above.

"That you, Doc, honey? Come to rescue me?" The question was accompanied by much giggling, both female and male.

Taking a single step backward, Doc looked up. Sure enough, perched on the porch railing sat Kate dressed in nothing but corset and pantalets. Behind her, his burly arms circling her waist in a most possessive manner, was a trooper of the United States Cavalry. Doc knew this to be true since the fellow was clad in his distinctive cavalry hat, boots and nothing else.

Doc salvaged his dignity, walking off without as much as a backward glance. Turning up Locust Street, trapped in the ever tightening cycle of a love-hate relationship with a volatile woman, he cursed himself as a fool and Kate as a harlot. He allowed his guard to slip.

A heavy blow across his shoulders sent him reeling to his knees. His first instinct was to reach for the .45 holstered in the shoulder rig. He didn't remember until his hand closed on nothing that Bat Masterson relieved him of it and his other pistol earlier that evening. He damned himself for forgetting to stop at the sheriff's office to retrieve the weapons and Masterson for not leaving them with the bartender at the Long Branch as was customary. Making Doc an example was not all Masterson accomplished that evening. It seemed he now made him a victim.

One of the assailants bent over Doc and began rummaging through his coat pockets, perhaps believing the single blow had put Holliday out of commission. The pain was bad, but not debilitating. As Doc felt the thief's hands on him, he realized the fellow had to be off balance. He would take advantage of the situation. Throwing off his attacker, he leaped to his feet. A right cross caught the assailant full on the side of the face and dropped him like a stone.

Doc took the typical boxer's stance, hands poised to deliver more punishment as he bounced on the balls of his feet. Only then did he realize it wasn't one man he faced, but at least four. Though the odds seemed against him Doc didn't lose heart, though he realized he'd lost the element of surprise. These men would expect him to fight back now. They would be ready.

Three against one was just too many for Doc to handle, though he did get in several more decent punches. The man he'd struck first was soon back in the fray as well, full of piss and vinegar, and ready for payback.

It wasn't until the clouds passed from the moon's face that Holliday got a good look at his attackers. "Flynn, Potter, Cary and Marais, I don't know why I'm not surprised." Sure enough, these were the men Doc trounced at Spanish Monte earlier. The two thousand dollars he won belonged for the most part to them.

"Where's that money you stole off us, Holliday? Where?" Flynn rubbed his jaw. "You know what's good for ya, you'd better tell."

"I'm no fool. I never carry that amount of cash on my person. It's locked in the safe at the Long Branch."

"Liar." Flynn drove in at Doc, the other three joining their partner in the rush, the combined momentum slamming Holliday to the ground, all the wind knocked from his body. Fighting to catch a breath, Doc lay helpless, unable to put forth any resistance as he was dragged into the alley between the Great Western Hotel and the burned out shell of a once popular saloon.

"Grab that bastard and get him up against that wall. I'll teach him manners. High and mighty Doctor Holliday. High and mighty Reb tinhorn sonofabitch."

Two of the three manhandled Doc up against the wall of the hotel, slamming him face first into the rough bricks, scraping off skin from forehead to chin in the process.

At last able to draw breath, he struggled and swore and for his troubles, got a vicious blow to the back at kidney level. He might have fallen but for the hands pinning him to the wall, spread-eagled. Rough hands tore off his coat. Locating the wallet and finding it all but empty of cash, there were more curses, threats and blows.

"Where is that money, Holliday, huh? Make it easy on yourself."

Doc recognized the wispy voice as Marais'. He was a bespectacled man of small stature and quiet manners. Holliday was surprised the little Frenchman would be involved in anything like this. Money was indeed a great instigator.

"I stole nothing from you," Doc spat. "The money I *won* is in the safe at the Long Branch."

Nothing Holliday could've said would have appeased the men at this point. There was no cash, Doc knew each of his attackers, and he was not one to keep silent about the assault.

It was also well known around town that Holliday's best friend was the stern faced deputy marshal and known head knocker, Wyatt Earp. Once the assault against the dentist was known, Earp wouldn't stop until he brought them all to justice. These facts were discussed, and it was the opinion of all save the little Frenchmen that Holliday had to be silenced on a permanent basis. As Flynn laid into Holliday with all that was in him, pummeling the slender man with blow after blow to his back and shoulders, Marais shrieked in despair.

Stop it! You'll kill 'im! I want my money back as much as you, but murdering a man was not part of the plan."

"Yeah, Flynn, you'll kill 'em," Cary piped up. He suddenly decided he did not want murder on his conscience, yet somehow felt it all right to hold a helpless man prisoner against the wall so Flynn—and if he tired, Potter—could beat him to death.

Flynn ignored his cohorts and renewed his efforts. Holliday barely felt the blows being rained onto him. The original dull made-him-want-to-vomit pain gave way to a general all over agony. Even his shoulders felt as if they were being twisted from his body. In spite of his best efforts to the contrary, Doc groaned aloud.

"Hey! What the hell's goin' on back there?"

At the shout, the beating ceased and a generalized panic ensued as the men took to harried flight, all except Flynn. "You ain't gettin' away this easy, Holliday," he hissed against Doc's ear. There followed a last blow to Holliday's side, this the worst of all.

Without the hands holding him up, Holliday slid down the wall, his legs too rubbery to support his weight. Grabbing him by the shoulders, Flynn slammed him to the ground and proceeded to jerk the gold watch and chain from his vest. "At least I'll get somethin' to remember you by."

Doc fumbled for the timepiece and managed to snag the last few inches of chain. For a second it was a tug of war to see who would come away the victor. With a final, vicious yank the thief managed to part the watch from its chain. Flynn got to his feet and dashed away with his prize.

John Holliday managed, with much concerted effort, to force his unwilling body into a sitting position. Shoulders rounded, head on chest, he stared down at all that remained of a cherished memory, a bit of heavy gold chain from whose end dangled a small watch fob, the figure of a rearing horse. Blood mingling with unashamed tears dripped from his chin, and he never noticed the gold links were embedded into the fleshy heel of his right hand. When his mother presented the timepiece to him on the occasion of his fifteenth birthday, it was with the following rejoinder: "Whenever you hold this watch in your hand, think of she who gave it and of the love and devotion with which it is imbued." It was his mother's final gift to him.

Gentle hands touched him and voices sought to reach him, and finally he raised his head. Staring into Wyatt's eyes, Doc held out the fragmented memory. "My watch, I want it back. I need it back. Help me, Wyatt?"

Earp's hand closed around Holliday's. "You can count on it, Doc."

Wyatt lifted Doc to his feet and placed his arm around his shoulder, steadying him. "Can you walk?" he asked.

Doc nodded, but as he attempted to put one foot in front of the other, he stumbled. Wyatt's firm grip kept him upright. "Lend a hand here, Creek."

At his left Doc felt Johnson's solid presence and another supporting arm. "Who did this, Doc?" Creek asked. "Was it them fellas you played Spanish Monte with tonight? Flynn and them?"

"Flynn stole my watch, that sonofabitch," he slurred. "Was him, Cary, Potter and that little Frenchman." With effort he raised his head to look at Wyatt. "You remember the little Frenchman, don't you, marshal? Maurice or Marais something."

Doc fought a rising panic. He couldn't quite remember the man's name though he'd known it well enough before. Confused, he pulled away from his friends' supporting arms and, angry, turned upon them as if they had something to do with his bewilderment.

"Leave me alone. Just let me be. I can do this by myself. I'm not some helpless child." He wrapped his arms about his hurting body and bent over, groaning into the pain, yet at Wyatt's approach he backed away, snarling. "Let me be, damn you."

Something wasn't right. Nothing was right. He couldn't put two and two together. Couldn't remember what the hell he was doing in this part of town in the wee hours of the morning. Couldn't remember why he hurt so bad. Couldn't understand why, when he touched the spot on his side that throbbed and burned, his hand came away sticky and wet. The smell of blood wafted up to him and nausea rolled in, engulfing him like a thick fog.

In an agony of confusion, he held the bloodied hand out toward Creek and Wyatt. Their faces froze in an expression of mutual shock, mouths gaping, eyes wide while their hands reached out to him as he fell.

Coming to took a long time, like surfacing from the deepest part of the ocean, fighting through a gray, murky sea one labored stroke at a time. He was in his own bed. That much he knew. Perhaps the other was all just a bad dream.

He'd always suffered from nightmares, especially as a small child. They were fewer now, but no less terrifying in their reality. But as he attempted to roll from the unaccustomed position on his belly to his side, the subsequent pain slammed home the fact that last night had been no dream. He cried out.

"Try not to move, John."

He recognized the lilting brogue of Doctor Thomas McCarty, the one licensed physician in Dodge City, Holliday's colleague and friend.

The sharp jab of a needle and slow comforting warmth spread through the pain. "You've suffered a stab wound to the right side and a grievous beating. Sleep now. Sleep," the voice coaxed, and Doc was ever so willing to obey.

A great commotion wrenched him from slumber, an argument of major proportions between Wyatt and Kate. Doc figured if he kept his eyes closed perhaps it would stop, but no. Even with his mind clouded by morphine, he had little trouble tracking the general gist of the squabble. Kate was ranting drunk and Wyatt, angry.

"It's my fault this happened. If Doc hadn't a come lookin' for me south of them damned tracks he wouldn't a got beat like he did and robbed, too. His ma gave him that gold watch. It means everything to him. None a this woulda happened but for me."

Wyatt's words were too quiet for Doc to make sense of, yet Earp's tone crackled with anger. He was attempting to boot Kate from the sick room. She was having none of it.

"Take your stinkin' hands offa me. This is my room. Mine and Doc's. It's you who don't belong here." There followed a great rustling of satin as Kate struggled to free herself, and a loud *slap*.

Without warning, Kate threw herself onto the prone and helpless Holliday, nearly smothering him as she showered wet kisses onto the side of his face, his hair, even the one hand that rested outside the blankets. Tears flowed as she begged his forgiveness. Frantic, clutching at the bedclothes and even at Doc himself, Kate cried as Wyatt attempted to pull her away.

The smell of her alcohol soaked breath and the stench of some strange man's scent upon her skin and clothing, turned Doc's stomach. With what little strength he could muster, he turned his face into the pillow.

Night had already fallen when next he woke. This time the room was blessedly quiet. Seated in the chair near the window, Wyatt appeared to be reading the evening paper. Doc was hesitant to disturb him, but a most appalling thirst made even swallowing difficult. He cleared his throat. Wyatt started at the slight sound, folded the paper, and laid it on the table. A small smile brightened his otherwise serious countenance. "You're awake."

He rose, picked up the chair and carried it over to the side of Doc's bed, sighing as he settled himself onto it once again. Without needing to be asked, he poured a glass of water from the pitcher on the nightstand and held it so Holliday could quench his thirst. "More?"

"No. Thank you," Doc replied.

Wyatt returned the empty glass to the nightstand. Reaching over, he took Doc's hand and turned it over, palm up. He then drew something from an inside coat pocket. With great reverence he placed the article into Doc's hand and closed the bruised fingers around it.

A huge lump formed in Doc's throat, and tears sprang into his eyes as he grasped the precious watch once more. His fingers traced the delicate filigree of the ornate case and he placed the timepiece to his ear. The reassuring tick was like the beat of a mother's heart. No words were sufficient to tell Wyatt what his gesture meant to a grieving son. However, in that moment the bonds of friendship, of loyalty, of brotherhood were such in John Holliday that only death would be powerful enough to tear them asunder.

Wyatt turned Doc's hand back over and looked at the battered knuckles. This time he grinned from ear to ear. "You took quite a toll on them that beat you. Speaking as your boxing coach, you did me proud."

"You caught them all then?" Doc's voice was a whisper, but Wyatt heard, nodding.

"Rounded all four of 'em up and an uglier bunch a black-eyed swells I never hope to see again. You marked 'em good for us, Doc. You marked 'em good." Earp squirmed in the hard backed chair, seeming ill at ease with what he was about to say. He leaned forward in the chair at last.

"Texas Jack told me what happened with Bat Masterson in the Long Branch, how he disarmed you, left you wide open to anybody with half a mind to rob you once you left the saloon." Wyatt slammed a fist against his thigh. "I told Masterson he almost got you killed and for what, to make himself a big man? All he did was prove himself small, small and petty. Bat's a damned fool kid."

Doc shifted painfully. "This was no one's fault but mine. I crossed the tracks searching for Kate. I let down my guard. It's my fault, not Kate's, not Bat's."

Wyatt shrugged. "I'd say you're bein' mighty generous, but if that's how you're callin' it..."

"It is."

"All right then. But Bat's still a damned fool kid and Kate's still a…" Wyatt glanced rather at Doc and Holliday hoped his frown proved negative enough to silence Earp on the subject. It was.

An hour or so past dawn, the morphine wore off, and Holliday felt wave after wave of sickening pain break over him. Trying to deal with it did not work, but Doctor McCarty materialized out of the gray mist, his hypodermic and vial of painkiller ready.

Through the clearing mist appeared someone else, someone dear. Cleva Moss removed her bonnet and next her gloves, which she placed inside the hat. Her movement was soundless, her smile sweetly sad. At John's bedside, she crouched down looking into Holliday's face.

The morphine had yet to kick in, and John was bathed in sweat, his considerable discomfort impossible to hide from one as perceptive as Cleva. Yet as he looked upon her, a lady he missed more than he dared admit even to himself, he managed to smile in welcome.

She reached out, brushing the damp hair back from his face. Desperate to touch her, to take her hand, he reached for her but the agony of abused muscles prevented it. Seeing his need, she took his hand in hers.

Cleva's attention now turned to John's injuries, and though he'd not seen the damage for himself, he felt it, each discolored bruise, each welt from neck to waist, the heavily bandaged knife wound, and he saw them now, each mark upon his flesh, through her eyes. John swore Cleva's gentle touch against his wounded side eased the hurt; maybe it was just her presence.

She stood away from him and removed her traveling coat, laying it across one of the straight-backed chairs. Then with great care she let herself up onto the bed where she gathered John into her arms. Easing his head up to rest in the notch of her shoulder, she held him close, crooning softly to him, stroking his hair and face, rocking him with all of a mother's tenderness.

Her essence was the same as he remembered. It was how she always smelled, of soap and clothing dried fresh in the sun and of fresh-baked bread. Cradled against her, he felt the reassuring beat of her heart. Perhaps it *was* her presence, perhaps just the morphine taking effect, but John felt warm and safe and content.

Cleva's voice lulled and soothed him as she related all that had occurred at the ranch since he and Wyatt had left. And she told him how terribly he was missed, he and the marshal. It seemed tears were in her voice then, and John wanted to comfort her, but he lacked the strength even to speak let alone reach out to her.

How long he lay comforted in Cleva's arms he did not know, but he fell asleep there, not waking until mid afternoon. It was Wyatt's face he woke to then. He glanced past the lawman, searching for Cleva, for any sign of her, for her hat and gloves, her coat. There was nothing. Something dawned on him then, and it pained him more than his injuries. Why it came to him he did not know, but that he knew it to be fact was indisputable.

"Wyatt?" His voice was so weak and strained, he almost did not recognize it as his own.

"Yes, Doc. How 'bout some water?"

Holliday nodded and took several sips from the glass Earp held for him.

"Wyatt, Cleva." He could almost not bear to say the words, but forced them out nonetheless. "Cleva Moss is dead."

Wyatt shook his head. "No, that's not true. It's just the morphine. Doctor McCarty said you might have dreams, see things that aren't there. Guess it happens pretty regular." Earp set the glass down on the table.

"Believe me or don't," Holliday said, "but I know it to be true. Send a telegram, Wyatt. Send a telegram and find out what happened. God help me, I don't want this to be so, yet I know it is."

"What makes you say Cleva's dead, Doc?"

"Is she here? Is she in town, in Dodge? Have you seen her?" Holliday pressed.

"No, I haven't, but that doesn't mean she's not here. I've been pretty busy, but I can check the hotels. If she's here, I'll find her." Wyatt's attempt at a reassuring smile went unnoticed by the agitated Holliday.

When Doc spoke again it was to a spot past Wyatt, off somewhere, as if he couldn't look at his friend as he spoke.

"Well, Cleva was here with me. I don't know for how long. Her bonnet was green with a white ribbon. Her gloves were white and her coat a ladies' traveling coat, sort of tan, perhaps made of light canvas. Her dress was yellow, with a row of tiny buttons like pearls up from the wrists. Her hair was done up, you know, her braid was pinned onto the back of her head, and Wyatt?"

"Go on, Doc."

Holliday looked at Wyatt and into his eyes, not flinching, drilling into the other man, securing his attention. "There was no scar."

Earp slumped back in the chair, body limp, arms hanging loose at his sides. He wore a most somber expression.

"You believe me, then?" Doc whispered.

Wyatt avoided a direct answer. "Soon as Mattie comes to relieve me, I'll send a telegram to Caldwell, to the marshal. That's the town closest to Cleva's ranch. If anyone knows anything, it should be the local law. Until then, you just try and rest." Earp patted Doc on the shoulder. To Holliday, it seemed Wyatt avoided looking directly at him. Perhaps the anguish he read there was too much for him to take.

Doc closed his eyes and even trying not to, he found himself sinking into sleep. This time there were no dreams, at least none of which he was aware.

A cool breeze fluttered the lace curtains, disturbing the deck of cards spread across the table. A bottle of good Irish whiskey sat unopened near the sill and sitting in the chair beneath the window was Mattie Earp, a near empty bottle of laudanum, Doc's laudanum, dangling from the tips of her manicured fingers.

She made a pretty picture in her pink frock, dark blond tresses a mass of pinned up curls, or would have under different circumstances. The woman sprawled in the chair, a book of poetry on the floor, head back, mouth gaping, in an opium haze and oblivious to Holliday as he called to her from his bed, the pain in his side and back reaching the point where he needed relief. Twisting and turning in his discomfort, he managed to become cocooned within his bedclothes, which didn't help his situation.

Minutes ticked by and the pain increased and the anxiety at being pinned in the bed by the snare of blankets soon turned to panic. Again and again he called to Mattie, but she remained oblivious.

Struggling made matters worse, twisting the bedclothes ever tighter around him, and the pain was now unbearable. He almost fainted from relief when the door opened, and Kate breezed in.

Sober, she took in the situation at a glance. Cursing under her breath, Kate threw down her reticule and went to Doc. Easing him up against her, she unwound him from his prison.

Stalking over to Mattie, Kate grabbed the laudanum bottle and tipped it up to the light. "Damn. She didn't even leave a spoonful left, but it's gonna hafta do." Hurrying to Doc she held him up and gave him the drug directly from the bottle. Water followed. Doc moaned into the pain, Kate trying to soothe him, all the while swearing and cursing the woman in the chair.

This hellish scene greeted Wyatt upon his return. The telegram he carried stuffed into his pocket.

"What's going on in here? Kate, I could hear you when I was comin' up the stairs. Mattie?"

"That stupid bitch of yours, she drank up Doc's laudanum. I got what little bit she left into him. He's doin' some better now." Kate stroked Holliday's cheek and his eyelids fluttered closed.

Doc slept for hours and fought the urge to wake up. His last waking experience had been none too pleasant, and he did not want a repeat performance. But Tom McCarty was there, and Kate as well as Wyatt, so his fears of being neglected were soon put to rest.

The physician encouraged him to open his eyes. "You need more fluids and I can't get anything into you while you're asleep," he'd chided Holliday when his patient seemed loath to be disturbed. "If there's anything you like to drink besides water, anything I can get a good amount of into you, tell me, but no coffee, beer, or whiskey."

Doc thought that didn't leave much he could think of, but McCarty had a suggestion. "How about sarsaparilla or some flavor of soda pop? They contain water and sugar, and I can't see anything wrong with that. What do you think, John?"

Well, to Holliday almost anything beat water, so he nodded. "Sounds fine." His voice came out a scratchy feeble croak, but after drinking as much water as the physician deemed satisfactory, Doc was allowed to drift back to sleep.

Wyatt was sitting next to him when he woke later, and Holliday was beginning to think he spent all his hours in those two small rooms. Guilt sort of nagged at him about that until Earp told him he'd just taken over for Kate.

The lawman seemed sad, more melancholy even than was usual for him, and Doc wanted to ask him if it was because of Cleva. He wanted to, but the words wouldn't come, and he let Wyatt bring the subject up in his own time. A half hour passed with no words between them, Earp just giving Holliday sips of water or soda and gazing out the window at nothing, as if working up the courage to speak. Finally he did so, but not before placing a hand on Doc's shoulder and turning his chair to face the man in the bed.

"About Cleva, Doc, you were right. She's, she's dead. It happened yesterday morning in Caldwell." Wyatt paused, swallowing hard.

Doc felt the blood drain from his face. Though he'd known what Wyatt was going to say, hearing the words still stunned and grieved him. "Go on," he whispered.

"Seems she was in town running errands. She crossed the street onto the boardwalk in front of the mercantile and collapsed. The doctor said it was a stroke. There was no pain. There wasn't anything anyone could do." Wyatt stared down at the telegram he held between his hands. Silent tears dripped onto the crumpled paper.

When Wyatt looked up at Doc, Holliday saw his own hurt reflected in the other man's eyes.

One question Holliday asked of Earp: "What had she been wearing?" Wyatt sent another telegram to Caldwell.

When Wyatt handed the telegram over to Doc he did so without a word. Holliday read the wire and then folded it and placed it into the book he'd been reading, *A Midsummer Night's Dream*. He never opened the book again.

John Holliday sat in the chair by the window, gazing down at the goings on in the street below. Nothing exciting was happening, but anything at all beat staring at the four walls of his prison another moment. He'd almost come to despise the green ivy spiraling its way to the ceiling on gilded wallpaper he'd once thought somewhat pretty. What had he been thinking? From his bed he could see a bit of the outside world, but mostly just the sky, the passage of the sun overhead and lazy clouds wafting by and the occasional bird in flight. The sun was soon to set, and he enjoyed that time of day best of all. Each evening offered a different palette of colors: bands of violets, pinks, reds and oranges like a multi-layered parfait. Sunset never failed to bring peace to his soul, troubled or otherwise, peace and even a modicum of happiness to his often joyless world.

Tom McCarty, however, was not happy when he arrived to examine his patient. "How did you manage this?" He asked.

"By *this* I assume you mean getting out of bed and walking over to take this seat?" Holliday replied.

To which the doctor countered, a scowl on his open, youthful face. "You shouldn't be out of bed as you well know. I thought you an educated man, John. Replace educated with exasperating and I'd agree."

McCarty set his bag down on the table and removed his stethoscope from within the dark recesses. Doc unbuttoned his shirt half way down, just enough to allow the physician to listen to his heart. McCarty warmed the instrument in his hand before placing the listening apparatus over the heart.

The organ thumped and banged with enthusiasm, and McCarty appeared satisfied.

"Is there still blood in your urine?"

Doc frowned at his colleague's lack of gentility. "No."

"Good. You just bruised that right kidney. For a while I was concerned it might be a laceration instead."

"I did not bruise my kidney. Those ruffians did the job for me."

"I stand corrected, John." McCarty smiled then had Holliday lean forward so he could listen to his lungs. "The bruises are fading. It's about time."

Moving the stethoscope back and forth over the same spot did not make what McCarty heard any better, nor did it change the facts. The physician leaned Holliday back into the chair and pasted him with a withering glare. "Why didn't you tell me you're consumptive?" he asked.

"When you first attended me I was in no position to offer up any information, Tom," Holliday replied, buttoning his shirt with exaggerated attention to detail.

"You could've told me since then. My God, man, I gave you morphine more than once and laudanum. That depresses breathing. I could've killed you. You might have told me, John. After all, I *am* your physician and I thought your friend."

"Only Wyatt knows. It is not common knowledge and I know you and I have patient-doctor confidentiality regarding this matter."

"Well, of course. You know I wouldn't tell anyone, John."

Doc reached with slow painful deliberation the few inches to the cigars sitting on the table and lit one. "How long do you think I have, Tom? A month? A year? Ten years?"

McCarty snatched the offending tobacco from his fingers, grinding the cigar out in the ashtray with a good deal more force than was necessary. "If you're tryin' to make a point that you don't give a damn…"

"Mind your own business, doctor. There's nothing you can do. There's nothing anyone can do."

Doc calmed down a bit, more angry at himself and at circumstances than at his friend. "You know that's true, Tom. Accept it. I have."

McCarty's Irish temper flared. "I didn't save your life so you could toss it away. I care even if you don't."

"Who said I don't care? I care more than you or anyone will ever know, but I am a lost cause. Tom, I do my best. If I seem cavalier about it, well it's just my way of accepting what has to be. You don't need to understand me. Just accept me." Holliday offered his hand.

Thomas McCarty's ire cooled as quickly as it flared and he shook Doc's outstretched hand, clasping it with affection. "I *don't* understand, but who ever said an Irishman had to understand an Englishman, even one so far removed from the Isles as yourself. However, if you're willin' to accept me with all my flaws, I can certainly return the favor."

"Agreed," John smiled.

CHAPTER 14

Hesitant footsteps stopping just outside the door to number 24 had Doc setting aside his book to reach the shelf beneath the nightstand for his pistol. He placed it beneath the bedcovers and waited.

A soft rapping was followed by the creaking of unoiled hinges. Doc's hand rested on the hidden .45, his thumb light against the hammer. The door gaped, and a face peeked through.

"Morgan Earp. How are you? Where have you been all this time? Come, sit down so we may talk." Holliday indicated the chair by the bed. He knew he looked like hell, courtesy of Kate's hand mirror, and Morgan's wincing expression. Self-consciously, Doc's hand went to the scabbed over scrape that covered the left side of his face. He hadn't been barbered in days, and dark circles beneath his eyes accentuated the pallor of his skin. In his own words, he looked like "death warmed over."

But the younger Earp didn't seem to mind Doc's look.

Morgan smiled and that smile lit his entire face. Morgan resembled Wyatt to such a degree that people who did not know them well often mistook the brothers one for the other. Doc always found it easy to tell them apart. While Wyatt gave the appearance of being in deep thought, Morgan always looked about to smile or laugh. What John Holliday was to Wyatt Earp, Morgan Earp was to Doc. He could make the dentist smile almost without effort and laugh out loud. He was delightful company and Holliday had missed him. Near the same age, a few months apart, the two had much in common, having spent many an hour at the poker or Faro tables, more often than not just talking and joking.

Morgan pulled up the chair giving Holliday an exaggerated once over. "You look used, Doc."

"Sorely my friend, sorely," Holliday replied, but smiled nevertheless, reaching out to shake the other man's hand.

Morgan noticed the bruised, healing knuckles. "Wyatt told me not to be too concerned about how you looked. He said wait until I see the other guys. Seems you gave those bastards a run for their money."

"I did manage to catch them unawares, but whatever damage I accomplished is due to your brother. He insisted I have boxing lessons and being Wyatt, he wouldn't take no for an answer." Doc sank back against his pillows, the memories not ones with which he was comfortable.

Morgan saw the change in his expression and switched subjects, holding something out partially concealed within his fingers. "I was in Deadwood, saw these, and figured they could keep you company while you play solitaire."

Doc looked at the gift Morgan gave him and was pleased he had been remembered. The box contained a deck of playing cards that, according to Morgan, "came direct from Paris, France." Gracing the back of each card was a quite unclothed lady. Well, they were sort of covered, a hint of gossamer silk here, a strip of lace there. Like a naughty schoolboy, Morgan gave rapt attention to the pictures, pointing out and commenting on each lady's attributes, or lack thereof, trying his best to get Doc's mind off his recent tribulations. Noticing the unopened bottle of whiskey on the table, Morgan suggested they toast the lovelies, to which Doc readily agreed.

Three whiskeys later, and Holliday was feeling no pain at all. The liquor had loosened up Morgan, and he was feeling his youth and the need to express it. All that kept him from getting Doc up and out of bed for a night carousing on the town was the appearance of stern faced brother Wyatt.

"Come on, Doc. The night's young and so are we. The ladies are waitin. Come on." Morgan reached out to get a hand on Holliday and succeeded in snagging one sleeve. Wyatt's iron grip on him prevented any further action.

"Damn, Wyatt, you are a spoil sport. Doc wants to go, don't'cha, Doc?"

Holliday nodded with a silly grin.

Wyatt stood near the door, arms folded across his chest. "How old are you two anyways?"

Morgan and Doc exchanged somewhat confused looks with Doc slurring, "Is that a trick question?"

"No tricks, Doc. Morgan, say goodnight to your pal and lope on off to chase skirts or whatever you had planned, but he's stayin' put."

Holliday and the younger Earp both gave Wyatt what they assumed in their somewhat drunken states to be disgusted, withering looks, but Wyatt proceeded to laugh out loud. So taken aback were the two by Earp's unusual show of levity, the younger men joined in.

Feels good to laugh, Doc thought as he blotted his watering eyes back across his sleeve

Wyatt got his laughter under control, revealing a stricter,

more mature older brother. "There'll be time for all that later, when Doc's feeling better, Morg."

Holliday affected a pout. "But, Wyatt, I feel fine. Honestly I do," he pleaded.

Exasperated, Earp grabbed Morgan by the arms and propelled him toward the door.

Morgan looked back over his shoulder at Doc and shrugged. "Later Doc. Hope you're feelin' better soon."

Kate must have passed the brothers as they headed down the stairs and out. Doc heard Morgan's shrill wolf whistle of appreciation just as she stepped through the door and into the room they shared.

"Come here, darlin'," Doc drawled.

If Kate expected to crawl in next to the recuperating Holliday for a good night's sleep, she was mistaken. Still feeling the effects of the whiskey, Doc was in a playful mood, and when Kate climbed into bed next to his warm body, her own very scantily clothed, he reached out for her. In the narrow bed there was little room for her to affect an escape, and she didn't put up much of a struggle. Healed or not, Doc's body was willing, and with the spirit equally so, the deed was well accomplished, and Doc's sleep came deep and contented.

Doc woke to find Kate gone and Wyatt looking forlorn, standing at the foot of his bed gazing out the window. Maybe he wasn't forlorn, perhaps Holliday read something into Wyatt's usual expression, but no, when Earp turned to face him, Doc found his first impression to be the truer. A sense of foreboding enveloped him.

"I'll be leaving town for a few days. Didn't want you to wonder where I'd gone. Also, I didn't want you to hear it from anyone else."

"This sounds ominous, marshal. Shall I be concerned over your well being?" Doc motioned for Wyatt to hand him a cigar off the table choosing to ignore the other man's frown of disapproval. Earp handed him the stogie and lit it for him without argument. Doc's sense of impending bad news escalated.

"It's ominous because I know you'll want to tag along and you can't. This'll cause you grief and I'm sorry for that." Earp ran a hand through his thick blond hair, a stall if ever Doc saw one. Holliday fidgeted, wishing Wyatt would just get on with what he wanted to say and not drag it out so.

Wyatt pulled the chair over and sat down, giving the wounded man the once over and not disguising the fact that he was doing just that. "You're not well enough to travel. A blind man can see that and I ain't blind." Wyatt cleared his throat. "I'm riding to Caldwell to take Cleva's body back to the ranch."

Doc felt as if someone kicked him hard in the gut. His world dropped out from beneath his feet and he stuttered, attempting to find the words to reply, but unable. He closed his eyes and saw Cleva's face as clear as if she stood there before him. How much he wanted to do this one last thing for her, to help bring her home, to help dig out the place where she would at last find peace, to do so with his own hands, to do something for her. How he wanted to rant at Wyatt and ask the whys and why nots, but he'd already been given the answers. The only faults he could find with his friend were his overabundance of logic and his damned straightforward thinking. Doc knew he couldn't make the trip, but that didn't make the not going any easier for him.

He stared out the window, yet saw nothing. "Take Morgan," he said. "It's dangerous out there, one man alone. He's good company, not as good as me, but he'll do. Yes, do take Morg." The voice with its soft Georgia drawl was nothing more than a whisper.

"I'll do that, Doc. Get better."

Holliday didn't turn around until he heard the door close, then he stared after Wyatt for many long moments, his thoughts blank. Then, slipping down under the covers, he buried himself beneath them, letting the tears come, knowing there was no one to hear.

For three solid days, John Holliday did little but sleep. No amount of coaxing got food past his lips, and he drank only when fluids were forced upon him. The curtains were closed and the shades beneath drawn.

On the morning of the fourth day, he asked Kate to bring him a hot cup of tea, please, if it wasn't any trouble. By noon he asked for and got a bowl of soup. No one understood what initiated the change. Doc would have been hard pressed to answer that himself. It was almost as if he'd mourned enough. Now it was time to get on with living.

In an odd course of events Holliday would never be privy to, that morning, on that fourth day after Wyatt and Morgan left—leaving Doc sinking into his depression—Cleva Moss was laid to rest in an oak grove on a hill overlooking the ranch she started with her family. In her resting place near them, she now slept at peace.

CHAPTER 15

With Wyatt and Morgan up in Deadwood during the cattle drives' off season, and Creek Johnson and Texas Jack back at their ranch in Arizona, Doc's time was taken up with his dental practice during the day and his gambling trade in the evening hours. Even Kate was out of the picture, a nasty spat driving a wedge between her and Holliday, perhaps permanent, perhaps temporary. She hightailed it out of town on the first eastbound stage, a curse on her lips and a small bankroll in her handbag. And although Doc's trade left him well occupied, he missed the companionship of good friends.

Waiting for a patient, he was surprised when the knock at the door of number twenty-four, The Dodge House, was light and muted. Holliday was expecting the blacksmith, and his knock was anything but delicate. The man was also two hours late, and Doc was of the opinion he would be a no show.

Shrugging into his work coat, straightening the lapels and buttoning the loose fitting garment as he walked, Doc made his way to the door, turned the key in the lock and opened it. Indeed the delicate hand that tapped against the door did not belong to Gunnar Schroeder the blacksmith but to a lady as petite as Schroeder was large.

"Clementine." Holliday whispered the name, as if to speak it aloud might cause the vision to disappear.

The lady smiled, holding her gloved hand out to him. He took it, pressing it to his lips.

"Will you ask me in, John Henry?"

"I will indeed, Miss Mosby." John drew her into his rooms, closing the door behind her, locking it, as was his habit. Pulling out a chair from the table by the window, he watched as she crossed the room, seating herself. The lady was resplendent in a peach organza frock in the latest eastern style. A matching bonnet framed her heart-shaped face and accentuated the auburn curls that peeked from beneath the lace and fabric confection, the sight enchanting Holliday.

"Exactly as I remember." He took the seat opposite her, amazed to see the lady, delighted, and yet a pall hung over his joy, dark and hazy. He brushed it aside and smiled.

"No, not exactly," he corrected. "You are lovelier even than my memories." Again the cloud, again the nagging fear.

Reaching the short distance across the table, he took both her hands in his. Confined in the gloves, they trembled like small birds, and were cold as he held them. "What brings you here?"

"Bold and to the point. You've matured since we parted company, John Henry." Her gaze met his and she was as bold in her look and what was behind her lovely green eyes, as he was in his thoughts.

"I, too, have matured in the last five years, much to the chagrin of my parents. They told me I was brash and indelicate, adding stubborn and headstrong for good measure. 'No well bred southern girl travels alone on a train through godless, friendless country,' to quote my father. But he'd forgotten something about me, John. I am no longer a girl. I'm a woman. He was correct about all the rest though." She hesitated for a moment. "I came for you."

Shocked, John dropped her hands and sat back in his chair, staring at her, not even realizing how impolite it was, how ungentlemanly. He saw her past and his, all the plans they made back in Georgia on his family's plantation and on hers bordering it.

First they were the dreams of children new in love, the parties they would attend together, the clothes she would buy, how jealous their friends would be of their life together. Then, later when the love deepened and each knew there could be no life for them separately, they spoke of the wedding, the honeymoon, his attending college, his practice and how they would move to Atlanta and be all things one to the other, and the children who would come later. All those memories came to mind, all the dreams that should have been fulfilled and would never be.

"Nothing has changed, Clementine." His eyes were sad and his voice as he continued. "I had no future then. I have none now."

Tears came into her eyes and when they fell she let them. "Your illness never changed how I felt about you. One day, one year or fifty, you are all I ever wanted. You are still all I will ever want."

John rose from the table, pushing his chair away, turning his back on her. She had taken the words from his mouth, from his heart. It was what they had always said to each other, back then, back when he had been alive.

"You never said goodbye to me when you left, John. I had no closure. At least allow me that." She rose from her seat, silk petticoats rustling as she came up behind him, her head barely reaching his shoulder. She laid a hand against his arm. "All these years apart, and it is still the same for me. Still and always the same, John."

He covered her hand with his. "I knew if I saw you before I left Georgia, I could never leave. Once I believed there was a chance I could recover my health, that I might beat this insidious disease and come home, come back to you." He shrugged. "That was all a pleasant fabrication, a dream, a fairy tale fed to me by my well meaning uncle and his doctor friends. It was a lie, Clementine. I'll never be well. I have nothing to offer you, not even myself.

"For the first year all I thought of was you. All I saw in my dreams was you. Such thoughts were driving me insane. I couldn't work. I couldn't think. I couldn't eat. One day, alone in my room, always alone, I came to a conclusion. There could be no more thoughts of you. If I was to live at all, to function at all, I had to let you go. I had to. And so I did, until today, until I saw you again and it all came back to me as if we'd never parted."

He couldn't stand it, couldn't stand that she was there in the room with him, so close, touching him. He groaned and turned to her, folding her into his arms. Bending his head, he kissed her with all the pent up longing, loneliness, and desire he hid from himself for five tortured years.

Their lovemaking was fierce, almost frenzied. John forced himself to slow down, reminded himself to be gentle, but their combined passion went beyond his control. Never had he been with a woman whose desire not only matched, but surpassed his own, and when he felt resistance within her body he tried to hold back, but Clementine pressed him forward.

Tears streaked her cheeks and he felt shame. "I hurt you,"

he whispered, covering her face with kisses, but she shook her head, lowering his face to hers with a hand behind his neck, kissing him on the mouth.

"You are all I ever wanted," she murmured.

The next few weeks were spent in a rapture of rediscovery, renewing, and strengthening what had been theirs years before. Nothing dampened the joy, the ardor of every moment of every day.

Not even an encounter with Bat Masterson was unpleasant, though as Doc noticed the man advancing up the sidewalk toward them one afternoon, he felt his gut tighten in apprehension. When John realized a meeting between them was inevitable, he took it in stride. Pasting a smile onto his face, he greeted Masterson.

"Good day, sheriff. I'd like to present Miss Clementine Mosby. Miss Mosby, this is the sheriff of Ford County, Bat Masterson."

Masterson took the lady's outstretched hand, looking at a loss as what to do next. Sensing his slight distress, Clementine smiled and nodded. "I am most pleased to make your acquaintance," she said. Withdrawing her hand, she linked her arm once again through that of her escort.

"No, it is I who am pleased." Masterson glowed, and Doc felt a jab of irritating jealousy. *Is it my imagination or is that jack-a-nape leering at Clementine?* Doc huffed. *What am I worried about? He may dress well, yet he lacks sophistication and is by no means a gentleman.* But when John met Clementine's adoring gaze, he realized all his worries were for naught. His heart soared.

"We're off for some lunch at Delmonico's then. Good day to you, sheriff." Doc tipped his hat and before Masterson found his tongue to respond, he and Clementine were half way down the boardwalk, talking and laughing, absorbed in each other.

Together in the suite they now shared at the Dodge House, the finest suite on the top floor with a view of the entire city and the vistas beyond, they lay content in each other's arms.

As this night was like all the nights that had come before, they whispered together of what lay ahead, made love and lay together, hands entwined and bodies touching.

Yet somehow this night differed from the others. Several times Clementine made as if to speak, but for some reason thought better of the idea, covering her hesitation with a sweet smile or some trifle of information. John was curious, but figured a lady often needed time to make her point in just the way, at just the precise moment. Besides, at this moment he was blissful, he was happy. She lay with her head in the hollow of his shoulder and he couldn't remember when he had been so at peace or when everything had been so right in his world.

Her hair splayed out around her in a halo of mahogany, spilling onto his chest and across both pillows, the soft lamplight highlighting its redness. Taking a lock in his hand, he reveled in the texture of it, like the finest silk and every bit as lovely.

"Clementine?"

She did not answer, but snuggled closer to him, one hand resting on his chest, against his heart, her soft breathing indicating sleep.

"I'm certain whatever it is you wanted to tell me can wait until morning. Good night, darlin'." He brushed her forehead with a kiss.

At first he thought his unaccustomed warmth was due to the heat of the evening itself coupled with the heat of Clementine's body, the length of her pressed close to him.

Careful, so as not to waken her, John eased back the blanket. The breeze coming in through the opened windows began evaporating the perspiration from him. That in turn led to shivers, and even the blanket pulled up again did not drive those off. His teeth chattered and he trembled in earnest, and then it began.

Not now. Please, God, not now, he prayed, even as the cough raged through him. Burying his face into the feather pillow, he attempted to smother the sound of his body's betrayal, but it was no use. Violent racking coughs tore into his fragile lungs. Fighting for life, he did not notice Clementine leave their bed and indeed their rooms. His head swam and he fell back onto the pillows, gasping, blood trickling from the corner of his mouth.

Her sweet face hovered over him, but there were tears in her eyes and fear. In spite of that, she stayed. Stroking his face and hair with a cool hand, she blotted the blood from his lips with the corner of one of her own handkerchiefs.

"That's quite a lady you have, John."

What time is it? He wondered. *What day? Where's Clementine?* "Tom?" the last was a spoken word and not a mere thought.

Doctor McCarty nodded. "I was just saying Miss Mosby is quite a lady, John. She's rarely left your side, let alone these rooms since you took ill." McCarty felt the pulse at Holliday's wrist. "It took all my Irish charm to make her go outside for a breath of fresh air. She was near as pale as you."

John blinked at the brightness of the light that poured through the windows. "Morning," he stated.

"Oh, it's morning, all right, morning of the sixth day since I was called in. You've had a rough go. Miss Mosby will be relieved you're awake. She's been worried, John. We both have."

McCarty appeared disheveled, like he'd missed more than one night's sleep.

"Will I live?" John asked, his voice hoarse, his throat raw.

"You're young and strong and that's in your favor. You have a lady who loves you. That's in your favor as well."

"Do not mince words with me, Tom." Holliday insisted.

McCarty pulled up the chair and sat down. "I believe you will survive this particular bout with time and a great deal of bed rest and care. How many more episodes your body can tolerate, that nobody knows."

John turned his head away and closed his eyes.

He woke to a dark room, though a hint of sunlight peeked in from beneath the drawn shades, pale and just coming dawn. He believed he was thinking okay when he swung his legs over the side of the bed, pulled on his trousers, and slipped into low-topped boots.

On the spare bed lay Clementine still clothed and asleep, breathing through parted lips, eyes closed and dark lashes long and lush upon her pale cheeks. With longing he reached out to touch her, but pulled back too quickly. The room spun and his vision darkened. He stood stone still, willing it all to pass away. It did. For the life of him he couldn't remember why he had to leave. But he knew he must.

Her hand caught his arm and held him with purpose. Her strength of body was negligible, but it wouldn't take much to keep Holliday from moving. As he looked down at her, puzzled, confused, she smiled up at him.

"Where are you going, John? You need to get back into bed. You need to rest, to sleep and get well." She guided him back to the bed, got him to sit at the edge where she removed his boots and pressed his body back onto the sheets. He offered no protests as she drew the blanket up, but continued to gaze at her, disoriented.

"I don't know where I'm going," he answered. He reached out for her, the one bright light in his dark, pain-filled world.

Taking his hand in hers, she kissed the palm and rested it against her cheek before laying it back on the covers. He closed his eyes, and it was many long days and nights before he opened them again.

John's consciousness existed far from the room in which his corporeal body lay, but he *was* with Clementine. Together again and always they laughed and whispered and made love, oblivious to time or place or the dictates of circumstance. To John Holliday this was no dream, but reality, his reality and nothing and no one could tear him away. The more he became involved in fantasy, the less involved he became in the real world, the one in which he truly belonged. His breathing and heart rate slowed, and it was so easy to drift and sleep and dream. So easy to put aside pain and worry, loneliness and loss, so easy to accept joy and love and happiness as his due, not seeing death waiting and lurking to claim even that little piece of feigned normalcy.

Morning came around again, and it seemed there had been no changes. Holliday slept on, peacefully ignorant of the darkening clouds that had settled over the room he occupied. Seated at the mirror, Clementine went through the motions of her morning toilette. In her hand the heavy boar's hair brush stroked through the mane of luxurious hair, a hundred strokes, two, three hundred, until the reddish mass crackled and glowed with vitality, unlike the reflection of the young woman in the mirror whose darkly ringed eyes and pale complexion told of her constant vigil at her lover's side.

She brushed until her arms ached with the effort before stopping to lay the brush aside and reach up again to her hair, aptly weaving the waist length of it into a thick braid, wrapping it into a bun at the back of her head and pinning it tightly.

"So lovely."

Clementine started at the sound in the otherwise almost

dead stillness of the room, her gaze focused in the mirror and in the image looking back at her. She smiled.

From his bed he'd watched for some time, silent, savoring the moments, those moments other men took for granted in their secure, healthy lives. He took great pleasure in his lady's routine, wishing it might go on for hours. Although it did not, John was not disappointed for he soon found himself the object of Clementine's attention, her hands cool upon his face, her lips warm on his, and her tears this time tears of joy. He smiled with all that was left in his worn out body.

Her returning smile was radiant. "Welcome home," she whispered. "I missed you."

A good week passed before Holliday was well enough to be out of bed for any length of time. He felt good, all things considered, but remained weak and tired. "As expected when a man has been literally at death's door," commented Doctor McCarty.

Once, during his recuperation, he almost asked Clementine what she wanted to tell him those many days before he took ill, if indeed she wanted to confide something to him at all. But he was easily sidetracked and exhausted so his unasked question went unanswered. At this juncture it seemed of little importance anyway.

John delighted in being well. Everything brought a smile to his lips, most especially the sight of Clementine, the feel of her skin, the scent of her hair. He reveled in her, reaching out to grab her close for a kiss or just to brush her face with the tips of his fingers.

Yet as he lay next to Clementine in bed, her head nestled in the crook of his arm, her expression, even in sleep contented, happy, a smile playing about her lips, the cold ache of reality seeped into John Holliday, into his mind, his heart, his soul. And he knew this, what he desired more than anything, this life with Clementine could not be. He coughed, muffling the harsh cackle with a handkerchief crushed to his mouth. The pain in his chest was nothing compared to that in his heart.

In the following days John became quiet and introspective. He talked little and laughed not at all. He was pensive and melancholy, and when he broke the silence, it was if life's fire had burned itself down to ash.

His voice was odd, almost not his own as if the words issued from someone else, or from somewhere else, each syllable agonized over, each word a sword point into his heart and hers.

"Nothing has changed, Clem. At least nothing has changed for the better. More than ever I know now I have nothing to offer you. I'm dying. I almost died those two weeks past, and you can't say that isn't the truth."

He paced the rooms, hands behind his back, face a confused mask of emotions. Although not looking at Clementine, he knew she followed his every move from where she sat, tiny and straight on the chair by the window.

"You deserve everything."

His voice quieter now, sad, almost a whisper, "You deserve everything and that does not include caring for an invalid husband. I can offer you nothing, not even myself. If I kept you here with me, if we married, even if you did not wind up hating me, I know in time I would hate myself for what I'd do to you." At last he stopped his frantic pacing and turned to face her. Falling to his knees before her, he buried his face in the folds of her skirt. "And forgive me. Promise you'll forgive me."

Lifting his face up to meet her gaze, she asked of him, "What do you want from me, John? Do you want me to say that it's all right? That I understand why you no longer want me? I *don't* understand. I love you."

Seeing her grief, her absolute despair, nearly caused
Holliday to forget his principles. Nothing at that moment
would have been easier than giving in to his own selfish needs
and desires, to tell Clementine how much he loved her, how
badly he wanted her, needed her, now and always. He pressed
a hand to his chest, grimacing. It hurt to breathe. It hurt to
swallow. It hurt to speak, yet he did.

"I *do* want you. You are all I ever wanted or will ever
want. That is why you must go on and have a life. You must
leave here and go home to Georgia. Be with your family. Trust
them to know what's best for you. Find a life, Clementine.
Make a life. Give me the knowledge that one of us will go on
so I can attempt to finish out what time is left to me without
the unholy guilt of two lives ruined."

She bent her head and kissed him, her passion hot, her
arms enveloping him. He returned the kiss, moaning with the
need of her, a need so fierce and deep, it threatened to shred
what little remained of his resolve. Pushing out of her
embrace, he struggled to his feet, swaying, his eyes closed,
and when she came to him to hold him, he prevented it.

"You can not change my mind, Clementine. Please pack
your things. The next train east leaves at 5:10 this evening."
He left the rooms he shared with her, pulling the door closed
behind him.

The twenty or so paces to Wyatt's empty suite were the
hardest steps John Holliday had ever forced upon himself.
Each footfall was an agony of indecision, no matter how firm
of intent he appeared in front of Clementine, and of
heartbreak. Fumbling the key in the lock he pushed through
the doorway and into the room. The air was stale and he
opened both windows before seating himself in the one chair
in the room. There he sat, unmoving, silent, and mourning.

At 4:30 pm he returned for her. When she opened the

door to him, it was all he could do to keep from dropping to his knees and begging her forgiveness. She never looked lovelier or more fragile as she stood before him, speechless, pale, her eyes puffy from crying, yet with her small chin held high. God how he wanted to hold her.

At the train he handed Clementine's luggage to the porter and walked her to the step-up. He took her small hand in his. As on that first day, the day she came back into his life with her heart upon her sleeve and her pride laid at his feet, her delicate fingers trembled within his.

"Forgive me, Clementine," he murmured. Those were his last words to her as he put her gloved hand to his lips and kissed it.

As he brought her hand to his lips for the final caress, his head bent low, she offered her own final declaration. "I will always love you."

CHAPTER 16

John Holliday felt the gaze heavy upon him, penetrating the haze of too much whiskey, too little sleep, and a broken heart. With much effort, he raised his head to meet it.

I should have known, he thought. *Wyatt Earp. Only he would have the audacity to force his way into my very mind.* Doc nodded a greeting to Earp as the other remained at the bar, perhaps expecting an invitation, perhaps just taking in the play. Wyatt nodded back, remaining stationary as he sipped a coffee.

For reasons unknown, Holliday felt disgusted with himself. He hadn't left the Long Branch in almost a week, by his own cloudy recollections. That meant he hadn't shaved, washed, or changed his clothing in as many days. His own stink, sweat, whiskey and even vomit, offended his senses though it seemed to have no effect on the saloon's clientele. He ignored it until now, until Wyatt Earp reappeared from his sojourn, his very presence enough to bring Doc back to himself, and Doc hated Wyatt for it.

A sharp remark from the gambler seated opposite Holliday snapped Doc's attention back to the game at hand. Charlie White, a former buffalo hunter turned barfly, accused Doc of cheating.

Holliday surged back from the table, eyes narrowing, face flushing, fingers going to the .45 in the holster at his waist. He tapped the ivory butt of the weapon, the action itself not particularly menacing, but coupled with the expression on the gambler's face and the increasing tempo of the tap, caused those at the table to pause in anticipation of what must surely follow.

Charlie White turned pale and smiled a sickly sort of grin, raising his hands in a show of apologetic diffidence. But Doc did not back down, and his voice rose harshly through the sudden stillness.

"That's right my yellow friend. Back down. You back right down. Don't you know who you're callin' a cheat? I'm Doc Holliday and you, my friend, will be just one more notch upon my gun. Go on, go for it. Go on!" he goaded the cowering White.

"I ain't heeled, Doc." the man cried out in mortal fear for his life.

Holliday lunged across the table at White who shrieked and fell over backwards in his attempt to get out of the mad man's reach. The other players sat dumbfounded, frozen to their seats in fear.

Doc felt hands upon him, rough hands, clamping his arms to his sides as he screamed in rage and fought with insane purpose. Not even Wyatt's voice in his ear took the edge from his anger. Earp dragged Holliday from the saloon. Then Wyatt took a moment to say something to Morgan Earp as they passed on the boardwalk.

"Don't ask. Just go in there and get Doc's winnings off the table. And bring his hat."

For most of a block Earp half carried, half dragged Doc down Front Street, Holliday cursing Wyatt. Frantic, Doc twisted to divest himself of his wrangler.

"I didn't know they taught such language in college, Doc," Wyatt gritted out under his breath. "Guess there are still some things I don't know about you."

At one point Doc tried to tear himself from Earp's iron grasp. Faced with a drawn back fist, Holliday thrust his chin forward, daring Wyatt to strike. Instead, the lawman jerked up on Doc's pinned left arm, nearly lifting the slim Holliday off his feet. Doc capitulated. However, it was the calm before the storm. The moment Earp released him into his hotel room, every bit of pent of fury came to the fore. Holliday went berserk.

Every empty whiskey bottle, and there were many, hit the floor with shattering force, lamps followed and chairs. Books flew from the shelves, several going out the window to land in the street below. Into the closet he went, tearing clothing off hangers, rending the fabric. The washbasin and pitcher hit the wall with a resounding crash.

Holliday stood amid the ruins, ashen, shaking, sweat staining his collar and dripping from his chin. He panted open-mouthed and felt dizzy and faint, due to the temper tantrum, but also due in no small part to the fact that he had scarcely touched anything resembling solid food in days.

Righting one of the chairs, Wyatt took Holliday by the arm and led him over, pressing down against his shoulders to get him to sit.

Beneath Earp's hands, Doc trembled. He did give in at last and sat, staring straight ahead, his expression vacant. Moments later he rested his arms on the table, lay his head down in the circle and closed his eyes. Sobs shook the frail body.

He didn't remember falling asleep, didn't know if it was sleep or unconsciousness, but when he woke, Wyatt was there sitting in a chair next to the bed in which Doc now lay. The remnants of uncounted cigarette butts littered the nightstand, and a cloud of blue smoke hung in the air.

Earp crushed out the last of the long line of quirlies in the overfilled saucer and leaned near. His appraisal of Holliday was frank. Doc cringed beneath the unwavering gaze. He knew he looked like death, skeletal, sick, wasted. He didn't need a friend to rub it in. When their gazes met, there was no smile for Earp, no pleasure in his unasked for company.

"I always wondered what you might be like if you ever got drunk," Earp said. "I believe I coulda lived without that knowledge." He leaned in close. "What are you tryin' to do, kill yourself?"

"Just like Wyatt Earp, straight to the point. Since you're bein' so honest, I shall be likewise. *Yes,* but like so many other things in my life at which I failed, I did not accomplish what I started out to do." This was the first time he admitted to himself he indeed wanted to die.

"What happened, Doc? What caused all this? What happened to you?" Earp pressed.

If Holliday noticed the concern in Earp's voice, on his face, in the expressive depths of the eyes, in the downward turn of the lips beneath the thick tawny mustache, it did not show.

"Don't ever ask me that, Wyatt. I can't talk about it, not even to you. I won't. Don't ever ask me again. If you do, it will be the end of our friendship and to you that might be a blessing." Holliday's gaze wandered to the table and to the one unbroken bottle in the entire room. It was a bottle of scotch. "I'd like a drink. Please."

Wyatt followed the gaze to the table and to the bottle.

Leaving Doc's bedside, he walked over and picked up the whiskey. "Is this your new best friend?" he asked handing the bottle over.

Holliday took the scotch, uncorked it, and drank. "It asks me no questions. It tells me no lies. It is indeed a good friend."

Wyatt shook his head in disbelief. "Oh, it lies all right. It tells you everything you want to know then doesn't let you remember. It listens, but offers no answers. It'll steal your soul, Doc."

Holliday, after another long swig from the bottle, nailed Wyatt with an icy glare. "There you are wrong, Wyatt. It can not steal what I no longer possess."

There was a prolonged and uncomfortable silence in the room, hanging like black mourning crepe from every corner. "I'll be leaving Dodge tomorrow," Doc said. "Things have turned cold for me here."

Holliday noticed a change in Wyatt, a look passed across his face, an expression of…could it be panic? It was brief and then gone, leaving Doc wondering if he had imagined it, but Wyatt's next words put the stamp of truth on Holliday's assumption.

"Stay a bit, Doc. Hell, Morg and me just got back. We've got lots to talk about and I'm sure Morgan will want to tell you all about the little lady he found for himself up in Montana. Stay, John. Give it a week. If, after that, you still want to leave, you'll have my blessings. I'll even help you pack. Stay, just a while."

There was, if not panic, at least alarm in Wyatt's statement. Words failed Doc and he opted for silence. Turning his face to the wall, he feigned sleep.

This time when John Holliday saddled his horse, packed his saddlebags, and prepared to leave Dodge City, there was no talking him out of it. As much as Doc knew Wyatt wanted, needed, some words of explanation, he could not give them. All Wyatt got from Doc as Holliday swung his tired thin body up into the saddle, was a promise to keep in touch.

"I will write, Wyatt. You have my word. I'll be following the Santa Fe Trail. If you need to contact me, wire ahead. I'll check each telegraph office I pass through."

Weary, Doc reached down to shake Wyatt's hand and then Morgan's. Wyatt remained silent. Morgan told Holliday to take care of himself in a quiet, unhappy voice. Turning the mare away, Doc headed due south.

Alone on the trail, Doc managed to keep his thoughts corralled and focused. The odd sip now and then of the fine bourbon in the small silver flask he carried in his coat pocket helped in that respect.

The sound of a horse coming up behind him at full gallop caused him little concern. His hand lay heavy on the butt of the holstered .45. He was ready to meet any comers. However, this rider was the last he ever expected to encounter.

"Doc, honey. Wait up."

Kate.

Riding by his side, flirting, fluttering her eyelashes, regaling him with stories of her escapades while they'd been apart, Doc assumed in hopes of making him jealous, she attempted to garner his attention. He ignored her, yet she continued her rambling, obnoxious patter. To block out the endless babble, Doc tipped the flask more and more often. Well lit by its contents, he found it easier to ignore the pain in his heart and the constant flapping jaws of the woman who rode, unbidden, beside him.

Doc bedded down in a cold camp, eating nothing, drinking nothing aside from small sips from the flask. Rolled into his blanket, smoking and sipping, he became aware of Kate's presence. Crouching down, she brushed her fingertips across his cheek.

Jerking away from her as if he'd been touched by a hot brand, Doc leaped to his feet and gave her a look of such utter contempt, she drew back in fear. He'd never given her reason to fear him until this moment, and that thought and Kate's reaction did little to comfort him. Crushing out the cigar beneath his boot, he went back to lie down on his pallet. Too exhausted to fight with her or fight her, he rolled away with his back to Kate, closed his eyes, and slept.

The whole long way to Trinidad, Colorado, Kate kept up her attempts to insinuate herself back into Doc's life. It was wasted effort. Finally, when he did speak to her, it was just to say thank you for a cup of coffee she almost had to force into his hands, or for a plate of food he barely picked at. His spirit was broken. His health soon followed.

He took ill before they reached Trinidad, barely able to stay in the saddle. And much to his discomfort, he found he had to accept help from Kate.

She got them rooms at a hotel and him a doctor. For over a week, they could not travel, he too ill and she not leaving him. At first he wouldn't eat, but she coaxed and cajoled and pleaded and until he took some nourishment. Something in him wouldn't let go of life, couldn't let go, a spark remained which drove him on.

He got well, and when he did, Kate rode beside him into New Mexico Territory.

Las Vegas, New Mexico was a right enough sort of town. It had everything to offer Doc Holliday including a dozen hot springs which catered to consumptives. In fact, the place was a haven for the prosperous, young tuberculosis sufferers of the time, and where a group of such gentlemen formed a rather tongue-in-cheek association titled The Lunger's Club.

Las Vegas also boasted many saloons and no dentist. However, Doc was not in the mood to hang out his shingle. Doc was not much in the mood for anything aside from gambling and drinking. Although he and Kate shared a tiny apartment and even slept in the same bed, their *marital* relations remained nonexistent.

In the early morning hours after Holliday spent the better part of the long night indulging in games of chance, poker or Faro, he'd fall into bed half dressed, drunk and too tired to think. Upon waking the next afternoon, he would find himself the subject of Kate's smoldering appraisal. In no uncertain terms, she berated him for his aloof treatment of her. Doc ignored her tirades, but being a woman of fire, she kept them up in any case.

Doc knew Kate wanted him back as her lover. He knew this because of her ploys, some subtle, some outright brazen. She baited him. She attempted seduction. She cursed him hoping to get a rise. She belittled his masculinity. She tried it all and in all she failed. However, Kate wasn't finished by half.

Coming back to the rooms at his usual time, close to dawn, Doc fumbled his key in the door and turned the knob. Something on the floor blocked his way and he pushed with some force before the door gave enough for him to step inside. Scattered clothing lay everywhere and not just Kate's, men's clothing, the dusty blue trousers and blouse of a U.S. Army trooper. Whiskey fumes fouled the close air.

In Holliday's bed, and oblivious to all but each other, were Kate and the cavalryman. For a moment, Doc stood frozen in the open doorway. He refused to believe she had stooped so low as to cuckold him in his own bed. After all, even Kate had her limits, but here was the proof of her fall in all its glory.

Doc felt nothing at first, not jealousy, but then something crept over him. There was still a man inside the shell he had become, a man with pride, at least that. And here he was, that pride wounded.

Closing the door behind him made no difference to the pair in the bed so rapt were they in their appreciation of each other. So Doc reopened the door, slamming it shut. The soldier stopped his attentions to Kate, sitting bolt upright in the tangle of sheets, blankets, and clothing.

Doc drew both ivory-gripped pistols, pointing them at the trooper whose florid complexion paled at the threat. Holliday was most pleasured by the fellow's reaction to him. It seemed even with a brain fogged by liquor and sex, the damned fool retained enough sense to feel fear.

"Get out." Doc ordered. "If I ever see you in this town again, you will wish this night had been your last."

The soldier was quick to comply. Gathering up his clothes, he tore from the room without a backward glance. Kate sat alone in the bed and to her Doc said nothing.

Laying his pistols on top of the dresser, he turned to the washstand and filled the bowl with water from the matching pitcher. He set about washing his face and hands, paying special attention to the manicured nails.

Drying his face on the rough towel, he noticed Kate's reflection in the mirror as she stood at his left shoulder, her dark eyes smoldering with rage. Yet when she spoke, she somehow managed to keep her temper, quite a feat for the volatile Hungarian.

"What do you see when you look in that mirror, Doc?" she asked. "Who do you see? Look. Look at yourself. Who died, Doc? Who died? My God, you even look like you're in mourning."

Gazing at his own reflection in that damned mirror, he wondered who did look back? Gone were the pale gray, blue or beige frock coats with the brightly patterned waistcoats and brilliant ties. In their place he now wore the same tired double breasted coat, a black vest, and a white shirt set off by a gray cravat. Less a mourner, he more resembled a shadow of his former self, a dark foreboding specter of the man he had once been.

Turning around he confronted Kate. "Who died? I did. I am a dead man. Oh, I walk and talk and breathe. Sometimes I even eat or sleep. Most of the time I just walk around inside this empty shell, a living breathing corpse." He smiled down at her, a sickly mocking smile. Even the life spark, tiny though it might have been, was in serious danger of being extinguished.

With all her might Kate slapped Doc hard across the left cheek, so hard it jerked his head to the side, but still the smile stayed on his lips. Again she slapped him, and again until the marks from her blows were vivid on his pale cheeks. At the last, she backhanded him, and the ruby ring she wore, an earlier gift from Doc, cut his lip. A single drop of blood beaded there and he reached up, rubbing the back of his hand across his mouth, smearing it.

Without a word, without a sound, he grabbed Kate around the throat with both hands, circling her neck, almost lifting her off her feet. Thinking to see fear in her eyes or at the very least hate, what he saw shocked and surprised him. It was elation. She worked long and hard to get a response from Holliday and at last was rewarded. It did not seem to matter to her *what* motivated Doc to act, to react, but only that something *had* motivated him, even if it was hate.

Instead of throttling her, he released his hold on her throat, picked her up, and threw her onto the bed still warm from her previous encounter, still warm from bodies and sweat and sex, and he was on her in a passionate rage.

And when he was through and she lay curled up to his back, one arm around his chest, her breath warm on his neck, he knew she had bested him. But he couldn't hate her, couldn't even be angry with her. She had made him realize life was meant to go on. No matter how much it hurt, it was still and all living.

Living meant a need for the more mundane things in life, and that included a source of income. There being no dentist in town, Doc determined to open a dental practice. He chose a spot on the north side of Bridge Street near the plaza, and for a time business was brisk. Then, due to the vagaries of life in a town such as Las Vegas, the need for dentistry dropped off, leaving Doc with a part-time business.

No problem there as the availability of saloons was more than a constant, it was a growing concern, and Holliday soon took up where he left off in Dodge City. For some hours during the day, he practiced at his dental profession. Late night hours were taken up by gambling. The latter was more profitable than the former, and soon cards took up more and more of Doc's time.

However, a damper soon ground Holliday's way of life to a halt. In March of 1879, a statute passed in the territory of New Mexico that made keeping a gaming table illegal. It wasn't long before The Territory of New Mexico versus John H. Holliday was heard in the San Miguel County District Court. Doc pled guilty and was fined $25.00 plus court costs for keeping a gaming table.

That and the continuing slow go of his dental practice led Holliday to take an offer when one was forthcoming. The source was unexpected, Bat Masterson. Masterson set aside his dislike of Holliday to ask Doc to join his posse of thirty-three men recruited by the Santa Fe Railroad to protect their right-of-way from Canon City through to Leadville, Colorado. Problems arose when the Denver and Rio Grande railway lines also claimed the above right-of-way. Legal battles were waged, but there was fear an out of court battle might also ensue. When the Denver and Rio Grande organized their own posse of good men and true, including local county sheriffs and Company B of the First Colorado Cavalry, the situation turned dangerous.

Doc, leaving Kate behind in Las Vegas, made his solitary way back to Kansas to join up with Masterson's Santa Fe constituency. The posse spent close to three months in Pueblo, Colorado and most of that time barricaded in the Santa Fe's roundhouse.

Many of the weeks spent in Pueblo were pleasant enough, if not very exciting. Doc spent much of his time playing penny ante poker, sleeping, or just shooting the breeze with the rest of the men. Poker stakes were kept low to prevent any high losses among the men who were all there voluntarily and for who knew how long. Friendly games among men kept cooped up together were a safe bet for all concerned.

Holliday had no problem with that and held court on a nightly basis. No one was averse to losing a couple of dollars to the gambler, and most held firm to the belief they were privileged indeed to have played against one of the best in the business, lived to tell about it, and had not lost their shirts in the process.

Not all was fun and games, however, and John Holliday was called upon twice to practice his first vocation, that of medical man.

The first incident amounted to little when James Sorensen found himself in the unenviable position of being deviled by an infected molar. Having caused him pain for some time, which Sorensen ignored, the tooth advanced to the stage of abscess. Reluctant, he made his way to Doc's cot where Holliday rested, cigarette in one hand and book in the other. Sorensen cleared his throat.

"You really a dentist, Doc? Cause if you are, I got a payin' job for ya." By this time, Sorensen's jaw was badly swollen, and he held a hand cupped around the offending side.

Holliday nodded, put his book aside and went in search of a good stout straight-backed chair. With his patient seated in the sunny doorway of the roundhouse, Doc settled down to business. Washing his hands and drying them on a clean white towel, he opened out his traveling case and searched through it for what supplies he needed.

It did not take much of a look inside the patient's mouth to locate the offending tooth. It was indeed infected and had to come out. So, with quite a crowd gathered, and the small James Sorensen, held in the chair by two burly volunteers, Doctor John Holliday plied his trade.

Much to the dentist's credit, the tooth was out in no time, the patient having little chance to let out so much as a yelp. To the patient's credit, he was a model. Although his eyes watered mightily, and he strained against the hands of his captors, James Sorensen did not utter a sound.

Dropping the rotten molar into a dish on the table, Doc turned back to his patient. "Rinse your mouth out now in warm salt water. Rinse, don't wash it too hard. You need to allow a clot to form. Do that five or six times a day for several days until it heals. I'll check it tomorrow." Holliday smiled and his patient seemed reassured.

Sorensen returned the dentist's smile. "Thanks, Doc," he mumbled. "What I owe ya?"

Holliday, washing his hands, put on a thoughtful expression before answering. "Nothing, James. You don't owe me a red cent. I shall charge the Santa Fe for my services. Seems fair, don't you think?"

Sorensen nodded as he rose from the chair, his hand once again cupping the wounded jaw. "Sounds fine to me."

The next incident was indeed an *incident*. Several of the Santa Fe men ventured out into town for a drink at the local watering hole. Finding themselves surrounded by a large contingency of Denver and Rio Grande supporters, they retreated in haste. Hasty or not, they were caught and several received a pummeling at the hands of the crowd. One man had his ear very nearly sliced off and once again John Holliday was called upon for his medical expertise.

Bleeding and scared white, Percy Shedrick was not the model patient Mr. Sorensen had been. Though on the large side, tall and muscular, his trembling and grousing started well before Doc had a chance to look at the injury, let alone touch it.

After some needling by his cronies and assurances by Holliday that the ear was not a lost cause, and that his *surgeon* would be as gentle as possible, Shedrick calmed down, aided by half a bottle of good scotch. However, he would allow no one to hold him. Something about being restrained did not set well with the man. So Doc, leery and cautious, proceeded.

After cleaning the ear well and disinfecting it, the dentist bent low and took the first stitch. Shedrick did not move, he did not so much as twitch, but at every single stitch swore with enthusiasm. Many stitches later, the ear was sewn on and Doc was tired of Shedrick and his cursing. Stretching out his stiff back, Holliday stood aside so the curious men clustered about could get a good look at his handiwork. After much back slapping and congratulations, Doc was able to wash up, put away his instruments and get to figuring how much he should charge the Santa Fe for this little bit of surgery.

The ear remained attached to the head and by the time Doc settled on a fee, the reattached lobe was already pink from circulating blood and John Holliday began to think that perhaps in his next life he'd come back as a surgeon.

The final incident hit closer to home, and involved two men who felt less than kind toward each other: Bat Masterson and Doc Holliday.

The evening so far had been pleasant. Doc won some and lost some at the poker game and decided to sit out the next several hands. Leaning against a post behind the dealer, he watched the play while smoking a cigarette. The conversation at the table got around to women, which was a common enough subject when a group of men had been deprived of the female comforts for too long a stretch.

A bronc buster by the name of Ken Spivey made the point that the best looking sportin' gals in all of Kansas had to be in Dodge. Holliday shifted, uncomfortable under that line of talk since he knew Kate plied her trade there and he hoped no one would bring up their connection.

For a while the conversation kept to a safe level as all the men agreed Sweet Cheeks Tate was by far the best looking soiled dove in all categories discussed including legs, bosom, face and hair, and of course, best posterior. Teeth were not included or discussed and Doc considered that a shame because he thought Squirrel Tooth Alice had the most interesting set of choppers he'd seen since dental school.

At the height of this florid and heated topic, Bat Masterson appeared. Standing right across the poker table from Doc, he listened for a few moments in silence, then let his pointed gaze rest on Holliday as he offered his own opinion on the matter of sporting women, prostitutes, and such.

"Well, seems I'll have to disagree with you men on the

most beautiful whore that ever set her dainty feet onto the streets of Dodge. That distinction would have to go to Doc Holliday's ladylove."

Doc felt his face heat and the cigarette dropped from his fingers. He returned Masterson's teasing expression with one of his own and it bore no resemblance to Bat's. The muscles in his jaw worked as he attempted to control his emotions. "Don't say another word, Bat. You'll regret it, I promise."

Looking cocky in the presence of the large group, Masterson replied, "What'll you do, Doc? Shoot me?" For emphasis he opened his coat, showing he was not armed.

Holliday mirrored the action, revealing a narrow expanse of navy brocade waistcoat and no guns. "I don't need a gun to teach you manners, Masterson."

Bat smiled, but continued to show his contempt for Holliday by being bolder and more precise in his words. "By Holliday's ladylove, I don't mean Kate Elder. No, not her at all, though she is deft at her trade if I do say so myself." Laughing, he took the taunts one step further.

"By ladylove I meant that sweet peach of a southern belle he squired around town some months back. What happened, Doc? Not man enough for a woman like that?"

Before he could go further, one of the men at the table spoke up. He was an older fellow, looked rough around the edges, but perhaps with enough sense to be indignant at the turn the talk had taken.

"Sheriff, there's no call for you to go on like that about a lady. We was talkin' whores and such here. I seen Holliday's woman, and she looked a fine lady to me. So you jest watch yer mouth. I might not be a gentleman, but I knows when to talk and when to shut up."

Although the old fellow's companions nodded in agreement, Bat kept right on with his tirade as he leered across the table at Holliday. "Was she good, Doctor? She looked good, all fresh and sweet. How about it, Doc?"

Holliday did not wait to see if Masterson had finished before tearing into his antagonist with undisguised fury.

In later discussions not a single witness could swear how the hell Doc Holliday made it around the table so fast to land the first blow against Masterson's mouth. Bat's head snapped back and blood flew from the split lips, spattering the two closest onlookers. Before the sheriff could bring his hands up to protect himself, Holliday landed two lightning punches to his gut, doubling him over.

When Masterson caught a breath and attempted to return the blows, he was out of steam, which rendered his punches ineffectual. Those Holliday didn't block. All in all, the fight lasted just moments and was quite one-sided.

Doc stood straight and still, perspiring and breathing hard, not from exertion but from the anger he still felt. Striking Masterson, bloodying the man, did little to temper the rage.

Somehow he found himself back in his own private bit of the roundhouse, seated on his cot. Someone saw to it that his hat hung from the peg on the wall and a cup of coffee, steam rising in a narrow spiral, sat on the tiny table he used for a nightstand. Looking up, he saw no one close by, but when he caught the eye of the fellow nearest him, Burke, a freight handler he knew from Dodge, the man nodded.

All Holliday felt like doing was to sleep. He felt exhausted, barely able to keep his eyes open. He figured if he slept he wouldn't think. He was wrong. Sleep came the instant his head touched the pillow and all through the long night he was tormented and tortured by dreams of things he could never attain or things he could never keep once within his grasp. Love, happiness, and life slipped through his fingers, all as elusive as the pot of gold at the end of a rainbow and just as much a fantasy.

Waking towards dawn, drenched in sweat and more tired than ever, John Holliday reached for the flask on the table. Draining it, feeling the warmth radiate out from his belly to his chest and then his extremities, oozing its way to his brain, he allowed the whiskey to work its magic. It swept away the feelings, the thoughts and the pain. It was a good friend, one who could numb his mind and bring him peace, temporary though it might be. Lying back and closing his eyes, Doc slept a black, imperturbable sleep.

After the fight, Bat Masterson cut John Holliday a wide berth. The clipped words exchanged between the antagonists were orders given and replied to. Whatever Masterson had been thinking when he'd baited Holliday without mercy was known only to Bat. But it got him nowhere and he accomplished nothing.

About the middle of June, the Pueblo County Sheriff, backed by over a hundred and fifty deputized locals, made their way to the barricaded Santa Fe roundhouse. Much to the disgust of many of Masterson's men, the head of the Atchison, Topeka and Santa Fe surrendered without fuss. No battle and little excitement, but then there was a decent paycheck at the finish. Masterson handed out approximately $10,000 to the men after shaking hands all around, thanking them for their perseverance and patience, all save John Holliday. His pay was handed over without fanfare, which was fine with Doc.

Without doubt, the best aspect of Holliday's excursion had been finding himself once again in Dodge City and once again in the company of friends. Neither Wyatt nor Morgan Earp had changed in his absence, though Morgan now had a common-law wife of whom he was more than passing fond.

The lady was a stunner named Louisa and although Morgan found her in a house of ill repute, she was indeed a lady, retaining none of the brassy behavior often a left over from a previous existence. She was sweet of nature, pretty in appearance, small boned, though somewhat on the tall side, dark haired, brown eyed, and shapely. She took to being a wife like a duck to water, and when she looked into Morgan's eyes, the love that shone out like a beacon made Doc's heart ache. Shaking off his own painful memories, he gave the new couple his heartfelt congratulations.

Wyatt seemed much the same as ever and appeared happy, and if Doc wasn't mistaken, relieved to see him. It pained Holliday to think he had caused a friend such concern for his welfare, and he saw to it that his behavior around Wyatt was exemplary, even cheerful. He surprised himself at how easy the acting came to him.

Spending a few days total in Dodge and finding his time well taken still did not keep Doc from his reveries. Every step he took, every place he frequented brought memories rushing back to him, both painful and joy filled.

Thoughts of Clementine flooded him and with those thoughts the knowledge she was lost to him forever and that he had been the cause. In his preoccupation he thought he caught a glimpse of her, but the sidewalk was a crush of people and when he managed to reach the spot in question, she wasn't there. He realized it could not have been her but mere wishful longing on his part.

As when he left her behind in Georgia those years past, now he must again steel himself from her; no more dreams, no memories, no thoughts of the lady whatsoever. John Holliday willed Clementine Mosby out of his existence. To remember was to die, and he chose to live.

CHAPTER 17

Pocketing his share of the railroad's $10,000, Doc hopped the stage and made his way back to Las Vegas, finding it little changed in his absence. However, change did come and soon.

The Santa Fe pulled into town July 4, 1879. On board the maiden trip were several men previously known to Holliday, including Dave Mather and Dave Rudabaugh. Doc thought the company kept a bit odd since Mather had been a lawman in Dodge and Rudabaugh a wanted man in several states. But this was New Mexico Territory and gaming made strange bedfellows indeed. Since Doc had no truck with Rudabaugh, his presence bothered him not in the least. However, he took pen in hand to alert Wyatt concerning Rudabaugh's whereabouts in case Earp was interested.

It appeared Wyatt was as little concerned about Rudabaugh as was Holliday and in fact, Earp's answering letter left small doubt Wyatt was getting fed up with the peacekeeping trade. He made brief mention of Arizona and the fact his older brother, Virgil, already called Prescott home.

Reading between the lines, Doc figured it a matter of time before Wyatt pulled up stakes and made his way west.

Though not happy in Las Vegas, Doc was at least content. Kate pretty much behaved herself, while the influx of railroad passengers caused business to perk up, both in dentistry and gambling, the recent gaming statute and fine little more than a slight inconvenience to the true sporting man.

However, there was a down side to population growth. More men in town meant more trouble and it wasn't long after the arrival of the railroad that a killing occurred. Mike Gordon was shot dead outside a dance hall on Centre Street. An argument with one of the girls coupled with a misplaced bluff at poker led the drunken Gordon on a shooting spree that ended in his own demise. Found mortally wounded, Gordon's death was ruled a justifiable killing by a person or persons unknown. Fingers pointed in Doc's direction, he being the most well known personage in town and the holder of a growing reputation, deserved or not.

The fact Holliday was two blocks away and in full view during the entire episode did not slow down the rumors. With no help from Doc this time, his reputation as a cold blooded killer soon became a bloated source of discomfiture to him. However, little by little, it came to matter less and less. The bolder and broader the lies, the fewer the men thinking it prudent to call his honest games otherwise, or tempt the fates by going up against him with a gun. Of course, there were still foolish men about, foolishness being an undeniable aspect of human nature.

Quite soon after the Gordon incident, Doc decided it was time to open his own saloon. Leasing a plot of land on the south side of Centre Street, Holliday contracted a carpenter to build an edifice, not imposing by any means, seventeen feet wide and thirty or so long, but more than sufficient for

Holliday's purpose. He also purchased a strip of property running alongside which offered him access to the back of the saloon and the gaming room entrance.

Living was going well. Life, now that was something else altogether. Days came and nights followed and both were well filled and busy. The new enterprise of the Holliday Saloon flourished with cash rolling in hand over fist. Still and all, Doc felt an empty, gnawing loneliness. He figured nothing and no one could ever assuage those feelings. He turned out to be wrong. On the morning of October 18, 1879, Wyatt Earp rode into town.

Sitting at the table nearest the door of his saloon, idly shuffling and reshuffling a deck of cards, practicing a bit of manual dexterity by bridging and fanning the supple deck, John Holliday was unaware someone of interest entered his establishment. A momentary lapse.

"This dive serve up any decent coffee?"

Rising from his seat so fast his chair crashed backwards onto the hardwood floor, Doc hurried to the bar, clasping the hand Wyatt held out and shaking it hard. He realized he must look like a grinning idiot but didn't care.

"My God, Wyatt. What brings you here? And yes, we have the best damned coffee in New Mexico. I've seen to that."

Over cups of the steaming brew and plates heaped with breakfast, the two friends talked. Earp spoke most of the time while Holliday listened, a pleasant turnaround for both.

"I got tired of Dodge. Guess it just toned down too much for me, got too civilized. I never was one to stay put very long, but Doc," Earp leaned across the small table, oblivious to the clutter of breakfast remains, and a great excitement suffused his face. "Come along, Doc. Come to Arizona. Virgil is already in Prescott, and Morg's supposed to meet up with us there. It'll be like old times, adventure, excitement. Everything we touch'll turn to gold. Okay, maybe not gold, but silver. Prescott is just a layover till we all get together. Then it's on to Tombstone. That's where the big bucks are."

Earp's excitement was contagious, like a bad cold, and it gave Holliday the same itchy feeling which signaled the possibility of trouble ahead. However, it was also contagious in a good way. For the first time since Dodge and Clementine, John felt life surge through his veins. He felt the future and maybe it did include him. Hope. He felt hope.

"I assume you are not thinking we become manual laborers, digging silver from the soil with pick and shovel?" Doc lit a slim cheroot and smiled at the picture that conjured.

"No, of course not. We'll be investors, in on the ground floor. We provide services, the miners provide the money. Doc, you won't even have to get your hands dirty." Wyatt chose a cigar from the holder on the table and lit up, waiting for Holliday to counter him.

"Dirty my hands? I should hope not, unless it's the dirt that comes from filthy lucre. But Wyatt, I have a business here. I'll need time to think things over. And of course, I must break the news to Kate about the possibility of a move. As things stand, she is quite comfortable here."

Wyatt pushed back and rose from the table. "You just take your time, Doc. We're pulling out of here tomorrow afternoon." Earp turned his back on Holliday and proceeded to the doors and out onto the boardwalk. If he expected a reaction from Holliday, he was not disappointed. A string of expletives fouled the air for a solid city block. Even as he ranted and cursed Wyatt for the bombshell he dropped, Doc knew what the outcome of their conversation would be. He knew it every bit as well as did Wyatt Earp.

When Holliday broke the news that Wyatt wanted him and Kate to accompany Earp and his wife to Arizona, Kate blew up.

"How can you leave all we've worked for here, Doc? How? You got your dental practice. You got your own place, your own saloon. You're the boss. Nobody tells you what to do or how to do it. Why do we have to give up all that to traipse after that damned lawman and his whore? Why?"

Even as Kate ranted, she tossed clothing into one of several suitcases open on the floor. She meant to follow her man no matter her loud, vocal reaction to his news.

Doc sat in the chair by the window, watched Kate, and endured her fury. At least it wasn't directed at him in a physical sense. He abhorred dodging hairbrushes, pots of makeup, and shoes. However, the fury of her words *was* directed at him and they stung deep.

"You're like a little lap dog. Gotta trail after the master soon as he snaps his fingers at 'cha."

That was the final straw. Doc leaped from his chair and confronted Kate, face to face. "You couldn't understand, not a woman like you."

He didn't know how to explain the way he felt without it sounding strange, unmanly, explain that in his life, all the life left to him since the diagnosis of his illness, there existed a very few people who offered him more than just going on with living, who offered him a future and hope. Of those, two were women, Clementine and Cleva Moss with both being forever lost to him. The others were the Earp brothers, Wyatt and Morgan, and he'd be damned if he'd lose them.

Giving up any thought of explaining motives or feelings to Kate, he offered her a choice. "Come along or don't. It doesn't matter to me."

From that moment on, Kate continued packing in silence. Her silence was a blessing.

Holliday turned the running of his saloon over to Zeke Burton, who, in his capacity as head bartender and sometime manager, could handle the business until Doc either returned to Las Vegas for good or to close out his affairs. Everything depended on what lay in wait in Arizona.

CHAPTER 18

For the most part, time passed pleasant enough along the trail. Kate came around and began to talk again, and for that Doc found himself grateful. Though at times the woman exasperated him beyond ken with her gossip and endless prattle, at least now that she was no longer angry, he did not feel as if he were sitting next to a keg of giant powder ready to explode at the merest provocation.

Six days into the trip, Mattie was attending to what she referred to as a "sick headache." Her traveling companions knew that to be a euphemism for giving in to her laudanum addiction and she spent the better part of the day in her wagon in a fuzzy, oblivious haze. The travelers decided to take a day or so off, not just because of Mattie, though that was a consideration, but because they could all use a break.

Doc spent the better part of the night sleepless due to an annoying bout of coughing. Rising from a warm bed in the wagon, he headed out beyond the encampment where his cough would bother no one but himself. He retrieved the bottle of whiskey from his saddlebags, downing a good half pint before the cough subsided. However, due now to his inebriated condition, Holliday found his legs too unsteady to support him, which made a return to bed impossible. Dragging his saddle over to the fire and grabbing up a couple of saddle blankets, he curled up on the cold, rocky ground.

Doc woke to the sounds of the fire being stoked and the fragrance of coffee on the boil. Sitting up, he scrubbed both hands through a shock of unruly, blond locks.

Wyatt tossed a handful of kindling onto the hot coals before turning his attention to Holliday. Rocking back on his haunches, he offered critical appraisal. "What the hell did you do to your hair? Looks like a field a dried corn stalks." Earp broke into an uncustomary, robust laugh.

Nonplussed, Doc continued to massage his scalp making no attempts to finger comb the hair into place. "*I* did not do anything. If you must know the entire sordid story, I'll tell you, but Wyatt, you must promise to stop laughing."

"Actually, Doc, now that I look closer," Wyatt got to his feet and walked several steps nearer, peering down at his friend from above, "now I see it closer, looks to me more like a big field of dandelions gone to seed."

Doc coughed, covering his mouth with a blood stained kerchief. The sound of the cough and the sight of the soiled handkerchief sobered Wyatt; further laughter died unrealized.

"Do you want to hear this story or not, marshal?" Doc asked, some slight annoyance creeping into his voice.

"Sure I do. This ought to be good." Wyatt crouched near the fire and poured out two cups of coffee. He handed one to Holliday who accepted it, taking a tentative sip before going on.

"We lost the one decent barber we had in Las Vegas. The fellow who took his place was more a sheep shearer than a barber. I'd seen his work and wanted none of it. I decided to just let my hair grow out until the right man came along for the job.

"Well, it got so I began to resemble a friend of yours, Wyatt, Bill Hickok, all this long hair curling every which-a-way. Kate got fed up. Said either the hair went or she did."

Doc paused to sip more coffee. "Since she was having a good week, and I would've missed her more than the hair...."

Wyatt finished the sentence for him, "you got shorn."

"Correct, my friend. And so you see the final results. Though this has grown out some. My hair was so short I resembled the working end of a bristle brush. Wyatt, the embarrassment I found myself subjected to was appalling. I couldn't stand to look at myself in the mirror let alone go out onto the streets."

Doc's imitation of a man in abject mortification, mouth beneath a flaxen moustache in a pout, eyes turned down, shoulders slumped, caused Wyatt's sobriety to fall by the wayside. He laughed heartily, causing Doc to smile.

"I'm so very glad I can offer you all the benefits of a good guffaw, marshal. In truth I'm happy I affect you in that manner. Someone should."

Doc threw off the blankets and got to his feet. Clothed only in a shirt and boots, though the shirt's long tails draped nearly to his knees, Holliday should have known the sight would be somewhat humorous to Earp in his present mood. Noticing Wyatt's difficulty in keeping a straight face, Holliday offered yet another explanation.

"Didn't want to wake Kate by dressing last night. My cough came upon me without warning."

Wyatt nodded. "I understand, but maybe you should get dressed now. The ladies might wake up and…"

Doc stopped Wyatt with a wave of the hand. "Pardon me, but ladies or no, neither Kate nor Mattie are schoolgirls or nuns, Wyatt, and they've seen their share of men's legs. Of course perhaps Mattie has never seen a pair to match these and maybe you're thinkin' you might fall short on the comparison." Doc struck a haughty pose, hands on hips, for effect.

Earp wiped watering eyes back across his sleeve. "Get dressed. Unless you changed your mind about goin' out for birds this morning?"

Doc appeared outside his wagon, fully clothed, as Earp finished saddling his horse. Hanging from the pommel by a leather thong was a long-barreled shotgun.

"What you plannin' on doing with that scattergun?" Doc asked as he walked over, tying a silk scarf about his throat. "Those poor birds don't stand a chance in hell with you blazin' away at them with that thing."

"Doc, they're birds. We're gonna eat 'em, not draw against 'em." Wyatt slipped a few more twenty gauge shells into the pocket of the jacket he'd tied on behind the saddle and swung up onto his horse.

Holliday remained skeptical. "Speaking as a medical man and a dentist, I would rather not have one of us bite into a nice piece of game bird only to come away with a broken tooth. Nor would I care to swallow small undigestible pieces of lead."

"What would you prefer I kill 'em with, doctor, a rock?" Wyatt grinned.

"A rifle," Doc replied, "but if that takes too much skill for you, then by all means use the scattergun. I myself prefer a head shot, clean, quick and quite a feat of skill. But then you do as you wish, Wyatt. You will anyhow." Holliday walked over to his horse, patted the mare on the nose and went about taking his time with the saddling.

Impatient to get started, Wyatt turned his mount and loped off.

Kate poked her head out from the wagon. "Comin' back for breakfast, honey?" she asked as she jumped to the ground and strolled Doc's way. "Biscuits, eggs and ham sound good?"

Holliday nodded. "Sounds wonderful, but give us at least an hour. Wyatt is in hunting mode, and it will take at least that long for him to flush the need from his system."

Kate raised her face for a kiss and he bussed her a quick one on the lips. Swinging up onto the back of his bay, Doc heard the first report of Wyatt's rifle. He urged his mount into a run. If Earp thought to keep all the fun to himself, he was mistaken. Doc was pleased Wyatt decided to make the hunt a true challenge by using a rifle, and Holliday was always up for a good challenge.

Wyatt was perhaps a quarter mile from camp. As Doc rode up expecting a smile and a plump bird, he instead found Earp standing near a grouping of boulders, a stricken look upon his face as he held his left arm out toward Holliday. The rifle lay forgotten on the ground.

Doc dismounted. "What happened?"

Without waiting for a reply since one was so slow in coming, Holliday seized Wyatt's arm to examine the area just above the wrist. The blood drained from his face. He didn't need Wyatt's whispered "rattlesnake" to confirm what he already knew.

"Sit down, Wyatt." Doc ordered. "Sit down now."

Earp complied, almost collapsing onto the ground.

Doc tore the silk scarf from his throat and tied it around Earp's arm just above his elbow, tight, but not as tight as a tourniquet.

"I shot a bird," Wyatt slurred. "It dropped into the rocks.

I reached in. Never heard the snake rattle. Never got a warning." A violent shiver took him.

Working fast, Doc pulled his knife from the sheath and a flask from inside his jacket pocket. Slitting Earp's shirtsleeve, he tore the fabric up to where the scarf was tied and then poured whiskey onto the bitten area and onto the knife blade. There was a single fang mark and a scratch indicating the strike of the other fang, but that one bite was sufficient.

Holliday took a swig of whiskey, swishing it around inside his mouth before swallowing. If he was to suck the venom from the wound, he sure as hell did not want to introduce any more bacteria into it. As a dentist, he was well aware of the filth contained within the human mouth.

"Hold still now." Doc incised an X across the bite, bent down and sucked venom from the wound, spitting blood and poison out onto the ground.

Holliday sucked and spat for what seemed forever, until Wyatt could no longer stand the pain and jerked his arm from Doc's grasp. Spitting once more, Doc wiped his mouth across his sleeve leaving a wide, red smear on the white cuff. The taste of blood was something he was used to, but that didn't make it any more acceptable or less nauseating to him.

Wyatt looked bad. He was breathing far too fast and was deathly pale. His fingers were as swollen as small sausages, and his hand and forearm half way up to the elbow were discolored black and blue.

Doc laid him back against the ground, resting the wounded arm down, allowing it to bleed from the site. If there was any more venom in the wound, let it bleed out.

Taking the pistol from the holster at his waist, he fired twice into the air hoping Kate, back at camp, would hear and know something was amiss.

Doc's plan worked, and within moments Kate arrived,

sliding down off the horse's back. Kneeling beside Holliday, she stared open-mouthed at Earp.

"What the hell kinda country is this anyhow, huh, Doc?" She rested her hand on Holliday's arm, looking into his face, then back down at Wyatt.

"An unforgiving one," he answered. "Get back to camp and bring blankets and more water. Whatever you even *think* I'll need. If Mattie's awake, tell her Wyatt needs her."

"Okay, Doc." In a flash Kate was on the horse and gone.

With extra blankets and the saddle from Wyatt's horse, Doc made the injured man as comfortable as possible, little enough under the circumstances.

Wyatt's discomfort was great, and his ability to breathe jeopardized by the snake's venom as he fought to draw air into compromised lungs. The wound stopped bleeding, and Doc bandaged it using several of his own cotton handkerchiefs.

Thirst was another torture. Wyatt used up one canteen, working on a second, but water was plentiful in these parts, the one blessing so far.

Doc was beside himself. Reading about snakebite and treating it were two different things. Thanks to an insatiable appetite for books, including one with an improbable name, *Trials and Tribulations of the Westward Trek,* which included the graphic and rather disgusting chapter, "Death along the Trail," he did have some small knowledge of what treatment entailed. However, book learning versus actual experience offered little comfort when the life of a friend hung in the balance.

Hours passed with Wyatt's arm continuing to swell out from his body, his pulse so weak Doc fought to locate the faint trill beneath his fingertips. The entire arm blackened and Holliday feared the limb to be lost.

Late in the afternoon, Mattie put in an appearance at
the makeshift camp. Doc was angry with her for her
tardiness and self absorption, and made no bones to hide
his feelings.

"You up to watchin' Wyatt for a couple hours so I can
get some sleep? I mean *watch him*. If you can't do that, tell
me and I'll send you back and bring Kate over."

Mattie nodded. "I'll watch him close. I swear," she
whispered. "You best get some rest, Doc. You look
mighty poor."

Nothing compared to how I feel, Holliday thought. "Wake
me if his fever goes any higher or he gets worse. Wake me in
a couple hours, anyway."

Getting to his feet, he stretched, working kinks out of his
long thin body, stiff from sitting on the hard ground for hours
on end. He walked over to where Kate had laid out blankets.
The air was cool, but a fire burned and the blankets were
warm. He drew them up and rolled himself into a knot. The
pain in his chest nagged a bit, but he figured it was fatigue.
Reaching into his coat, he took out the flask and a few sips
later found the pain hazy and sleep close by.

He woke to the smells of dinner cooking, stew and
biscuits and coffee on the boil. Opening one eye, he noticed
Mattie still seated at Wyatt's side. With a damp rag she cooled
his face, and the sound of her singing floated softly on the
still air. Holliday had never heard the woman sing and her
voice was sweet and high pitched, more girl's than woman's.
She carried a tune, and carried it well. Angling himself up
onto one elbow, he asked her how Wyatt was doing.

She stopped singing and turned toward him, blushing,
embarrassed to be caught in her lullaby. "The fever's about
the same I guess, but he's been talkin' a lot and not makin'
sense. Seems he hurts all over and can't get comfortable,

neither." Her pretty face crumbled, and tears came into her eyes. "He isn't gonna die is he, Doc?"

Holliday rolled out of his blankets and got to his feet. Again he stretched and realized the ache in his chest was gone, but the one in his empty stomach deviled him. Ignoring it, he went over to check Wyatt and without bothering to meet Mattie's anxious gaze, he answered her question. "He won't die." Doc hoped his statement did not prove premature.

After Doc had removed his scarf from Wyatt's upper arm, he slit the shirtsleeve all the way to the shoulder to allow the limb to swell without constriction. It proved a good precaution. The arm was swollen, hideous. One of the women, in all probability Kate, padded it from beneath with a folded blanket.

Laying a hand against Wyatt's forehead, Doc noticed the fever had not elevated much, but allowed the feel of one's hand was not an exact science. Earp was delirious and Holliday felt the beginnings of despair.

Sitting next to his friend, he drew up his knees and rested his head in his hands. Depression washed over him in brooding waves, and he closed his eyes and wished he remembered how to pray, but hypocrisy had its limits. Instead, he wondered what he could have done differently, faster, better. He wished he were a physician instead of a dentist. However, wishing, like praying, accomplished nothing. Wyatt's voice jolted him from his self-deprecating reverie.

"You sick, Doc? You look sick," Wyatt murmured and Holliday's darkness lightened a fraction.

Doc managed a small smile at the recognition. "I'm not sick, just hungry and worried. Doesn't take much to make me look ill, however. More to the point, how do you feel?"

Wyatt's eyes closed and it took more than a moment for

him to settle on a precise adjective. Not surprisingly, it was an expletive.

"I'd say that is a most apt description, my friend," Doc replied. "Would you like some water?"

Wyatt nodded, and Holliday gave him a long drink. "Anything more? A smoke? Some coffee? I see Kate's brewed a pot, and hers is always to your liking, black as coal, thick as tar, and enough to float a boat."

Earp shook his head no.

"Some whiskey, perhaps? Spirits have been known to ease discomfort." Doc already held the flask in his hand, but Wyatt signaled his answer by turning his head away.

"I'm right here if you need me." Doc drew the covers up around Wyatt and got to his feet.

At the fire, Kate handed him a plate of food. He dug in without hesitation and found after a decent meal his outlook was a bit more upbeat. Wyatt's condition appeared to have stopped deteriorating, and that was good. He was taking in fluids, and that was good. He was somewhat clear minded, and that was a plus. Tomorrow would tell.

After eating and downing half a pot of coffee, Doc decided Kate should go back to the original camp with Mattie. The animals needed tending and all the travelers' belongings remained there, unguarded.

"You need anything, Kate, fire off the rifle and I'll be there in a moment. And watch out for Mattie," he warned. "Her ability to function on a good day is taxed, and today has not been a good day."

Alone with Wyatt, the sun setting in a glorious blaze of magenta darkening to purple and gray, Doc built up the fire and settled in for a long night. Grabbing up a saddle, he placed it close to Wyatt's resting place and there made up his own bed.

With the setting of the sun, the night soon cooled. Doc was glad for his heavy, shearling coat. He covered his patient with another blanket. Wyatt groaned and Holliday wished he would take a bit of whiskey. What with Earp not being a drinking man, it would take only a little to afford him some relief.

Doc tried again, this time pouring the liquor into a coffee cup, not to disguise it *per se*, just thinking maybe Wyatt might be more apt to drink some if it wasn't from the flask. Placing it to Earp's lips and using his most persuasive voice, he urged the suffering man to drink, "just take a little, Wyatt. It'll help the pain. I swear it. I know. Please."

Earp drank. He took about a shot glass full and refused more, but in his condition and with his intolerance to drink, the effects were almost immediate. The tormented body relaxed, and the mask of pain on the puffy face softened, becoming more human and more recognizable.

Sitting close, Doc swallowed down what was left in the coffee cup. He was tired, but not to the point of needing sleep.

Usually ensconced in a smoke choked room during the nighttime hours, Holliday was fascinated to be outdoors for a change. He enjoyed watching the fire crackle and spit as it chewed into the odd green chunk of wood, colors changing, flames leaping high or spiraling down.

All night he drank the coffee Kate left for him until he was down to the bitter dregs and he tossed the last of it aside. He rolled cigarette after cigarette and the breeze caught the smoke and wafted it off and away. Not far to the east, a coyote called. It was answered off to the west and soon the calls came closer together and were interspersed with the barks, yips, and growls of canine communication.

Doc relaxed into his saddle and looked up at the cloudless sky, covered horizon to horizon with a multitude of stars sparkling like so many diamonds.

A flock of birds appeared, obscuring the view. At first Doc believed them to be birds, but what birds flew at night other than perhaps owls or nighthawks and those not all together in so great a number? Bats, they had to be bats, and Holliday was amazed. He'd seen them massed in Texas once, but even in Texas where everything is the biggest, the loudest, the best, there had not been so many. This group contained a thousand, tens of thousands. As a whole, they swooped and turned and vanished as they'd come, with no fuss, like a great living shadow. Again the stars appeared, and John Holliday gave thought to all he'd missed in the crowded, noisy saloons, yet knowing that is exactly where nights would find him once the opportunity again presented.

About an hour before dawn, Wyatt turned restless. His fever spiked and he couldn't stand even the weight of the blankets against his skin.

"I can't take it. I just can't anymore." Wyatt tried to sit up, but when Doc pressed him back to the pallet, his hands against Wyatt's shoulders, Earp yelled in anguish at the touch against the raw nerves of his skin.

"Damn it. Damn it all." Though it took effort, Doc willed himself calm and by the time Kate arrived, breathless, on horseback, he knew what his action must be.

"I heard a scream. Thought you'd need me, Doc."

Holliday nodded and his sense of relief must have shown in his expression for Kate brightened a little.

"Bring laudanum. Hurry, Kate."

Without comment, the woman was back up on her horse and the sound of pounding hooves came fainter until they were gone altogether.

Doc watched Wyatt deal with the devil, tossing in agony Holliday could but imagine. Checking his watch by the fire's glow, he was amazed that less than fifteen minutes had passed since Kate's departure. It seemed like hours.

Holliday snapped the case closed. "Where are you, Kate? Where?" As if in answer, a shout penetrated the darkness, and Kate rode up to the campfire, disheveled, but Doc thought never more attractive.

Grabbing the bottle from her hand without so much as a thanks, Holliday poured laudanum into a spoon, put it to Wyatt's lips, and tipped it up. Another spoonful followed the first and then water to wash away the vile taste.

Doc rocked back, watching and waiting for any sign the opium had helped. Moments ticked by. Wyatt stopped struggling at last and for a lucid moment gazed at Holliday. A slow, deep breath followed. Wyatt closed his eyes and slept. Drug induced or otherwise, sleep was sleep, and for now the pain seemed at least tolerable.

Doc gave in to his own exhaustion, exhaustion so overwhelming he sat, trance-like, before the fire, a boneless bundle of clothing, a body without form or substance.

Kate's hands were on him, her voice soft and coaxing as she got him up and to his pallet. "Rest now, Doc."

He laid back and closed his eyes. She felt his forehead for fever, but seemed satisfied that it was merely the regular elevation of his temperature and little more. Pulling the blankets up, she patted them into place.

Doc caught her hand. "Thank you, Kate," he whispered. "Thanks."

Instead of rising, she squeezed her body onto the narrow bed, put her arm around his waist, her head on his shoulder and snuggled close. He woke some time later to Kate no longer at his side, but hovering over him.

"He's awake now, Doc."

Doc sat up, groggy, rubbing sleep from his eyes and wishing he had a cup of strong coffee, but that could wait.

Wyatt seemed to be bearing up under the pain although the laudanum must have worn off. Earp's expression appeared more relaxed and when Holliday laid a cool palm against his forehead, Wyatt allowed the touch without comment.

"Do you feel better?" Doc asked as he reached for Earp's right hand to feel the pulse in the wrist, the beat even and strong.

"Don't hurt so much," Earp replied in a strained voice, "but my arm. I can't feel it. I'm not gonna lose it, am I?"

Wyatt needed reassurance that Doc wanted to provide. He stroked Wyatt's open palm, hoping for a reaction. "Can you feel this?"

"No."

Holliday turned to Kate and beckoned her near. "Have you anything with a pin? Anything at all?"

The woman undid the broach that closed the neck of her shirtwaist and handed the small cameo to Doc.

Turning back to Wyatt, not allowing him to see what he proposed, Doc pricked Earp's palm with the pin.

"I felt that." Wyatt's face, swollen and lined with fatigue, creased into a relieved smile.

But there was no one more relieved than John Holliday. "You won't lose your arm, Wyatt," he promised. "Sleep now. Just sleep."

The rest of the day Earp slept, waking only to drink and to take a little nourishment in the form of broth. Slowly the arm took on its normal proportions and contours, though the discoloration would last a fortnight or longer. Full feeling returned gradually .

Almost a week passed before Holliday figured Wyatt well enough to stand the strain of moving on. He drove the Earp wagon and Kate drove theirs, with Mattie spelling Kate if she grew too fatigued. Doc wanted to make some progress and he didn't mind if progress was slow with few miles covered. He felt it was time to get going. Wyatt agreed.

The first day Earp rested in the back of the wagon, but that was short lived. When the small caravan stopped for the noonday meal on the second day, Wyatt made his discomfort known. "I'm seasick. I know that makes no sense at all, but Doc, I feel bad."

Holliday knew his passenger spoke the truth. Earp looked green about the gills and all attempts at walking without a seaman's rolling gait appeared beyond his means.

"Seems they don't call these wagons *ships of the plains* for nothing, Wyatt."

From then on, Wyatt sat up front on the driver's seat next to Doc, a boon to all concerned. Although Holliday had not complained, his neck and shoulders were stiff from the constant turning to speak to his ailing companion.

So the friends talked and smoked as Doc drove the team and time passed most agreeably. Wyatt continued to heal, and by the time the group reached the outskirts of Prescott, Earp was all but well. When he attempted to thank Holliday, Doc wanted none of it.

"Your recovery, my friend, is all the thanks I require."

CHAPTER 19

November 1879 found the Earp/Holliday party at their destination, Prescott, the booming capital of the Territory of Arizona and a bustling metropolis of miners, merchants, and free enterprise. Doc Holliday felt right at home.

Doc was anxious to meet the older brother of his friends and expected to be, if not accepted by Virgil, at least treated with courtesy. However, that remained to be seen.

Even before preliminary introductions took place, Doc felt himself the object of Virgil Earp's cool and almost haughty appraisal. As much as he tried to keep a nonchalant demeanor, rolling and lighting a quirly as he pretended to observe with interest those passing along Prescott's main thoroughfare, Doc's complexion flushed warm under the elder Earp's sidewise glances. As Wyatt walked over to make the introductions, Holliday tossed the unsmoked cigarette into the street and turned, a half smile upon his lips, to extend his hand.

Virgil's handshake was firm, but there was nothing behind it. His blue eyes, identical to those of Wyatt and Morgan, offered a cold reproach. Doc's sincerely offered greeting, "I am most pleased to make your acquaintance, Mr. Earp," hung in the air like an unanswered question. Making matters more uncomfortable, Wyatt excused himself and disappeared down the boardwalk and into the hotel lobby. Doc figured to speak to his friend about his act of desertion when next he got the chance.

Not one to allow an opportunity to pass, Virgil cut to the chase. "Don't think you can hide what you are from me, Holliday. I've heard about you, quick tempered, fast on the draw and eager to prove it, and a drunkard to boot.

"Might be you got Morg fooled, but he's just a kid, and maybe even Wyatt don't know how things stand, though that's not somethin' I expected from him."

Virgil leaned in close to Doc who resisted the urge to step back out of the line of fire, instead holding to his ground. "Don't try to pull nothin' on me," Virgil warned. "I'm on to you."

Doc had taken enough from Virgil Earp. "If I was all you think I am, Mr. Earp, you'd be lyin' dead in the street. No one has spoken to me the way you have without retribution swift and certain. That does not mean I've murdered in cold blood, only that I demand respect." Deep within his chest, Holliday felt a cough rumble. Taking out a handkerchief, he held it in his hand, just in case.

"A reputation is difficult to live with. You should know that. You should also know that most reputations are based on someone else's lies.

"I can't prove myself to you in a day. I don't want to prove myself to you in any case. You are the brother of my friends, and I accept you for that. I respect you for the same reason, but do not push me, Mr. Earp, because some things you've heard about me are true."

Tipping his hat to a dumbfounded Virgil, Doc turned and followed Wyatt's route down the street to the hotel. Showing no emotion was difficult. Inside he was torn, both angry and hurt. Having to prove his worth to an Earp never crossed his mind. Again the rumbling in his chest, and this time the cough erupted. Covering his mouth with his kerchief, he coughed for a long moment before continuing on.

Thinking to spend some time in no company other than his own, Doc saddled his horse and rode south toward Granite Creek. Although he mentioned a bit of target practice to Kate when she inquired as to the reason behind his solo venture, the explanation was a cover. Why he felt reason to camouflage his single, albeit slight selfish, desire to be alone, he did not know, except that perhaps it was Kate's penchant for feeling neglected whenever he did not desire her company, especially for anything so petty as a man's need for some time to himself. It became easier to lie than to explain one's motives.

The ride itself was nothing short of blissful and cool mountain air, blue sky as far as a man could see, and birdsong to lighten even the darkest of souls, and the water. Dismounting, Doc tethered his horse to a low branch, tossed his hat to the ground and sat crossed-legged at the edge of the crystal stream. Closing his eyes, he listened as the water lapped at the bank. Holliday breathed in the freshness of late fall, cleansing his mind of past hurts and present problems. He was reminded of Georgia and home, and for the first time in too long, John Holliday felt at peace.

Peace did not last long, shattered by an uncontrolled fit of coughing that left Holliday sweating, shaking, exhausted and unable to gain anything more than faint breath. Climbing back into the saddle seemed an obstacle far from reach, and staying in that saddle for the lengthy ride back to Prescott an unreachable goal.

Night fell and caught Doc unprepared. Ill equipped to spend the night out, he suffered the tortures of the damned, shivering in the cold while hacking bloody sputum into his last remaining clean kerchief. Holliday made his body as small as possible against the weather and prayed for dawn.

The sun had risen some hours earlier, but the bright light of a new day did little to affect Doc, other than offer some warmth that hardly dented the bone-numbing cold he carried into day from a miserable night. Sitting up against a large rock, he accepted the warmth of the sun-heated stone, dozing, head down against his breast.

Shouting and the commotion of horses racing unchecked into the clearing woke Holliday with an unpleasant start. He drew his .45, thumbing back the hammer. Sighting the weapon was another matter altogether, as his sleep-bleared eyes failed to focus until Wyatt crouched almost in front of him.

Doc eased the Colt's hammer down and holstered the weapon. He slumped back, pressing the bloodied hanky to his lips to stifle yet another cough.

The concern on Wyatt's face wrenched Holliday's heart, and the hand his friend rested against his shoulder said more than words. It was then Doc realized Wyatt, too, held a pistol. Looking somewhat self conscious, Earp dropped the weapon into his coat pocket.

"I...we," Wyatt indicated the approaching Virgil Earp with a tilt of his head, "thought you'd been shot, Doc." Earp's gaze traveled down Holliday's shirt, the part visible beneath his opened coat spotted with blood, both dried and fresh, but with no bullet holes.

It was Doc's turn to feel self conscious. "I wanted some time alone. Never figured the cough might come on me with such vengeance. I didn't mean to cause consternation in anyone." Extending a hand to Wyatt, he accepted help getting to his feet. Though his legs felt rubbery and his head swam, he felt a great relief at being *rescued*. He smiled. Wyatt returned the grin.

Virgil Earp holstered his .44 and stalked over to the pair. There was fire in his gaze and anger in his voice. "This some sorta game, Holliday?" he growled.

"I assure you, sir," Doc replied, his voice raspy, "this is no game."

The older Earp appraised Holliday, not hiding the fact he was doing so. Doc ran a shaky hand back through unkempt hair. Though glad he had a friend who cared enough to make certain he was safe, he despised the fact Virgil Earp believed he was owed some sort of explanation. However, whatever Earp saw must have indeed assured him that no game was intended as no more disparaging remarks were forthcoming.

Doc walked over to where the water ran swift and clear and hunkered down at the edge scooping up handfuls and drinking. Rinsing the stained kerchief in the water, he used its wet coolness to scrub away some of the lingering lethargy he could not shake.

Straightening up, he felt dizzy and reached out to grab for the tree he thought to be within his grasp. It was not, and he fell half in and half out of the water, retaining consciousness just long enough to feel embarrassed at his plight.

He woke with his head propped up on a saddle and swathed in horse blankets. His dripping coat hung draped over an infant fire Virgil stoked to life. Not realizing Doc was awake, the elder Earp questioned Wyatt concerning Doc's condition.

"What's the matter with him?" Virgil inquired, angling his head back to where Doc lay.

"Consumption, he has consumption," Wyatt replied.

"Consumption. Well..."

Wyatt changed a subject he felt little comfort discussing, and for which Doc was grateful. "Wish we had some coffee. The wait might be long,"

Wyatt crouched at Doc's side, but Holliday feigned sleep, unwilling to acknowledge he knew his friend had broken a trust, even if it was to a brother.

"I'll ride to town and get some supplies. Won't take long." Virgil did not wait for Wyatt's reply. The sound of a horse kicked into a fast trot faded quickly, and Doc no longer needed to pretend sleep as it overtook him without warning. Warm and comfortable, he slept until the smell of boiling coffee tickled his senses awake. Again it appeared he was the subject of the conversation as the brothers sat near the fire.

"Seen him sick like this before, have ya? Appears you knew what to do for 'im right off," Virgil said, sipping the hot fragrant brew.

Wyatt nodded, but it was some time before he answered. "Yes, I've seen him like this. Worse."

"Worse? Seems a man couldn't be much worse without dyin'," his brother observed.

"He *is* dying," Wyatt confirmed, emptying the coffee onto the ground.

Doc's sense of betrayal doubled.

"He known long?" Virg asked.

Another long pause followed before Wyatt answered. "Yes."

"Guess that might explain a few things," Virgil offered and if Doc wasn't mistaken, and he prayed he was, there was just a hint of pity in Virgil's tone.

Wyatt countered his brother and this time there was no pause. "It explains nothing, Virg. He won't set things straight with you. He'd never do that. Guess he just figures you should know how it is with him, like Morg and me know. I was around for the start of it all, the lies, the truths. You ever feel the need for what's true, come to me, just ask.

"Virg, you know I'd be the last one to tell you who to like or who to trust. All I'm sayin' is I trust this man with my life. He's my friend. What you do or what you decide is your business."

Some of Doc's hurt at what he perceived as betrayal on Wyatt's part, eased. What did he expect Wyatt to do, lie to his own brother? No, of course not. He wished the questions had not been asked in the first place, but since they were...

Wyatt sat at Doc's side, cross-legged, blowing on a cup of the fresh, hot coffee to cool it to drinking temperature. Noticing Holliday was awake, Wyatt asked if he'd like some. Doc nodded, attempting to take the cup from Wyatt, but his hands shook too hard. Earp held the cup for him while he drank.

Doc slept for some time, but even a sound sleep did not offer respite from the cough, though it wasn't bad enough to wake him for the first hour or so. When it erupted into a full blown episode, the cough tore through Doc's battered lungs, the force of which spattered the already soiled kerchief he pressed to his mouth. He cast about frantically. Wyatt was nowhere to be seen, but Virgil sat stoking the fire and staring at Doc with an expression akin to concern. "My coat, the flask," Doc managed to say between spasms.

Virgil searched through the drying jacket. Locating the flask in one of the pockets, he had the top off before reaching Holliday's side. He held the container out, and Doc took it in trembling hands, getting it to his lips with difficulty. Though

Virgil saw this, he made no move to assist. "Sorry, Holliday," he mumbled, hands clasped behind his back.

Exhausted, Doc fell back against the saddle and closed his eyes. For some time he felt the elder Earp's presence as Virgil hovered near, but he chose to ignore it, instead expending all his waning energy on not coughing.

A good hour passed before Doc woke and he felt a good deal better for the nap. The Earp brothers were down at the creek, heads together, talking low, so Holliday decided to try out his legs. No longer dizzy, he did feel weak, but that was doubtless hunger.

Wyatt turned at his approach. "I'd rather you didn't get quite so close to the water this time, Doc. Took hours to dry out your coat from your previous encounter."

Holliday frowned and with malice aforethought, strode over to stand next to the Earps at the water's edge. "For future reference, Wyatt, sarcasm is not your forte. Please leave that to the experts."

Wyatt nodded in agreement. "I'll do that, Doc. Uh, you hungry? Virg and I were just about to open up a couple cans of beans." Wyatt clapped a hand to the dentist's back, careful not to use too much force.

"I am starving and so, in spite of the lack of cuisine offered at this fine establishment, I accept your offer."

Virgil and Wyatt exchanged shrugs. "Guess that means beans are okay with him," Wyatt said.

After a meal of warmed frijoles and thick slices of bread cut from a loaf, the three men sat drinking coffee and smoking, quite content with full stomachs and silence.

* * *

There remained much to do in the time left to Wyatt and Virgil before the day came to pull up stakes and head to Tombstone, so Holliday saw little of Wyatt, which he regretted, and Virgil not at all, which he did not.

Feeling some better, Doc opted for an evening in the finest saloon in town, seeing what the play was like and getting a sense of the place. Play was good and high rollers a plenty with many eager to test their skills against a sporting man of Doc Holliday's talent.

As usual, Kate was at his side, refilling his shot glass if the need arose, or getting him a beer or something to eat if that was his desire. Kate loved the nightlife and as the hour grew later and later, she never noticed the passage of time. Into his game and on top of it, neither did Holliday. Two out of three pots were his and as always, he was loath to quit while a winning streak was on him.

Night turned into day and still Doc beat the odds, winning handily. Hunger came and went with little note and the need for sleep also went unanswered. Later the other players fell by the wayside due either to exhaustion or sudden lack of funds.

Gathering his winnings with a broad smile, quite pleased with himself, Doc offered Kate his arm, and together they walked the couple blocks to the hotel.

Holliday took time before climbing into bed to order up a hot bath in which he luxuriated, soaking in the warm water until it became too cool for his liking. Climbing out and toweling off, he got into bed next to an already slumbering Kate. Rolling himself into the blankets, he found sleep without difficulty.

Twenty-four hours later he woke, not realizing the hour

or the day, just knowing that one moment he'd fallen asleep, and the next he was sitting up, wide awake with that damned piercing pain in the right side of his chest. So white he was, the pain written across his face, Kate ran for the doctor.

Doc woke to the pain in his chest relegated to a bruised feeling where the physician had inserted a long, thin needle between his ribs and into the abscess deep within his right lung to drain the excess fluid. He felt no need to cough, either, and that was indeed a blessing. He moved his eyes, not feeling the desire to move much else. Surprised when his gaze met Wyatt's, he smiled.

"Need anything?" Wyatt asked.

"Water would be nice," he replied. "I'm a bit dry."

Holliday drank until he was no longer thirsty then lay back on his pillow waiting for whatever it was his friend wanted to say, if anything.

"I came by earlier to tell you Morgan just blew into town. He can't wait to see you. Guess he might have to. I didn't know about this, Doc," he said.

Holliday brushed aside his friend's apology. "There was no way you could know, Wyatt. It came up on me suddenly. Although I would love to see Morgan, I would hate for him to see me incapacitated. Perhaps, perhaps we might give it a day. I'll be out of this bed by tomorrow afternoon and we can meet for supper at the restaurant downstairs."

"Sounds good, then. Tomorrow afternoon, say around five." Wyatt got to his feet and stretched before walking over to the windows and closing them down, each in turn, preventing the entrance of night's cold air into the sick room.

Doc mentioned Kate, asking Wyatt if he knew when she

might return. As soon as the question passed his lips he wished he had remained silent. Wyatt scowled and once more Doc was reminded of how little his best friend and his mistress had in common, aside from him, and there in lay the rub.

"Kate's a jealous female, period," Wyatt said. "And that's the worst type."

Doc sighed. "You argued."

Wyatt shrugged. "We argued. I asked why she didn't send for me with you so bad and all. 'We didn't need you, Wyatt,' she said. Maybe that's the truth and maybe not. Still, she mighta sent word."

"Kate believes she is all things to me," Doc explained. "She knows that isn't true, yet continues to delude herself. Kate will never understand my need for someone else, someone who provides not just companionship, but kinship, a closeness not connected to physicality at all, but spirituality. She is indeed jealous of you, Wyatt. And she has reason to be."

The next afternoon found John Holliday feeling better than he had in ages. The discomfort in his chest was all but gone, and the tiredness plaguing him all too often in recent weeks seemed to have vanished. His physician gave him a clean bill of health, all things relative, with the stipulations he not overtax himself and get plenty of rest.

Doc had all the intentions of following doctor's orders, but like most good intentions, they fell by the wayside.

His reunion with Morgan was warm, and with so much catching up to do, the friends spent a late night out on the town. Virgil gave up early, leaving Wyatt, Morgan and Doc to howl at the moon, the three doing so in some of the many fine, and not so fine establishments lining Whiskey Row.

Partying went on into the wee hours of the morning when

Wyatt figured Holliday had done enough. He hadn't mentioned the dentist's operation to Morgan because Doc asked him not to. So Wyatt took upon himself the task of being the wet blanket.

"I'm done in," he complained, yawning. "Lots to do tomorrow and I need some sleep. Come on, boys, let's call it." Wyatt draped his arms around his companions, both of whom looked at him as if he'd lost his mind.

"Wyatt you act like an old man," Morgan said gazing at Holliday as if for confirmation. "What's with him, anyways, Doc? Actin' like an old man. I expect that from Virg, but Wyatt?"

Holliday pushed Wyatt's arm off his shoulder and chuckled. "Morgan, let's just you and I find something more to occupy our time. We don't need this, this," Doc searched for the right term with which to peg Wyatt.

"We don't need this ole stick in the mud." Sick and tired of being sick and tired, Doc was elated at his newfound energy, but worried somewhere in the back of his mind that it could not last. He meant to make the most of it while he could.

Wyatt, however, would not be denied. "Come on. One last drink down at the Fox, then," he coaxed, slinging his arm once again around Doc's shoulder as he steered the way toward the door.

The two willing younger men went along, Doc singing at the top of his lungs some ribald song about a woman named Dora. Morgan convulsed in laughter at the lyrics. Caught up in the moment, Wyatt allowed himself to be dragged, not only to the Fox, but also to the Biltmore and the Old Irish Pub.

Standing outside the hotel early the next morning, wrapped in a heavy coat and smoking a cigar, John Holliday greeted a green-around-the-gills Wyatt with a smug smile. It was clear his friend was in the throes of a nasty hangover, though his drinking consisted only of beer, and in Doc's rather fuzzy recollection, little enough of that.

Wyatt stated his opinion of the grinning Holliday in a raw voice. "I hate you, Doc."

Holliday continued smiling his bemused, irritating smile. "I reciprocate your feelings, Wyatt. Are you on for some breakfast?"

At the very thought of food, Wyatt's stomach lurched, "Coffee. I am in the mood for coffee, and if you order bacon or sausage or anything else swimming in grease I'll— Let's just say whatever I do *will* include you, Holliday."

CHAPTER 20

Preparations for the move continued and the closer the time came to leave, the more Doc felt torn. His winning ways at the poker table continued unabated with more high rollers streaming in daily. He had amassed a tidy sum indeed, and had no desire to break the streak quite yet. When he spoke to Wyatt about perhaps the move being delayed for a week or so, his friend looked disquieted.

Wyatt tapped the ash from his cigar off against the saucer of his coffee cup. Doc knew by the stall, short lived though it was, the answer he sought from Earp would not be forthcoming.

"You see, Doc, it's like this…" Wyatt looked uncomfortable.

Holliday shook his head. "Don't concern yourself, my friend. I never should have put you in such a position knowing the family is preparing to leave on time."

Earp appeared relieved by Doc's understanding of his situation. He motioned the waiter over and ordered another pot of coffee.

"If it was just me, you know I'd wait, but Virgil's keen on Tombstone. It's almost like he's afraid the parade'll pass us by if we don't make tracks." Wyatt filled Holliday's cup before topping off his own with fresh aromatic brew. "He's anxious. Wants to get in on the bottom floor."

"Let's hope his anxiety is not ill directed and the floor ends up dropping out from beneath him."

Wyatt's expression soured. "You don't think much of Virgil, do you?" he asked, leaning forward, waiting for Doc's answer.

"More to the point, Virgil thinks little of me," Holliday countered. "You can't understand, can you, Wyatt, how your friend and your brother tolerate each other only for your sake?"

The sour expression faded and a slow easy grin took its place. Wyatt relaxed. "Oh, I think I understand what it is you're sayin', Doc. It's about the same as how your friend and your woman tolerate each other, and just barely, for your sake."

Holliday smiled. "Touché, Wyatt. Well said. Now, may we drop this subject before it becomes tiresome?"

Earp nodded.

"Expect me to arrive in Tombstone in a few weeks, more or less, depending upon my luck at the gaming tables. Until then I expect to be updated now and then. If I am delayed, I shall let you know." Doc plucked his gold watch from the pocket of his waistcoat, flipped open the elaborate case and made much of checking the time. Satisfied it matched that of the restaurant's wall clock, he slipped the Waltham away, patting the round outline the watch made in his pocket. The timepiece held many memories, not the least of which centered on the man seated opposite.

Pushing back from the table, Holliday retrieved his hat from the chair next to him and rose to his feet. Donning the black Stetson, he extended his hand to Wyatt.

Earp got to his feet and clasped the outstretched hand. "What's this, Doc? A bit early for goodbyes, ain't it?"

"No, my friend, it is the perfect time. I've come to dislike, no, I've come to despise goodbyes, so give the family my fond regards. We shall meet again in Tombstone."

Doc's luck continued for more than a few weeks. But then something occurred, not of his making, which brought his good fortune to a grinding, irksome halt.

Prescott decided it was time to crack down on gamblers and gambling, giving Doc Holliday an awful sense of *deja vu* going back to his days in Las Vegas, New Mexico Territory. It seemed civilization did indeed have its drawbacks, some of which put a definite damper on the way in which Doc Holliday spent his evenings and made his living.

However, Doc's practice of dentistry continued on a roll, due in no small part to the enthusiastic praise of Holliday's physician, Doctor Matt Mercier. Doc's saving of Mercier's molar with an expertly crafted gold crown had delighted the physician as did the lack of discomfort involved. Not only did Mercier sing his colleague's merits to any and all who would listen, he also offered Doctor John Holliday the use of his own offices whenever Holliday wished to pursue his calling.

Holliday's dental practice boomed as gold crowns became the ultimate in status symbols among the well heeled miners and businessmen of the town. But even the most promising of booms goes bust, and so it was with Doc's practice. Holliday thought the slump in dentistry a prudent time to plan a quick trip to Las Vegas to finish his business there.

Not surprisingly, a disagreement found Kate and Doc at odds. Prescott bored Kate, especially since Doc had become more dentist than gambler, his switch of occupations somewhat curtailing Miss Elder's nightlife.

"I want company, Doc," she complained, turning her back to Holliday to allow him to fasten those top hooks she could not reach on the low cut bodice of Holliday's favorite red velvet dress.

Doc brushed aside the dark curls and fastened the hooks with ease, grateful for his small hands and manual dexterity. Kate turned around, pressing close, her heaving bosom effectively displayed.

Doc raised an eyebrow. "Your obvious attempts at seduction fall on deaf ears, my dear," he drawled, "though I will admit the view is tempting indeed." He allowed his gaze to linger along the line of her *décolletage*.

Angry, Kate attempted a slap that Doc blocked, catching her gloved hand in his. "I won't play into your hands, Kate." He turned away, walking over to the window where he picked up a cigar and lit it, drawing on the thin cheroot with obvious satisfaction before settling himself into a chair.

"I rather enjoy my new status in this town. I find it quite to my liking to be addressed as *Doctor* Holliday and to count among my friends those of high standing in the community."

"So now I embarrass you, is that it, Doc? I ain't good enough to be seen with you any more?" Kate smoldered. Doc recognized all the signs. An eruption of monumental proportions loomed on the horizon. "Them hoity-toity friends of yours, that Richard Elliot and John Gosper, them bores. How do you stand 'em, Doc?"

Kate flounced over to the bed and sat down in a huff. For a moment, Holliday thought she just might break into tears, but no, that would ruin her artful makeup.

"Richard Elliot owns the Accidental Mine and John Gosper happens to be the secretary of state and acting governor of the Territory. Both are articulate, witty men with, I might add, valuable connections. And to answer your question, Kate, yes, there are times when you embarrass me, your nocturnal activities being less than ladylike. There are also times you complement me to perfection. However, lately the latter moments are few and very far between."

Doc beat a hasty retreat before Kate's tantrum began in earnest. When he returned, he was greeted with stony silence, much to his relief.

Kate's packed bag sat inside the door, her traveling cloak folded on top. "I'm leavin' on the first stage south this afternoon," she admitted.

Doc crouched down and drew his own leather valise from beneath the bed, lifting the heavy packed bag onto the coverlet. "I shall walk you to the depot since I leave on the eastbound stage myself."

If Kate hoped Doc might attempt to prevent her leaving, she now knew that would not be the case. For their remaining time together, she ranted and cursed him while he refused to be riled by her behavior, which only added fuel to Kate's fire.

However, Doc, being in a good mood, was impervious to Kate's ire. He looked forward to winding things up in Las Vegas. Cutting the New Mexico ties cleared the way to Tombstone and a new start.

Carrying Kate's bag in one hand and his own in the other, Holliday accompanied her to the stage depot. "Maybe we'll meet up again, Doc," she said as she settled herself onto the hard wooden seat of the coach and reached a hand out to him from the window.

A gentleman to a fault, he took her gloved fingers and pressed them to his lips. "If the fates allow," he replied, smiling up at her. The smile was too wide, the expression too teasing. Abruptly, the woman pulled her hand from his.

"Goodbye, Doc," she said as the driver cracked his whip and Kate's stage lurched forward.

Shrugging, John Holliday handed his bag up to the driver of the eastbound Star Line Stage and settled his lanky frame onto a seat by the window. When he smiled this time, it was genuine.

Las Vegas had changed in the months Holliday had been away. More people meant more buildings, more buildings meant more equity in his own property. He would make a tidy profit on the saloon when he sold out, which, after paying off his debt to the builder, he did.

Doc made his way to Old Town for a visit with a past acquaintance, Leo Harrigan, the owner operator of Harrigan's Irish Pub. Holliday had no inkling of what or who awaited him in the dim saloon through whose elaborate double doors he now passed.

There was a roar of gunfire, and a bullet whipped past Doc's hip, with another going far wide of his shoulder. Dropping into a crouch, he pulled his .45, aiming at all that was visible of his attacker: a dark silhouette edging out from behind the bar, long barreled pistol extended. Two rapid shots and the threat to Doc's life was over.

Slowing standing upright, Holliday walked over to the prone figure and watched as a patron rolled the shooter onto his back. Holliday kicked the still smoking .44 out of reach, though the gunman looked ill prepared for any further trouble. One of Doc's bullets had grazed the side of the head, digging a gouge into the dark hair, while the other creased the left arm. Neither appeared life threatening, though the scalp wound bled profusely.

"Charlie White. I'll be damned," Holliday whispered.

"You know him, Doc?" Leo Harrigan stepped around the bar, a short, double-barreled shotgun steadied across one arm. Seeing the shooter down, Harrigan broke the shotgun and removed the shells.

"I know him, Leo," Doc replied, holstering his gun. "We met in Dodge, at the Long Branch. He accused me of cheating at cards when, in fact, he was the one cheating. I embarrassed him in public. It appears he never forgave me."

Before the week was out, Charlie White left on the eastbound stage never to be heard of again in the west. Even though White failed in his attempt to kill Doc Holliday, he succeeded in wounding him, nevertheless. Another gunfight, another rumor, another story blown out of proportion, Charlie White could not have hurt John Holliday more.

Doc left Las Vegas bound for Prescott with a great deal of money in his saddlebags and a heavy heart, the leaden feeling exacerbated by the unwanted interest of his fellow stage passengers. While no one came right out and said anything to him, he felt their curious gazes upon him when they thought he wasn't looking, the men and even the woman, though she seemed a lady. He expected more from her. Finally he could stand it no longer and took his leave of the coach in Flagstaff, opting to rent a horse and take his chances alone.

Staying the night in town, he left the next morning. Though the day was sunny, it was still late spring and the mountain weather remained cold and somewhat freakish in nature. He dressed warmly and carried plenty of provisions; anything was better than being the object of fear or curiosity or both. And he had his own thoughts to keep him company.

His one worry concerned his mount. The animal seemed a good one, but Holliday was not used to his habits and hoped the big gelding proved a horse to be counted on in a pinch.

Two nights spent out in the frigid mountains, and Doc thought the reasoning behind his foolish endeavor rather flawed. The temperatures were bone-chilling and frequent snow squalls became almost constant companions. He was cold. He was tired from sleeping on the ground and not sleeping. Wolves howled all night, turning the horse skittish and giving his own nerves a turn.

Grumbling at his own lack of sense, Holliday saddled his mount. The animal snorted and danced and made the work take twice as long as it should have. But the horse, like the man, was anxious to put the night behind him and get moving.

Toward evening, Holliday found himself in a small settlement. Several shacks lined a street of sorts. There was a saloon. Hungry and cold, always cold, he tied his mount up in front of the watering hole and stepped inside.

The saloon wasn't bad for all its lack of outer embellishments. The bar was a beauty of polished mahogany, while the large mirror, taking up most of the wall behind it, offered a panoramic view of the squat room.

Tables were scattered haphazardly about, and the place was crowded. Obviously, it was *the* place to be for many miles around, even boasting hostesses, a couple of whom were not bad on the eyes. And the smell of cooking food made the traveler's mouth water. He was no cook, subsisting on undercooked bacon, barely warmed beans, coffee thick as sludge, and hardtack.

Finding a table, he sat down, signaling for a hostess. One of the pretty ones sashayed over to his table, smiling down at him, and he realized she wasn't quite as pretty as first thought.

Her too-red lip rouge was smudged, and there were lines around her mouth and eyes from age, overwork, alcohol or a combination. Her ample breasts, threatening to overflow the top of her tight bodice, were white as uncooked dumplings and when she bent over to take his order he was appalled by the blue veins that snaked across the pasty flesh. The complete picture nearly took away his appetite. Ordering from the rather limited menu, Doc waited impatiently for the food to arrive.

Gambling was in full swing, but he wasn't interested in a game. This place was too far out in the sticks for any players of worth to show up, though, of course, *he* was here and he could clean up if that was his desire. However, he desired nothing but food and a bed within four walls and a bit of warmth.

The food was good and there was enough of it. The beer he'd ordered was cold which would've been fine any other day save this, so Holliday ordered coffee. That warmed him, and soon he was drowsy and in dire need of a bed. But first he had to tend to his horse and that he did, finding a stable, paying for a good currying and some oats, then it was back to the saloon and a bed upstairs. He walked in carrying his saddlebags and was pointed to room number four.

Almost asleep on his feet, Doc stumbled to the top of the steps, turned right and found the room. There was no lock on the door. Inside stood an iron bedstead, a small table with a lit kerosene lamp on it, a washstand, and the hostess from downstairs wearing a come hither look on her painted face and nothing else. Holliday froze in the doorway, at first surprised and then angry. He held the anger in check.

"Not this evening, ma'am." Reaching into his waistcoat pocket he tossed two silver dollars onto the bed. "For your trouble," he added.

The whore seethed, but said nothing as she gathered up her clothing. Not bothering to dress, she pushed past Doc and out into the hallway. More and more Holliday wished he had stayed on that damned stage.

There was no chair to prop in front of the door to bar it from the inside, so Doc placed the small table there after moving the lamp over to the washstand. It would keep no intruders out, but would give notice if someone tried to enter. He splashed some cold water onto his face, brushed his teeth and then climbed into bed fully clothed, not even bothering to remove his boots. The saddlebags lay at the foot of the bed and his right hand rested on the .45 in the shoulder holster.

When morning rolled around and he had not been molested, Doc was shocked, but very much relieved. Grabbing up his gear, he made haste out of the room, out of the saloon, and out of the small town.

The day proved uneventful at first. The temperature warmed, the heavens were brilliant with azure sky and cotton wool clouds. Doc let down his guard.

He was jumped just as he headed into a stand of Ponderosa pines by two men with Winchesters and the whore from the saloon. He couldn't say she looked better in the light of day though the no face paint was an improvement and the jacket buttoned up to her chin did cover a multitude of sins, and veins.

"Hand over them saddlebags and we'll let 'cha go on yer way," the whore said, and Doc realized why his refusal of her favors the night before had caused her anger. She meant to rob him then, and it was certain her failure had not set well with her companions.

Beside her, the two men whispered in collusion. The older one Doc figured was no doubt the whore's pimp rode a bit closer, the Winchester held steady as he approached. He scrutinized Doc before coming to a conclusion.

"You'd be Doc Holliday." He crowed, delighted at his own acumen. "I see'd you once in Dodge City." Then, as if suddenly aware of what he'd just said, the fellow backed his horse up a couple steps.

Doc replied with sarcasm, knowing the three would have no idea of his meaning, "Ah, now dawn comes up over Marble Head."

They did not understand and stared dumbly at him, turning to look at each other in confusion before turning back to Holliday.

"Watch yerselves. It's said he's fair righteous with those guns a his." This was from the younger man. "I heared he's kilt a dozen men, more even."

Holliday sat his horse unruffled. No one had made a move, but there were two rifles on him, cocked. He'd just wait a moment. Something had to happen. When nothing did, he goaded the three hoping for some sort of action to which he might respond.

"If you like, we could ride into the next town and have our photographs taken together, sort of a memento of the occasion."

Still no one budged, and Doc figured now was the time to make his own move since they seemed so mesmerized by his presence. Just as he thought to draw his Colt, the woman's horse moved in front of the pimp's, she was having some difficulty controlling the animal. Perfect timing allowed Doc to draw and wing the younger man before the pimp could maneuver around the whore and get off a shot.

The wounded thief's horse reared, throwing the man to the ground, and the pimp's shot went wild. The whore was still having difficulty controlling her own mount, and the animal bumped the pimp's horse as he levered a round into the Winchester for another shot. However, Holliday used the time well, and in the confusion, he was off without a backward glance.

The gray gelding proved his worth as he dodged trees and held his ground across the uneven woods, taking direction from Doc's hands on the reins, knees against heaving sides as man and horse outdistanced and out rode any who might have followed. The rest of the day, Holliday spent in reflection as he berated himself for losing touch with his instincts and allowing his mind to wander. He also realized he'd supplied yet more fodder for the grist mills of the rumor mongers and storytellers, imagining in vivid detail the embroidered tale his trio of would be thieves would weave concerning their encounter with Doc Holliday.

He rode into Prescott, weary, stiff-muscled, and more wary than when he had ridden out on the stage. Of course his little run in with Charlie White beat him back to town causing his hard won standing in the community to plummet. As much as he hated to admit Kate had been right about his *hoity-toity* friends, they proved untrue at best. With bruised ego in tow, he prepared to take leave of Arizona's touted territorial capital.

While preparations were underway, Doc's prodigal paramour returned, regretful of her quick temper and wanting to accompany Holliday to Tombstone. Doc figured wherever the stage had taken her had not lived up to Kate's expectations and so, once again and for better or worse, she desired to hitch her star to his.

Doc never enjoyed traveling alone, and so he forgave Kate her trespasses, though not without shamelessly allowing her to wheedle her way back into his good graces. When he left Prescott, it was in her company. Tombstone lay ahead.

~END~

Watch for ***Holliday in Tombstone*** by
Susan M. Ballard.
Doc Holliday's story continues.

About the Author

Susan M. Ballard shares a small ranch in Pearce, Cochise County, Arizona with her husband, Brian. She is a member of The Western Writers of America and the Ranching Heritage Association. Her work, both fiction and non-fiction, has been published in *Wild West, Out West, Voice in the Desert, War Journal* and *Chronicle of the Old West*. Susan is a regular contributor to *The Tombstone Times*. **Borrowed Time** is her first novel.